Murder, She Meowed

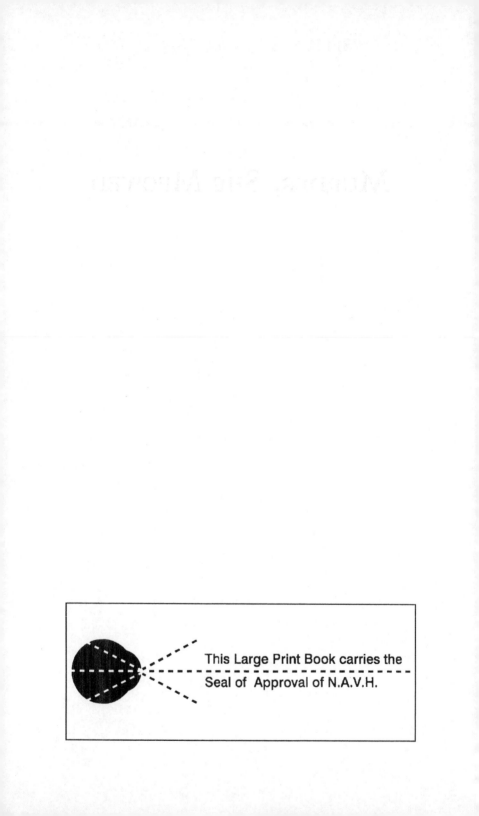

This Large Print Book carries the
Seal of Approval of N.A.V.H.

A PAWSITIVELY ORGANIC MYSTERY

MURDER, SHE MEOWED

LIZ MUGAVERO

THORNDIKE PRESS
A part of Gale, a Cengage Company

Farmington Hills, Mich • San Francisco • New York • Waterville, Maine
Meriden, Conn • Mason, Ohio • Chicago

GALE
A Cengage Company

Copyright © 2019 by Liz Mugavero.
A Pawsitively Organic Mystery.
Thorndike Press, a part of Gale, a Cengage Company.

ALL RIGHTS RESERVED
Thorndike Press® Large Print Clean Reads.
The text of this Large Print edition is unabridged.
Other aspects of the book may vary from the original edition.
Set in 16 pt. Plantin.

LIBRARY OF CONGRESS CIP DATA ON FILE.
CATALOGUING IN PUBLICATION FOR THIS BOOK
IS AVAILABLE FROM THE LIBRARY OF CONGRESS

ISBN-13: 978-1-4328-6438-5 (hardcover alk. paper)

Published in 2019 by arrangement with Kensington Books, an imprint of Kensington Publishing Corp.

Printed in Mexico
1 2 3 4 5 6 7 23 22 21 20 19

For my Shaggy Dog.

*You were my favorite hello
and my hardest good-bye.
You are forever in my heart —
my lifetime dog.* XO

CHAPTER ONE

Stan Connor hated tears. They were the one emotional act she felt completely ill-equipped to handle, whether they were her own tears or someone else's. When it was her little sister crying, it was worse. And when she was the cause, it was nearly unbearable. Even when Caitlyn was being a drama queen.

"Caitlyn, please stop crying." Stan looked helplessly at her Maine coon, Nutty, who sat on the middle of the coffee table in Stan's comfy little den, watching the histrionics with a barely concealed sneer. He was much better at handling this stuff. Mostly because he had no patience for it. He usually flicked his tail and walked away, but apparently even he didn't want to miss this.

"H-how can I stop crying?" Caitlyn paused, ripped a couple of tissues from the box on the table, and blew her nose loudly. "You're being so *unreasonable!*"

Stan resisted the urge to pull her own hair out by the roots. She wished the doorbell would ring, or for a fire alarm to sound, or heck, even a tornado warning — not that they got many of those in Frog Ledge, Connecticut. Anything that would save her from her sister's drama would be helpful. "I'm not being unreasonable," she said, trying to sound reasonable. "It's a lovely thought. Truly. I just don't want a traditional bachelorette party. Not everyone who gets married has to have a bachelorette party!"

This set Caitlyn off into a fresh set of wails. "But they *should*! Especially when their sister wants to throw it for them! Don't you get it, Krissie? I'll never have another chance to do this ever again. You'd really deprive me of that?"

Now was not the time to point out, for the millionth time, that Stan hated being called Krissie. Or that Caitlyn's life wouldn't end if she didn't throw her sister a bachelorette party. In Stan's opinion, they were overrated, cheesy, and completely unnecessary. A waste of time and dollar bills.

But she'd always been one to buck tradition, while her sister ran into it headlong.

"How about we go out for drinks or something? Or we can go into New York and go to a piano bar? Or a spa?" Stan latched

8

on to that, knowing her sister loved being pampered. But in this case, Caitlyn didn't react. "I really don't need a big production. The wedding is in three weeks. There's so much to do. This doesn't mean I won't throw you a bachelorette party," she hastened to reassure her sister. Caitlyn and her boyfriend Kyle were also engaged. Their wedding had a longer tail, though, because she was planning for a huge shindig even though it was her second time around. Their wedding date was set for December. "You can have whatever you want," Stan said, aware of the semi-pleading note in her voice. "I just don't want the same things."

It sounded like a reasonable argument to Stan. Nutty, now bored with the conversation, flicked his bushy tail, hopped off the table, and strolled out of the room, probably to sprawl across the kitchen floor and wait for dinner, a subtle reminder that this nonsense was cutting into his eating time. He hated when dinner was late.

Maybe Stan could use that as an excuse to stop talking. Time to feed the cats and dogs. She started to rise from her seat on the couch, but Caitlyn's death stare made her sink back down. "We're not done, huh," she said.

"No, we are *not* done!" Caitlyn cried. "I

can't believe you're making me go through all this to do something for my own sister! Who's marrying the man of her dreams. It's not like you'll be doing this again, Krissie. You and Jake are total soulmates. It's a once-and-done thing. Not like my stupid first mistake." She sniffed. "I don't care what you say. We're throwing you a bachelorette party. And that's that." She crossed her arms defiantly. "You don't want me to get Mom involved, do you?"

Stan's head, which had started to hurt at the beginning of this conversation, now throbbed. No, she didn't want her mother involved. She could see her chances of winning this argument slowly spiraling away into a black hole. Better to cut her losses and let Caitlyn do her thing. If she laid down some ground rules, it wouldn't go too far off the rails.

How bad could it be?

"Fine," she said, throwing up her hands in defeat. "Fine, fine, fine. Plan a bachelorette party. But I want it to be here in town. And nothing crazy. Not a ton of people, no cheesy guys, none of that."

Caitlyn let out a squeal and vaulted to her feet. She rushed across the room and threw herself on top of Stan, hugging her. "Thank you! You won't be sorry! We're going to have so much fun, you won't even believe it. You'll wonder why on earth you didn't want to do it in the first place. I'm going to call Brenna right now and start planning. And Nikki! And Izzy, and Amara . . . there's so much to do. Thank you, Krissie!"

She raced out of the room and into the hall. A minute later, Stan heard the front door slam.

Stan dropped her face into the pillow. Scruffy, her schnoodle, padded over and nudged Stan's arm with her nose. The dog's sweet brown eyes were anxious. She always knew when her mom was stressed.

Stan raised her head and met Scruffy's eyes. "She thinks I won't be sorry. But guess what? I'm already sorry."

Chapter Two

"I don't know why I told anyone in the first place." Stan poured a generous portion of wine into her glass, the snap of her wrist causing some of the red liquid to splash on the kitchen counter. "I mean, seriously. We should've just disappeared for the weekend and eloped, then come back and had a huge party. Maybe we should still do that." Stan looked hopefully at her best and oldest friend, wanting approval and encouragement. "Right? Shouldn't I?"

Nikki Manning surveyed her for a long minute, then burst out laughing. "Nice try, Connor. Your mother would have bodyguards on you before you even closed the car door. You don't think she's anticipated you trying that? You don't think she's got people watching the house right now, ready to spring into action at your first false move? You should know your own family better than that."

Stan grabbed a sponge and wiped up the wine spillage. Nikki was exaggerating, of course, but not by much. Her mother would, at the very least, track her down if she tried that. Stan resisted the urge to look out the window to see if she could spot someone doing surveillance.

She'd called Nikki after Caitlyn left last night, desperate and hoping her best friend could help keep her sister in check. Nikki had been expecting the call. Caitlyn had already called her from the car. She wasn't wasting any time or giving Stan a chance to change her mind. So Nikki, being the good friend that she was — and since her boyfriend was home to care for their foster dogs — had jumped in the car and driven the hour to console Stan. Nikki's plan was to stay a few days and help Stan thwart Caitlyn's plan.

"You know, all this talk about how your wedding is *your day* is crap," Stan said. "None of this is going to be mine, is it? I mean, with my mother and sister both living in town now, and my mother's wedding done, they're all over me." She slumped miserably in a chair at her kitchen table. "I want to get married at Jake's pub. I want a small ceremony with our close friends and the pets. And a big party after. Then I want

13

to go on our honeymoon. That's all I want."

The honeymoon part, at least, was not up for discussion. They'd booked their tickets for two weeks in Ireland before they'd made any of the other plans. Stan wanted to skip ahead to that part.

"Okay," Nikki said. "I don't see why you can't have that, even if you do have to sustain the torture of a Caitlyn-planned bachelorette party."

"Oh, you don't, eh?" Stan took a gulp of wine. "You've met my mother, haven't you?"

Nikki grinned. "On second thought, I guess it might be more of a production."

"You think?" Stan muttered. "Despite the fact that I've had everything planned for months, she told me the other day she's put a hold on three churches on the green and will determine which one is the *most elegant.*" Stan accentuated the last two words with air quotes. "Because I can't possibly get married at a bar. It's *just not done.* I told her that's not what I want, but she has no intention of listening to me. My wedding was all planned. I just needed a dress. But apparently there's a whole other plan going on around me that I'm not even a part of. I don't even know how she manages to pull this stuff off."

"But wait," Nikki said. "She knew about

14

your plans to get married at the pub. You told everyone right after you guys got engaged. You've been planning this all winter. How is she going around you?"

"Because she's Patricia Connor, and she always does exactly what she wants. Besides, she told me she wasn't listening in the first place," Stan said. "According to her, she was waiting for me to come to my senses. But now she's realized that I haven't, and I probably won't, and she has to take over and launch her evil plan."

"Huh." Nikki got up to refill her wineglass. "Yeah, I guess you're screwed. And no chance of other people bumping her out of all these holds, I guess, since it is Frog Ledge, not New York City. I'm sure she has a lot of influence over a church. Especially since she's the mayor's wife. What does Jake's family think of all this?"

"They're pretty easygoing. I mean, I think Jake's parents would love the whole church wedding, but at the same time they recognize that it's not what we want."

"Listen. Don't let this all ruin your wedding. You get to marry Jake. I know how happy that makes you," Nikki said. "Right? I mean, the ceremony is what it is. You'll still do the party at the pub, and that will be what everyone remembers. Especially with a big Irish family like his."

Despite herself, Stan smiled. "Yeah. You're right. I'm so lucky. I can't believe I'm marrying Jake." It had been like a fairy tale when he'd proposed to her during the Frog Ledge holiday stroll over Christmas. He'd caught her completely by surprise when he'd popped the question inside her newly opened pet patisserie, Pawsitively Organic. She'd been more than happy to say yes.

Ever since she'd met Jake nearly two years ago, right after moving to Frog Ledge, she'd been hopelessly in love with him. Even from the beginning when she tried to convince herself she wasn't, or that it would never work, or couldn't last. From the moment she'd walked into McSwigg's, Jake's Irish pub in town, she'd felt like she'd finally come home.

And Nikki was right. She wasn't letting anything get in the way of that happiness. This was the start of the rest of their lives, and she wouldn't let a silly evening with some cheesy stripper or an argument over where the ceremony would be held ruin the most important thing — how they felt about each other.

"Okay. Point taken, Nik. I'm not letting any of them ruin this. So, Caitlyn and my mother can do whatever they want — well, within reason — and I'm going to enjoy myself no matter what. Because it's not the day that matters most, it's everything that comes after. Right?"

Nikki nodded enthusiastically. "There you go. You just keep that attitude and everything will be fine."

"What attitude?"

They both spun around as Jake walked in, Duncan and Gaston bounding next to him. The Weimaraner and Australian shepherd went to work with Jake every day at the pub, while Scruffy and their pit bull Henry usually hung with Stan at the patisserie.

"Hey! I didn't even hear the door." Stan got up and walked over to Jake. He hugged her tight, enveloping her in his familiar warmth. He smelled like outside. And faintly of French fries. "Done at the pub early today?"

It was Thursday, and Jake was taking the night off, which meant he spent the day at the pub doing prep work so his staff could run the place easily and effortlessly later. Stan had closed up Pawsitively Organic at four today, leaving her the afternoon with Nikki and the evening with her fiancé. Stan and Jake had planned to go out for dinner. And probably talk about wedding plans. Theirs, not Patricia's.

"Yeah, the lunch rush wasn't really a rush today so we got a lot done early." Jake kissed Stan, then headed to the fridge. "So what attitude? Hey, Nikki," he added, waving at her.

Nikki saluted him from her chair. "Stan's attitude. Her positive, uplifting attitude toward her family," she said with a wink.

"Uh-oh." Jake uncapped his bottle of water and took a swig. "What's going on now?"

"They're just trying to run the show. Nothing we hadn't expected." Stan tried to shrug it off. "My sister threw a fit when I told her I didn't want a bachelorette party. So now I'm having one."

Jake laughed. "You expected anything less?"

Apparently Stan was the only one who kept underestimating her family. "I guess I thought I could talk sense into her." Stan sighed. "I was wrong."

"Of course you were. There was no way you were dodging that bullet. Plans have been well underway for a while."

Stan stared at him. "They have? And you knew about this?"

"Sweetie. The whole town does." Jake regarded her with a touch of pity.

Stan whirled on Nikki. "What aren't you

18

telling me?"

Nikki raised her hands in a gesture of surrender. "Hey. I'm not in charge here. I've tried to have input where I could because I know what you like. Frankly, it didn't matter. Caitlyn is calling the shots, and everyone else is going along with them. Mostly because they've been threatened to within an inch of their lives about what will happen if they don't."

Stan paled. "That doesn't make me feel confident."

Nikki shrugged. "I promise I'll try to buffer you as much as I can. Okay?"

"Fine. Great," Stan said. "I guess that's all I can hope for."

"Right. So, what are you doing tomorrow night?" Nikki winked at her.

Stan paled. "Tomorrow? That's when she's planning it? She knew all along she was doing this whether or not I agreed to it, didn't she?" Stan shook her head. "Man, this is what I get for trying to think the best of people. When? Where?"

"Jeez. I can't tell you everything. I just wanted to give you a heads up of when it was," Nikki said. "You cannot let on that I did. Seriously, Stan. She'll have my head. She wants to catch you completely off guard."

Stan looked at Jake. He barely managed to hide his smile behind a cough. "It's going to be fine," he said. "Really, Stan. How bad can it be?"

CHAPTER THREE

Since she couldn't sleep anyway wondering what her sister had in store for her, Stan was up and out of the house early Friday morning, Scruffy and Henry by her side. She had a lot of work to do, and since she was going to be whisked away on some crazy outing later, she figured she needed a head start.

Stay positive. Stan knew she should feel blessed and lucky. Her sister and her friends loved her enough to do this for her, right? Some people didn't have anyone who wanted to throw them a party. Still, if she didn't know her sister so well, she might not be so nervous. If Nikki was running the show, she'd feel much more comfortable. Nikki understood her. It was why they'd been friends for so many years. But Caitlyn? She meant well, but she and Stan were definitely very different people. Even though moving to Frog Ledge, divorcing her banker husband, and falling for a down-to-earth chef had tamed her a bit, Caitlyn still tended to think about things as a high-society girl. She liked fancy parties, expensive venues, showy displays. She was her mother's daughter, through and through.

Stan, by contrast, was not.

She pulled into the parking lot of Izzy Sweet's Sweets, rolled the windows down for the dogs, and promised them she'd be right back. Stan hurried inside, mouth already watering for one of Izzy's lattes. Izzy's was her favorite place in town. Well, next to the pub and her own shop. But she'd fallen in love the first weekend she'd moved here, when Izzy had joined the contingent of neighbors welcoming Stan to town. She had brought a basket of her gourmet chocolates, coffees, and teas. She and Izzy had also hit it off and become fast friends.

"Morning Stan!" Betty Meany, the town librarian, waved frantically from a table in the corner. Betty was a tiny little thing with a personality larger than the whole town. She dressed like a boss too — always wearing the latest styles, her hair trendier than most of the millennials in town. Today she had a red beret perched on top of her short, spiky white hair, the one splash of color in her otherwise black ensemble.

"Hi Betty." Stan waved back and got in line. Izzy and her longtime employee, Jana, worked the counter, Izzy taking the orders and Jana busy behind the machines. Stan never knew where to look first. The pastry cases were brilliant in the morning, overflowing with freshly baked Danish, muffins, cinnamon buns, and other goodies. But the chocolate cases made Stan swoon.

Izzy had the best chocolates imported from all over the world. She'd recently started selling her chocolates and gifts online, in addition to opening the town's first bookstore in over twenty years. Which meant she was incredibly busy and also enjoying way more success than most people around here had ever thought possible.

But the café was Izzy's first love, and Stan knew it was a point of pride for her. When she'd first opened, some of the town's old-timers pooh-poohed the idea of a foreigner opening some fancy coffee shop. Frog Ledge was not a town known for its diversity or gourmet food — a lot of locals preferred greasy-spoon diners and burger joints — and Izzy's caramel skin, long braids, and exotic background had turned quite a few heads. But she'd made a go of it. The college in the next town provided a steady influx of customers, and as word got out in the general area, more and more locals ventured in. Now, Izzy's place was to mornings in Frog Ledge what Jake's pub was to evenings.

"Morning, sunshine. What'll you have?" Izzy grinned and tossed her braids over her shoulder as Stan stepped up to the counter. Stan could feel the happiness vibrating off her. Stan knew it was mostly because of Liam McGee. Izzy had been seeing Jake's cousin secretly for more than a year when their relationship was "outed" last Christmas. It had been just what they needed to kick things up to the next level. Liam had moved to town and was living with Izzy, helping her run her businesses. A successful writer, Liam kept his own hours, so their lifestyles had gelled nicely. Liam had, surprisingly, settled into small-town life without missing a beat, something Izzy had worried about since he'd lived in New York City most of his adult life.

Stan hadn't seen her friend so happy since she'd met her.

"I'll take a salted caramel latte. With almond milk. And do you have any of those espresso bean muffins?"

"You bet. I made a small batch and saved you one." Izzy winked and disappeared out back, returning with Stan's treat in the bag.

"How's the wedding planning going?"

"Good. There are two weddings being planned. My version, and my mother's. In case you want to jump in and take one." Stan grinned. "It'll be fine."

"Keep talking, sister. All of this is a great reason for me to never have a typical wedding," Izzy said.

Stan's eyes widened. "Are you . . ."

"No. Not that I know of, anyway." Izzy shrugged. "It'll happen when it happens. Why mess with a good thing, right?" Her gaze drifted past Stan.

Stan turned and saw Liam sitting at the counter, facing the street. He had his laptop and a coffee, and was clearly off in his own little world writing, but he looked happy sitting here, in this tiny town, in his girlfriend's café.

Frog Ledge had that effect on people, though. Stan was a living example. It coaxed even the most big-city people in and kept them there. For Stan, it was all about the people. For others, it was a change of pace from the hustle and bustle of the city. Either way, there was a magic to this place. And Liam clearly felt it. He and Izzy were perfect together. And the thought of Izzy being an official member of the family made Stan so happy she could cry.

"True. I'm still thinking of kidnapping Jake and eloping," Stan said, turning back to the counter.

"I'll kill you," Izzy warned. "Never mind me, the rest of the town will probably help me do it. Everyone here needs to see you two get married."

"Jeez, why is that so important to everyone?" Stan asked.

"Because everyone loves both of you," Izzy said. "Now move along. I have customers."

"I'll see you later." Stan picked up her bagged muffin and moved to the other side of the counter, where Jana was putting the finishing touches on her latte. "Thank you," she said, grabbing the cup, and then moving through the tables until she'd reached Liam. "Hey."

He glanced up, pulling out his earbuds, and smiled. "Morning, Stan. Gettin' your fix, yeah?"

"Absolutely," Stan said. She loved Liam's accent. He'd spent most of his youth in Ireland. Liam's dad, Jake's uncle Seamus, had moved there when his sons were young. "How are you? How's life in Frog Ledge?"

"It's amazing," Liam said, his gaze traveling to Izzy behind the counter. Izzy saw him looking and winked.

"Well, good. I keep missing you when I go

to the pub."

"Yeah, I try to stop in a few times a week and help keep my cousin in business." Liam grinned. "How's the shop?"

"It's good. Really good, actually. I can't believe how well it's doing."

"I can. You're talented. And you love animals. It's the perfect combination," Liam said. "I don't know how the town ever got by without it."

"Well, thanks," Stan said, touched. "I'll see you later."

Stan left the café with a smile. Liam's praise meant a lot to her. She'd always liked Jake's cousin. He was smart, observant, and down-to-earth. He called things as he saw them. And she knew praise didn't pour out easily from him. But she knew he was right. She had a lot to be proud of, such as starting her own business from scratch on a whim, watching it gain traction, and finally seeing it become one of the town's favorite places. It was all part of the Frog Ledge magic.

Chapter Four

When Stan arrived at Pawsitively Organic, which was around the corner from Izzy's café — Frog Ledge's downtown was about two square miles — Brenna McGee, Jake's little sister and Stan's employee, was getting out of her car. She had two grocery bags with her and waved enthusiastically at Stan, nearly dropping one of them.

"Morning!" Stan hopped out of the car, the dogs at her heels, tails wagging joyfully at the sight of their auntie. "Need some help?"

"No, I got it, thanks. What a beautiful day! Isn't it?" Brenna turned her face up to the early morning sun and sighed. "I love spring."

"It is a beautiful day," Stan said, taking a moment to look around. Spring had fully — finally — kicked into gear in Frog Ledge. The temperatures were steadily on the rise, and flowers were blooming all over town.

Stan, who had never been much of a gardener, was even itching to add some flowers to both her yard at home and the shop. She was thinking pansies for the shop.

But the best part about heading into the summer months, in her opinion, was the farmers' market that would soon spring up on the town green, with its robust display of the best veggies. And all the summer berries. She loved summer berries. Most of her treat recipes in these months were planned around which berries were in season. Her organic farm suppliers were already sending her updates about what was new this season, and she couldn't wait to start creating new recipes for the patisserie, as well as the meal plans that were part of the shop's offerings. It was something she'd dabbled in before she'd opened her shop, and it had taken off like a rocket the past few months.

She'd been a little surprised by how many people wanted "real" meals for their furry friends. Apparently canned dog food was so yesterday. Orders for meal plans centered around organic, wild-caught salmon, grass-fed, local beef, and locally raised turkey were constantly pouring in through her new website, which Brenna had worked with a designer to create over the winter. That wasn't even including the townspeople who picked up weekly meals for their dogs. With that and the treat baking, she and Brenna were busy all the time.

Which was a good problem to have, but sometimes it got overwhelming. Caitlyn helped too — she did the books for the patisserie, and she jumped in on the baking when it was particularly busy — but Stan knew it was time to start adding staff.

It was also time to give Brenna a bigger role in the business. Brenna had been with Stan since the beginning, when Stan was baking a few batches of treats from her oven at home, and she had been instrumental in getting the patisserie open. She'd turned down other jobs to work with Stan because she believed in Pawsitively's mission, and because they worked well together and were friends. And now, almost relatives. Brenna, like her big brother, wanted to stay close to home, and this was a perfect way for her to do what she loved and do it among family and friends.

So, Stan figured it was time to make her a full partner. And then she needed to get serious about hiring a couple of bakers and counter people.

She and Brenna could make that decision together once they'd settled on their partnership. She'd been thinking about it for a few months, but events over the winter followed by the flurry of wedding plans had derailed her expansion plans a bit. But spring was the perfect time for new beginnings, and this way Brenna could run the show while Stan was pulled away with the business of getting married. And taking a honeymoon. No small feat given that she and Jake both ran their own businesses and were extremely protective of what they'd created.

She'd tell her tonight, she decided. If she survived this party.

"So, hey — do you want to get a drink tonight?" Brenna asked casually as she followed Stan into the shop and dropped her grocery bags on the counter.

Stan suppressed her smile. *Here we go,* she thought. She considered messing with Brenna and telling her she had plans, but that was the one problem with small towns like this. Everyone knew what everyone else was doing. All the time. And if she had plans tonight, half the town would know what they were. And if she *pretended* to have plans and hid in her house, the other half of the town would know that.

"Sure," she said. "What time were you thinking?"

"How about right after we close? I know

you probably want to go over to the pub later." On the nights when Jake had to work, Stan usually went over and had dinner with him. It was important to them both that they stay connected despite the crazy hours they both kept.

"Sure. That sounds good," Stan said, pretending not to notice the look of relief on Brenna's face at her easy agreement. "I'll have to run the dogs home."

"Yeah, no worries. Okay, I'll start baking." Brenna unloaded her bags. "I got stuff to make the cheddar cheese and apple pup-cakes. We haven't had those in a while. And those are Junior's favorite, so I thought we could make them the special for today and name them after him."

"That's a sweet idea." Junior was Izzy's senior dog, the newest addition to her family, which included two other pups — Baxter and Elvira. She'd taken Junior in last year after his owner had to give him up, and lately he'd been in ill health. Stan knew Izzy was worried about him. "We have the farm delivery coming today. I'll take care of that."

Every Friday, the local farm delivered Stan's grass-fed meat for her meal plans. She didn't eat meat herself and always felt a stab of guilt, but she knew the farmer and felt good about his practices. The meat was high quality and the animals were treated humanely, and since the dogs and cats she fed weren't supposed to be vegetarian, it was the right thing to do.

Scruffy and Henry heard the truck lumbering into the parking lot before she did. Both of their ears perked up. They knew the sound, because they associated it with their farm delivery guys who always gave them treats. The boys were right on time.

CHAPTER FIVE

"Morning, guys!" Stan held the back door open wide so her deliverymen could get their packages inside.

"Morning, Miss Connor! Hi Bren!" Perry Puck, one of the newer farmhands at Spring Hill Farm, shot Stan his famous grin, flashing lots of white teeth. For the life of her, Stan couldn't figure out how a kid like Perry Puck had ended up working on an organic farm in Frog Ledge instead of modeling for *GQ*. He was model material, with his perfectly mussed blond hair that fell strategically over one sea-foam green eye. The physical labor he did at the farm complemented a body that clearly spent many hours at the gym. He had a way of looking at women that was designed to make them giggle or blush, regardless of age.

Despite all this, Perry had a serious girlfriend — Brenna's best friend, Andrea, who was used to his flirty behavior.

According to Brenna, Andrea wasn't bothered by it.

"Morning," Brenna said, glancing up from where she chopped veggies with a particularly sharp-looking knife from Stan's new set. Perry pretended to cringe as he passed her, eyeing the knife dubiously.

"Keep moving!" Wallace Ames, the senior farmer, commanded when Perry lingered a moment grinning at Stan.

"Sure boss. Moving." Perry winked at Stan and obeyed.

Wallace came in behind him, shaking his head. "Mornin' Miss Connor. Sorry about that."

Stan laughed. "No need to apologize, Wallace." She glanced over to where Perry dropped the first box on the counter next to Brenna and began unpacking the first load. Brenna giggled at something Perry said.

"He's harmless," Stan assured Wallace.

"Mmm-hmm." Wallace didn't sound convinced. He sounded annoyed. Stan knew that Wallace thought his younger coworker wasn't serious about anything except fun. Wallace, on the other hand, was a serious farmer, second in command at the farm. He had a strong commitment to organic farming and was proud of the quality goods they sold. "Where would you like this? It's your turkey order."

"Perfect. You can drop it on the counter over there. I have to freeze some of it." She glanced at the list Wallace had handed her. "So, Perry has the beef, and do I have some veggies too?"

"Coming right up," Perry called. "I have to get them from the truck." He patted Brenna's shoulder on his way out. "Anything else you need, boss?" he asked Wallace. Despite Wallace's obvious contempt for him, Perry seemed to take it all in stride.

Wallace shook his head. "No, but hurry up. We have three more deliveries that need to get to where they're going by eleven."

"You got it." Perry hurried outside.

"I'm sorry to tell you I could only bring half your beef order," Wallace said. "Okay to get the rest to you early next week?"

"That's totally fine," Stan said. "I was going to freeze some of it anyway. So, you're busy then, huh?"

"Yes ma'am," Wallace said. "We're busier than we've ever been. Got lots of new customers on the schedule this year, and Roger is planning on hiring more staff for the barn. Rumor has it he's planning to open six days a week now, 'stead of four."

Roger Tate owned the farm and ran a

small market out of the main barn. Which must be doing pretty well if he was planning to be open six days.

"That's great news," Stan said. "Job security, right?"

Farming, while still one of the main occupations on the eastern side of Connecticut, was much more challenging today than in the past. With today's organic standards, heavy-handed federal and state oversight, and fewer people interested in the grueling hours, farmers definitely had their work cut out for them. The ones who were still in it were die-hards. Stan had gotten quite the education since moving to Frog Ledge, including a stint helping at one of the neighboring dairy farms last year. She had nothing but respect for the farmers — especially the ones producing healthy, organic products.

"Guess so," Wallace said. "Want me to unload this one?"

"No, it's okay. We'll take care of it," Stan assured him as Perry staggered back in under the bulk of two more filled-to-the-brim boxes of veggies. "My goodness, these carrots are huge!" She pulled a bunch out of the top of the box and waved them at Brenna. "Sorry. Veggies excite me," she said to Perry, who was watching her with an amused look on his face.

"Hey, everyone's got their thing." Perry deposited the boxes and turned to Wallace. "Ready to go?"

"Yup. Miss Connor, can you sign please?" Wallace handed her the delivery slip. "Oh, and can the dogs have a treat?"

"Of course." Stan scrawled her name and handed the slip back to him while Wallace fed Scruffy and Henry a couple treats from his pocket. She watched curiously as Perry went over and whispered something to Brenna. She nodded furtively, clearly not wanting to discuss whatever he was saying in front of anyone.

"Have a good day, ladies," Wallace said. "Come on, Romeo." He walked out the back door, letting it slam behind him before Perry could grab it.

"What was that about?" Stan asked Brenna after they'd gone.

"What?" Brenna asked.

"You and Perry. Whispering."

"Nothing," she said, a bit defensively, Stan thought. "He's asking for my help picking out a present for Andrea. It's their six-month anniversary next week."

"I see. How does Perry like this job? It doesn't really seem like . . . his cup of tea."

Brenna shrugged. "He needs the money

for school. And he likes it well enough, Andrea says. He likes any kind of physical work. And he doesn't mind getting dirty. I think he wishes the other guys were nicer to him, though. They kind of treat him like an outsider because he doesn't fit the farmer ideal."

"That's too bad." Stan knew what it was like to feel like an outsider, thanks to her former life in the corporate world. Although by all appearances she'd fit the mold, she'd never really felt like she belonged. Which was a good thing, she realized later, because it wasn't the kind of world she wanted to stay in. "Wallace doesn't seem to have a lot of patience for him."

"No. It's kind of mean, I think," Brenna said. "But what can you do? I guess Perry can fight his own battles. He's survived it so far."

CHAPTER SIX

The morning flew by from there. By the time Stan and Brenna unpacked and sorted all the meat and veggies and got some trays of fresh treats in the oven, it was time to open. Henry and Scruffy took command of the front door, greeting their neighborhood friends and begging for extra treats from anyone who was willing to provide them. A constant stream of neighborhood dogs, as well as some unfamiliar faces passing through town whose pet parents had heard about the patisserie, kept them busy, and by the time they closed the doors at five Stan had barely stopped all day. She sank down into one of the chairs in the café area after Brenna locked the door, desperately wishing for a cup of coffee, then remembered she and Brenna were "going out for a drink."

Stan wondered where they would take her. She wasn't dressed for this at all, but maybe

Brenna would let her change when they stopped by her house to drop off the dogs.

"Want to split this?" Brenna appeared with one of Izzy's muffins that was left over from the day's delivery. Izzy supplied Stan with coffee and human pastries so the pet parents could enjoy treats with their dogs. "That way we'll have energy for going out."

"Sure." Stan accepted half the muffin.

Brenna's phone dinged. She glanced at it, then set her muffin down on the table and hurried out back. "Be right out," she said, closing the door to the kitchen behind her.

Stan frowned. Whatever she was doing back there was noisy. She heard banging and a muffled curse, then a giggle. "You okay?" Stan called, getting up from her chair.

"Fine!" Brenna called back. "I'm good. Stay where you are. I'll be right there."

What on earth was she up to? Stan sighed and settled back in her chair, figuring she'd play along. She gave Scruffy and Henry each a treat. "You guys ready to go home soon?" she asked.

Scruffy wagged. Henry gazed at her from his spot on one of the beds. Nothing much excited Henry. Except food. Henry was sweet, gentle, and extremely loyal — completely opposite from the vicious dogs that pit bull critics portrayed. He'd saved Stan's life when she first met him, so of course she had to adopt him from the town pound.

Stan glanced around, impatient now. What was Brenna doing back there? Stan grabbed her own phone and texted Nikki: *Can we get this over with already??*

Nikki's reply was a laughing emoji. *Stand by.*

"Ugh. Standing already," Stan muttered. She got up to collect the dogs' leashes so when Brenna returned they could head out.

But then Brenna came out of the kitchen, smiling like the cat who'd eaten the canary.

"What's going on? You almost ready? I think I'm getting old. I'm kind of tired," Stan said. "If we don't go soon I might fall asleep on you."

"Why don't you go drop the dogs off? I forgot to clean up the last of the baking mess," Brenna said apologetically. "That way we don't have a mess tomorrow. I'll be quick, and then you can come back here and pick me up? Or we can take my car if you're tired." She ushered Stan toward the front door, herding the dogs with her before Stan had a chance to disagree.

"Should I change?" Stan asked.

"Maybe jeans," Brenna said, surveying Stan's brand-new polka-dotted sundress, a consolation prize for having to endure her sister's torture. "It might get chilly tonight. Be back in half an hour? That'll give me plenty of time to put the kitchen in order."

Stan agreed and drove home. She got the dogs settled, fed everyone dinner, and went upstairs to change and freshen up. What she really wanted to do was put her pajamas on and sit on the couch, but that was not an option.

Tomorrow night. No matter what, she promised herself.

She called Jake. "Just reminding you I'll be out on the town tonight," she said when he answered.

"How could I forget about the big night?" he asked.

She could hear the smile in his voice as well as the clink of glasses. She pictured him with the cell phone crooked between his ear and shoulder, flipping glasses as he removed them from the dishwasher and slid them back into their overhead rack.

"I'm kind of exhausted," Stan said. "I wish you and I were snuggling on the couch together."

"We can do that when we both get home," Jake promised. "It's a crazy night here anyway. I gotta run, babe. You have fun, okay? I love you."

"Love you too," Stan said. He disconnected. She changed into a pair of jeans, a sweater, and her black boots, ran a brush through her long blond hair, and freshened her makeup. That was as good as it was going to get tonight.

Stan headed for the door. "See you guys soon," she promised her four-legged friends, then hurried out to her car.

When she arrived at the shop, it was dark. She frowned. *Weird.* Unless Brenna was waiting out back. She put the car in park and texted her.

Brenna texted back: *Come in, almost done. I locked up the back, but the front is open.*

Stan gazed at the shop, dark except for the hall light, and wished Brenna would just come outside so they could go. But she was only prolonging the inevitable. She got out of the car and headed for the door.

When Stan pushed the door open, the lights came on. She stood still for a moment, blinking at the brightness, trying to comprehend the crowd of people crammed into her shop. More than half the town seemed to be packed in there. She had to hand it to Caitlyn — she still had the element of surprise. No way did Stan expect everyone to show up at her shop. She figured they'd rented a bar or something so

44

they could really get rowdy.

But no, they were all here. And in the time she'd been gone, they'd decorated. Streamers and balloons and glittery tablecloths decorated the shop, making it hard to remember that it was a pet patisserie. Two long tables lined the side wall, crammed with food. The doggie seating area had turned into a makeshift bar that appeared to have every kind of liquor anyone could possibly want.

"Surprise!" everyone chorused.

Nikki and Caitlyn were right in front. They ran up and hugged Stan. Char Mackey, one of Stan's first friends in town, was right behind them, tugging Stan's mother along. Char and her husband Ray ran the Alpaca Haven Bed & Breakfast down the street from Stan's house. They took turns hugging her and passing her off: Betty Meany, and Lorinda, who also worked at the library, waited for their turns. Miss Viv, Jake's uncle Seamus's longtime companion. Jake's mother. Stan's friend and neighbor Amara Leonard. Mona Galveston, the town's former mayor. Abby from the general store. Even Brenna's best friend Andrea, Perry Puck's girlfriend. Jake's other sister, Sergeant Jessie Pasquale of the Connecticut State Police, looked about as thrilled as Stan to be part of this. Izzy had Jessie's wrist clamped firmly in her hand, probably so she didn't bolt. Still, she gave Stan a big hug when it was her turn.

"Welcome to the madness," Jessie said with a wry grin. "Try to keep it low-key. I really don't want to arrest anyone tonight."

Stan laughed. Her mother approached and gave her an extra squeeze. "I'm so happy for you, honey," she sang. "We're going to have such a good time putting on this wedding!" Patricia Connor nodded approvingly as everyone clapped and cheered.

We. Stan tried not to grimace. So much to be thankful for, she reminded herself. Including the fact that she actually had a relationship with her mother now — something she hadn't thought possible only a year ago. "Thanks, Mom."

"So, what do you think?" Caitlyn asked, as everyone broke into little groups and began chatting among themselves. "Since you were giving me such a hard time about going to a bachelorette party, I figured we'd bring the party to you."

"Clever," Stan acknowledged. "Thanks for this, Caitlyn. It's amazing." Maybe she'd underestimated her sister. What better place to have the party than in her own shop?

"It wasn't just me," Caitlyn said modestly.

"Izzy was in charge of the food, and Nikki and Brenna helped a lot."

Izzy marched over. "Go eat," she urged. "People are waiting for you to start the food line."

"I will. Wow, Izzy. That's a lot of food!"

"Char and I made it with a team of helpers," Izzy said proudly. "So many people pitched in. Jake's mom, too," she said.

Stan caught Jake's mother's eye across the crowd and blew her a kiss. "You guys are all so awesome," she said.

"You might change your mind about that later," Nikki said softly in her ear, but she winked as she pulled away.

Stan didn't ask what that meant. She wanted to enjoy her food and a couple of drinks first.

CHAPTER SEVEN

It wasn't long before the party was in full swing. Brenna happily took over as bartender, which she'd been doing at McSwigg's for Jake since she finished college. Andrea and her roommate Marcy clustered around the bar with Brenna. Marcy looked out of place, but she was trying to make the best of it. She was a short, chubby girl with a round, freckled face and frizzy red hair. She looked too young to be out of college, Stan thought.

"So, you guys made sure Jake was in on this too, huh? I'm guessing he supplied the booze?" Stan asked Caitlyn as she loaded up a plate with Char's famous seafood gumbo. Char was originally from New Orleans, but then she met and fell in love with Ray and decided to give up her warm, fatty-food-filled life to become a New Englander. Although she'd managed to bring quite a bit of her old way of life —

and food — with her. It was one of the trademarks of the B&B. People came from all over for three things: Char's southern hospitality, the alpacas that lived on the property, and the food. Not necessarily in that order.

"Jeez, this was a real town project," Stan said.

"Of course, sugar," Char said. "Jake's got the best booze in town! Also, he loves you and wanted you to have a fabulous time. And, he had an in with the police to make sure we had the permits to do this here." She winked.

"And something like this, the whole town has to know about," Caitlyn chimed in, throwing her arm around Stan's shoulders. "You should know that better than anyone, since you're such a small-town lover now."

"You seem to be loving this small town just as much as I do," Stan said. "Which I have to admit, I never would've believed if anyone told me."

"I'm full of surprises," Caitlyn said.

"Sure are. So. Is this . . . everything?"

Caitlyn smiled. "More or less. Have another drink."

Stan did, and sampled the food while she circulated around the room to chat with everyone. She had to admit, it was lovely to have the party in her shop. Another happy memory for this place.

"Having fun?" Jessie slid into the chair across from Stan that Brenna had just vacated. It was the first chance Stan had gotten to really talk to her other future sister-in-law.

"I am. Thank you for coming," Stan said. "I know you probably like these things even less than I do."

Jessie grinned. "Surprisingly, it's something we have in common. I definitely would've pegged you as into all this."

Stan raised her glass to touch Jessie's — full of sparkling water. She never drank. "Nice to know I've been able to change your opinion about me."

When Stan came to town, she and Jessie hadn't exactly hit it off. It had taken Jessie a while to trust Stan, especially when she and Jake got involved. Jessie wasn't much for "outsiders," and she'd been convinced Stan was going to head back to her other life once the small-town thing got old and break her brother's heart.

But over the past year they'd gone from reaching an uneasy truce to becoming friends. Which was nice, given they were going to be part of the same family soon.

"So, what do you think? Can we sneak

out?" Stan asked, only half kidding.

Jessie sighed. "Don't I wish. No offense," she added hastily.

"None taken. Believe me."

Nikki came over and leaned down, slinging an arm across Stan's shoulder. "Need a refill?" She pointed to Stan's half-full glass.

Stan glanced at it. "I don't know, do I?"

"You might." Nikki nodded down the hall, where the kitchen door had opened and Izzy and Caitlyn came out, pushing a giant cart. With a giant cake. Definitely a Caitlyn cake, with giant pink and white tiers. And it was clearly fake. Which could only mean one thing.

"Oh, man." Stan covered her face with her hands. "I knew it was too good to be true. She couldn't resist."

Someone had turned the music loud, and "Uptown Funk" reverberated through the store. Everyone cheered as Izzy and Caitlyn rolled the cake in, doing a few dance moves along the way, and came to a stop right in front of Stan. Even Patricia cheered and hooted, which Stan thought was the weirdest thing ever.

"All right! Time for the main event," Caitlyn called, clapping her hands. The music cranked louder, and she rapped on the side of the "cake."

51

Stan held her breath. All eyes were riveted on the cake.

Nothing happened.

Caitlyn and Izzy looked at each other, Caitlyn raising her eyebrows in a question. Izzy shrugged, wide-eyed.

Stan glanced at Nikki. "What's going on? Should we, uh, cut the cake? Is it really a cake? I thought it was fake."

Without answering, Nikki rose and went over to confer with Caitlyn. The clapping had faltered, but the music still pumped through the room.

From across the room, Char yelled, "What's the holdup, honey?"

As the crowd egged her on, she marched over and yanked the top off the cake. "Listen, mister. Get your act together and get out here!" When she got no response, she frowned, then peered inside . . . and gasped, jumping back so fast she nearly overturned the chair behind her, her hands flying up to cover her mouth. The look on her face was not good.

That's when Stan saw it. Just the slightest bit of red, seeping out of the edges of the fake cake. She squinted, trying to figure out what it was, hoping she was seeing things. Her gut telling her she wasn't.

"What the heck?" Caitlyn demanded,

making a move toward the cake, but Nikki grabbed her arm and held her back.

Jessie was up from her chair and heading for the cart, Stan close on her heels. "Shut that music off," Jessie commanded, and the room went silent except for a low murmur traveling through the group as everyone tried to figure out what was going on.

"Just wait," Jessie said to Stan, but Stan ignored her and they reached the cake in tandem. Stan had no idea what to expect, but when she looked inside her stomach clenched, and she wished she hadn't eaten all that rich food. The first thing she saw was blood. A lot of it. And a knife, jammed inside a folded-over body. Even though his face was partially obscured because of the awkward position, Stan recognized the shock of blond hair and the chiseled, perfect face.

Perry Puck. Her farm delivery guy. Stabbed to death inside her bachelorette cake, wearing only a pair of red satin underwear.

CHAPTER EIGHT

Stan lifted her head, her gaze meeting Jessie's. She could read the expression on her soon-to-be-sister-in-law's face. A combination of *you've seriously got to be kidding me,* and *I need to take over and get this crime scene secured.*

Andrea jumped to her feet, pushing through the crowd. "What's wrong? What's wrong with Perry?"

"Andrea. Please stand back," Jessie instructed, immediately going into cop mode and using her body to blockade the cake. "Stan, do you know this guy?" she asked in a low voice. "Does she mean Perry as in her boyfriend?"

Stan nodded, unable to find the words.

"What happened?" Caitlyn gasped, trying to see around them. Behind the bar, Brenna seemed rooted to the ground, her face ashen, not speaking. The room turned into chaos as everyone tried to figure out what was happening, shoving at each other to get closer to the action.

Jessie started barking orders as she pulled her cell phone out of the pocket of her jeans. "I need you all to stay put. And stand back from my crime scene. No one leaves. Got it?" She turned away and spoke into her phone. "Lou. I need a team out at Stan's shop. And I need the medical examiner."

Andrea started to wail, desperately trying to push past the people in her way to get to the cake, to her boyfriend. Nikki, always cool, calm, and collected under pressure, expertly stepped in front of her. She took Andrea's arm and brought her over to the bar, where Brenna jumped into action and came out to console her friend. Marcy looked like she was about to lose it too. Stan hoped Brenna could keep it together.

Stan stepped away from the cake and backed up against the wall. Perry Puck. The dynamic, flirty farmhand who'd always seemed in such good spirits even when his coworkers were giving him guff. What on earth was he doing stripping for her party, first, and how had he ended up stabbed in her cake?

Stan's mother rushed to her side. "My goodness, Kristan, what's happened? Who's in that cake?"

Stan shook her head, barely able to speak. "The person they hired as a stripper."

"What happened to him?"

Stan shook her head, unable to answer. She knew if Jessie heard her she'd freak out. The rest of the room, already anticipating bad news, fell completely silent. Then Emmalee Hoffman burst into tears.

All eyes turned toward her. Betty went over and hugged her. "Emmy, shh," she said. "It's going to be okay."

"That's — that's Perry in that cake," Emmalee wailed. "He's Tyler's friend!"

"You knew him too?" Stan asked.

Emmalee nodded miserably. "He worked for me for a while. And he's been friends with Tyler most of his life." She drew in a shuddering breath. "Is he . . ."

Before she could finish her question, the sound of sirens outside drew everyone's attention as two state police cars pulled up. Trooper Lou Sturgis climbed out of the first one, followed by a cop Stan didn't recognize. Lou yanked open the door to the shop. Stan could see Trooper Garrett Colby, the town's K9 handler, get out of the other car.

Jessie moved through the crowd to Lou, pulled him aside, and started giving instructions. Stan could see her motioning toward the back of the shop. The second cop from

Lou's car followed her hand gestures and disappeared around the back. The rest of them came inside. Lou followed Jessie to the cake, peered inside, then winced.

"Ouch," he said. "Helluva way to go."

"I don't need the commentary," Jessie muttered. "Just take photos. Let's get everyone organized outside so you can start talking to them." She looked around for Caitlyn and motioned her to come over.

Stan saw her sister's hands were shaking. Her face was ashen and she looked like she no longer thought bachelorette parties were a good idea. Jessie dragged her partway down the hall so they were out of earshot. Stan crept a little closer so she could hear.

"Did you hire this man?" Jessie asked.

Caitlyn nodded.

"How did you find him?"

It took her a minute to find her voice. "Brenna told me to use him," she said. "She's friends with his girlfriend." Caitlyn's eyes drifted to Nikki and Andrea in the corner and she winced. "She knew he was working a side gig and she said he'd be perfect."

"When did you last see him alive?"

"About an hour ago. Brenna and I let him in, showed him the cake and let him get ready, then came out here to eat and make sure everything was rolling along. I told him we'd be back soon, to be ready."

"So, when you went back to get the cake, did you notice anything wrong?"

Caitlyn shook her head. "We just figured he was in the cake, as planned. I think Izzy said something, but he didn't reply. We — didn't think anything of it." She looked devastated.

"Did anything look out of place back in the kitchen? Could you tell if anyone had come in? Was the door locked?"

Caitlyn thought. "I don't know if the door was locked. I didn't stop to look around, but nothing looked out of place. It didn't look like there'd been a struggle or anything. I don't know." She bent her head, but not before Stan could see tears brimming in her eyes.

"Why don't you go outside," Jessie said to her. "Stan, you too. I need to show the ME's guys in." She nodded to the door, where a van had just pulled up, followed by an ambulance. The medical examiner's office, who would whisk the body away. Out of the shop, thank goodness.

Stan shuddered. She couldn't believe that this had happened in her happy place. How would she ever come into the patisserie again and not remember this? How would the rest of the town?

CHAPTER NINE

Stan stood near the shop door, trying to keep an eye on what was going on inside. Jessie and Colby had disappeared out back to take photos and gather evidence. It was an official crime scene given that was where Perry had been killed.

Trooper Lou and the new cop she'd never seen before systematically worked through the guests, speaking to everyone before letting them leave. They had their work cut out for them, trying to keep people from speculating and making sure they got to everyone. She knew for legal purposes they had to get everyone's contact information, even though it seemed redundant since Jessie knew everyone in the shop.

A few minutes later, Jessie came outside. She still wore her party clothes — which meant jeans and a jacket — but she looked every ounce the cop. A total switch from just a few hours ago. It always amazed Stan how Jessie could extract herself from a seemingly normal situation full of people close to her, especially one that she'd been a part of, and become so detached and businesslike so quickly.

It was what made her good at her job, Stan figured.

Now Jessie grimly faced the crowd of partygoers, all anxiously awaiting what came next. "Okay, people," she said. "I'm sorry to say the victim appears to be Perry Puck. I know a few of you knew Perry. When was the last time anyone here saw him?"

Emmalee Hoffman looked around, clearly not wanting to be the first to speak, then cleared her throat and stepped forward. "I saw him last weekend. He and Tyler were going out and he came over to pick him up."

Jessie nodded. "Did you see him tonight?"

Emmalee shook her head no.

"Anyone see him tonight? Before the cake?" Jessie asked. "Aside from Caitlyn and Brenna?"

More head shaking.

"He was here this morning," Stan said. "Doing the farm delivery with Wallace Ames."

"What time was that?"

Stan thought back. "Had to be around eight."

"And no one saw him since then?"

Silence.

Jessie blew out a breath in frustration. "Anyone know how to get in touch with his family?"

"I do."

Stan glanced up in surprise as her mother stepped forward, scrolling through her cell phone. "I'm friendly with Gabrielle. His mother." She recited a number that Jessie scrawled in her notebook. "But they're out of town," Patricia added. "There was a meeting this week she couldn't attend because of her trip."

"You're right. They aren't home. And I don't think they would care anyway."

Stan turned to see Andrea standing behind them, face streaked with tears, arms crossed against her chest. "You'll have to ask Sydney. I already called her. She's on her way," Andrea added.

Jessie approached her, not wanting the whole town to hear the conversation. "What do you mean they won't care? And who's Sydney? What do you mean you called her?" Stan could see the red creeping up Jessie's neck. The last thing she would've done would be to invite more people to the crime scene.

"His sister. She and her husband Jason

live in town. Her married name is De-Roche. But his parents — they won't care because they were really m-mean to him." Andrea's voice quavered as the tears threatened to start up again.

"Define mean." Jessie's tone left no room for nonsense. Stan felt the hair on the back of her neck stand up.

"Just what I said. Mean. They treated him like crap because he didn't do what they wanted."

Stan watched Jessie's face as she processed and filed that information in her mental filing cabinet. "Colby. Find the parents' address and go out there anyway."

Colby nodded and headed for his police car.

Stan looked at her mother. "You know the Pucks?"

Patricia nodded. "I met Gabrielle at a charity event a few months back. She's been a lovely friend. I feel terrible for her." She pursed her lips together. "Perry was supposed to take over the family business. They had high hopes for him."

"Family business? What was it?" Stan was surprised. If Perry had a cushy family job, why was he hauling around beef and stripping at small-town bachelorette parties?

"The Pucks own Greenery," Patricia said.

"The organic markets."

"Get out!" Stan loved Greenery. There was one near the dress shop she'd visited a couple weeks ago. She'd stopped in for lunch. That was the closest, and it was about an hour outside of Frog Ledge. She knew they had a larger presence out in Fairfield County, the richer area of the state on the New York side. "So why —"

"That's not really a conversation for today, dear," Patricia murmured.

But it had to be, didn't it? Greenery was a very upscale chain. Stan was willing to bet there was money to be made there. And given that Patricia and Gabrielle Puck had bonded, there had to be a level playing field status-wise. Char was the only person Patricia considered a friend who didn't come from old money — a lot of it. So, the question of why Perry Puck was trying to make extra money jumping out of cakes in his underwear was sure to come up in Jessie's investigation.

Rivers and Menoso, from the medical examiner's office, arrived and unloaded their stretcher. Trooper Lou excused himself from his interview and went to open the door for them.

"Hate to tell ya, but the body's in the cake," he said, pointing.

"You've gotta be kidding," said Rivers, peering inside.

"Man, nothing like this ever happened at the bachelorette parties I've been to," said Menoso, hands on ample hips. She had thick black hair and a lilting Spanish accent.

Rivers shook his head. "Let's get this done." He looked like he'd rather cut off his own arm than try to wrestle the body out of that cake.

Stan didn't blame him.

It took about a half hour before they had finished extricating the body and taking photos. They wheeled Perry's covered body out of the shop just as Jake and Scott, Brenna's boyfriend, arrived.

Jake zeroed in on Stan and went to her. He pulled her tight against him. "Aww, babe," he said softly against her ear. "I'm so sorry. Are you okay?"

"I'm fine," she said, but even as the words left her mouth she started to cry, grateful he was there so she could have a minute to fall apart.

Jake led her to his truck and opened the passenger door so she could sit. He stood next to her, still holding on to her hand.

"What happened?" he asked. "Or do I even want to know? I've heard bits and pieces from the town criers already."

"I have no idea," Stan said miserably. "Everything was going fine. We were just hanging out and eating. Then the stupid cake came out and all hell broke loose. I knew this stripper stuff was a bad idea! Why doesn't anyone listen to me? And why on earth was my farm delivery guy stripping for me? Good Lord, that would've been awkward come tomorrow."

Jessie came outside again, holding a plastic bag. She spotted Stan and Jake and walked over to them. Stan swallowed back the bile that rose in her throat as she comprehended the bag's contents. There were still traces of blood on the knife in the bag.

"Sorry," Jessie said. "But I need to know if you recognize this."

Stan turned away. It wasn't hard to identify the knife that had been on her counter earlier today. The one Brenna had used earlier to chop carrots and then later, to cut the freshly delivered beef into chunks for freezing. Wordlessly, Stan nodded.

"It's yours, then? From the kitchen?" Jessie pressed.

"Yes."

"Okay. Thanks." She started to walk away, then turned back. "You know we're going to have to close you up for at least tomorrow."

"I know. Honestly, I don't want to be back here tomorrow." Which made her feel worse. The tears filled her eyes again and this time they spilled over.

Jake pressed her head down onto his shoulder. "Do you still need her?" he asked Jessie quietly. "I'd like to take her home."

"Yeah, you can go. Can you talk to Brenna before you go? She's pretty shaken up, and I know she wants to wait for Andrea before she leaves."

"Yeah, this guy was her friend, wasn't he?" Jake sighed and rubbed a hand over his face. "This is crazy."

"Yeah. I remember when this town was quiet. And boring. I used to wonder if I should get a more exciting job. I should've just kept my mouth shut," Jessie said.

CHAPTER TEN

Before Jake could talk to Brenna, a sleek, black BMW X4 that looked brand new zoomed up to the front of the shop. Sydney Puck DeRoche and her husband Jason, Stan presumed.

Sydney was out of the car almost before it stopped, racing to the door, no small feat in her heels. Since Jessie had gone back inside, Stan got out of the truck and went over to Sydney. Before Stan reached her, Andrea saw her and came over.

"Sydney. I'm sorry to call you like that, but I wasn't sure what else —"

"Andrea!" Sydney wailed, flinging herself at Andrea, who looked a bit surprised, but she went with it, awkwardly patting Sydney's back as she sobbed.

Stan hung back a bit, not wanting to intrude. Jason stood there awkwardly, shellshocked. He looked like his life had just been upended and he didn't know how to handle it.

They must have come from somewhere fancy. Jason wore a suit and tie, and Sydney a little black dress. Stan had seen him before. She couldn't quite place him — people met during traumatic moments always looked out of place in a normal environment, she thought — but he looked familiar.

Stan stepped over to Jason. "Hi. I'm Stan. I own the shop."

He nodded. "Jason DeRoche. I bring our dog in every Saturday. He's a boxer named Charlie."

"That's right! I knew you looked familiar," she said. "Forgive me. I do know Charlie. He likes peanut butter treats best."

"Wow," Jason said. "That's pretty good that you remember that sort of thing."

Stan shrugged. "It's my job. Clearly I'm better at remembering dogs than people." She hesitated in the awkward pause that followed. "I'm so sorry for your loss," she said quietly. "It's shocking."

"Thank you," Jason said, his face falling back to shell-shocked. "I don't quite know what to do. My wife is devastated." They both looked over at Sydney, who still clung to Andrea like she was drowning.

Sydney looked . . . expensive. Her chin-length amber-colored hair had a slightly disheveled look that Stan knew cost a couple hundred dollars at a top salon. Her simple black dress was not cheap, and her heels were Manolos.

At first glance, Sydney was totally different from Perry. Granted, Stan had only seen Perry in the dirty jeans and work boots he wore for his farm job, but she still had trouble picturing him and his sister sitting at a fancy dinner table together.

"Excuse me," Jason said to Stan. He walked over to his wife and tried to comfort her, but she seemed to barely notice he was there.

"Are you sure?" Sydney kept repeating, her words barely understandable. Andrea nodded miserably.

Jessie, who'd seen the new arrivals and came outside, walked over to them. "Mrs. DeRoche? I'm Sergeant Pasquale with the Connecticut State Police."

Sydney stepped back and looked Jessie up and down, swiping at her eyes. "You are? Where's your hat?"

"My . . . I'm out of uniform because I was attending the party," Jessie said impatiently. "Let's go over here to talk." She pulled Sydney over to one of the police cars, opened the passenger door, and offered her a seat. Sydney shook her head.

Stan couldn't hear what Jessie was saying, but she presumed Jessie was asking about Sydney's parents and giving her the bad news. Especially when Sydney started sobbing again, big snuffling cries. "How can my brother be dead?" she wailed, loud enough for the whole parking lot to hear.

Jason paled and looked at Stan. "Did she say . . ."

"I don't think I'm supposed to —" Stan began, but Sydney had wrenched herself away from Jessie and ran over to them.

"Jason. I need to go to the hospital where they took my brother. I need to see him." She grabbed his arm and pulled. "Now! Andrea, will you come? Please?"

All heads turned toward Andrea, who was holding onto Marcy's arm seemingly for dear life. Brenna hovered nearby also, looking worried. Andrea's face went white.

Jessie was about to protest, then thought better of it. Stan wondered if she had more questions for Andrea, with whom she'd already spent a lot of time, or if she wanted to talk to Sydney more.

"I . . . I guess so," Andrea said, looking at her friends to save her. But Marcy, for one, looked just as shell-shocked as she did.

"I need to see him," Sydney kept repeat-

71

ing as Jason led her over to their car. He tucked her into the front seat, opened the back door for a reluctant Andrea, and climbed into the driver's seat. Then the fancy car zoomed out of the lot.

CHAPTER ELEVEN

Stan looked at Jessie. "So what next?"

"We've got more to do here. Why don't you all clear out? I'll be in touch about when you can open again. Stan, I'll need a key."

"Shoot. My bag is still inside. Behind the counter."

"I'll get it." Jessie disappeared inside.

Stan looked around at her small circle of remaining friends, all waiting anxiously. "You guys should go. Seriously. We're going home." She looked at Jake, who nodded. "Nik, you're staying the night, right?"

"Of course she's staying," Jake said. "She's not driving all the way back to Rhode Island tonight."

"I guess it's decided, then," Nikki said. "As long as I'm not in the way."

"Never. Brenna's coming back with us too." Stan glanced at Jake's little sister, who looked like she was still in terrible shock.

Scott had his arm around her waist.

Jessie came out with Stan's bag. Stan fished inside and found her keys, and took her shop key off the ring.

"Thanks. I'll get it back to you as soon as I can." Jessie pocketed the key and turned to go. Then she turned back. "Stan, I'm sorry this happened."

"Thanks, Jess," Stan said, blinking back tears. "Me too."

Char came over and grabbed Stan's hands. "Go home and get some rest. I'll see you tomorrow, honeybunch." Char pulled Stan against her enormous bosom. "You let me and Raymond know if you need anything tonight, you hear?"

"Thanks, Char." Stan extracted herself and turned to her mother and Izzy. "You guys go on. I'll talk to you both tomorrow too, okay?"

Izzy looked worried. "Call me if you need anything," she said. "I have no idea what else to say."

"That's plenty." Stan hugged her.

"I'm coming over," Patricia declared once Izzy and Char had left.

"Mom, it's okay. You should get home to Tony," Stan said. Her mother had married Tony Falco, Frog Ledge's mayor, a few months ago and they were still in their honeymoon phase.

"No, I'm coming." There was no arguing with Patricia when she was like this. She and Nikki headed to their cars, while Jake opened the door of his truck for Stan. Duncan and Gaston were in the back, heads hanging out of their respective windows, barking at passersby.

The night was quiet. The sky was clear and full of stars. She could hear shouts of laughter, dogs barking, and other small-town sounds in the distance. It was surreal to think of the tragedy that had occurred a few feet away.

"We'll be right behind you," Scott said.

Stan climbed back into the truck. She'd barely shut the door when she burst into tears, accompanied by noisy, gut-wrenching sobs. An ugly cry, her sister would call it. But she couldn't help it. Jake climbed in on the driver's side and hugged her, letting her get it all out while the dogs watched anxiously. When Stan finally ran out of tears, she wiped her face and leaned back.

"You know what the worst part is?" she asked.

"What?" Jake reluctantly let go and started the truck.

"I feel terrible about Perry. But I feel worse about my store. That's *my* store. That brings everyone so much joy. And it's been ruined. And I feel even worse that I'm thinking about that when someone is dead."

"Stan." Jake reached over and squeezed her hand. "It's perfectly normal to feel that way. It doesn't mean you're not thinking about Perry. And we'll get the store put back to rights. I promise."

Stan gazed out the window, watching the town pass slowly by as they drove the short distance to their house. "I know. But I feel like I need to *do* something, you know?" She looked at him. "I feel so violated."

"I know," Jake said quietly, pulling into the driveway. Scott and Brenna pulled up behind them.

Patricia and Nikki waited on the porch. Jake gathered the dogs while Stan unlocked the door and greeted Scruffy and Henry, who both waited anxiously. They felt left out, given that the other dogs were still out with their humans.

Everyone filed inside, Stan moving almost robotically, kicking off her shoes, dropping her purse, greeting the cats. Nutty immediately twined around her legs while Benny, her orange cat, bolted from the room when he saw all the people descending on the house. Benny was still pretty shy. He'd lived with an elderly lady before her death last year, and toward the end they hadn't had too many visitors. He was still getting used to people and dogs and all the other activity in their household.

"You guys want coffee?" Stan asked, leading them down the hall.

"Sure. I'll make it," Nikki offered. She busied herself at the coffeepot, choosing from Stan's vast selection and measuring the beans into the grinder.

Jake put the dogs out in the backyard and returned to the kitchen. He grabbed a couple of extra chairs from the dining area and set them around the kitchen table, which was smaller and cozier, and seemed the right place to be tonight. He ushered Brenna to a chair. She looked utterly lost. Scott sat down next to her.

"I have to call Andrea," Brenna said suddenly. "I bet she's not okay." She looked at Jake, her eyes wide and wet. "Do you think she's okay? I hope Sydney will take her home."

"Of course she will," Jake said. "Did Marcy drive her to the party? Or is her car still at the shop?"

"I don't know. They came late. I didn't even notice how Marcy left." Brenna exhaled. "I wasn't paying attention. Oh my God. Who would've done such a heinous, awful thing?"

Stan and Jake exchanged looks. Stan knew they were both thinking the same thing. If Andrea had come late, had she detoured into the kitchen first through the back door? Had she not been as laid back about her boyfriend's side gig as Brenna thought? It had probably been Jessie's first thought, too, which was maybe why she'd spoken to her for so long tonight.

Patricia spoke up. "I feel terrible for the family. What a tragedy. And I'm sure the circumstances will be difficult for them."

"By circumstances you mean he was stripping?" Stan asked.

Patricia nodded. "It's not exactly what most people hope for their children, is it?" she asked wryly.

"Mom. Why was Perry stripping and working at the Tates' farm if his parents own Greenery and he was supposed to run the business?" Stan asked.

All eyes swiveled toward Patricia.

"What's Greenery?" Nikki asked from the counter, hitting the button on the coffee maker.

Stan waited until the grinding ceased and silence settled over the room again. "It's a fancy organic market. A small chain here in Connecticut," she answered, still watching her mother.

"I don't know all the details, Kristan. I'm not that close with the family. We only just met a few months ago. But it was my understanding that Perry was . . . less serious about his future than his parents hoped. I think they were forcing him to take some responsibility outside the family business."

"So if they were forcing him to make money elsewhere, they can't really complain about how he made it, right?" Stan pointed out.

Patricia shrugged. "I'm sure they saw things differently. And I'm only guessing at most of this. But I would imagine they were practicing tough love. I'm not sure that's the route I would've gone with you girls had things been different, but each family has its own way of doing things. Not that we had a family business, but neither of you girls were expected to work a number of jobs to get through school. Of course, my biggest problem was your independent streak, Kristan. You never cared about family money."

Stan noticed she said this with an admiring tone rather than the derogatory one she may have used even just a year ago. They had come a long way in their relationship.

Jake noticed it too. He squeezed her hand.

"So this guy was on the outs with his family, then?" Nikki leaned against the counter, arms crossed, as the coffee sputtered and dripped into its pot behind her.

"I'm not sure he was on the outs. I simply think they laid down the law," Patricia said. "From what it sounded like, they hoped it would have more of an effect on him than it seemed to."

That fit with the Perry Puck Stan had come to know. The one who brushed off Wallace Ames's cutting remarks and continued to smile his way through the day. Carefree, happy-go-lucky.

And now, dead.

She felt sad for this boy — he was just a boy, really — and wondered who on earth would've been so angry with him that he or she could commit an act of violence on that level.

"Did you know all this, Bren?" Jake asked.

"Andrea told me some of it," Brenna said. "Perry and I were friends because of Andrea, but we didn't really get personal. I've hung out with them a few times, and when he started delivering to us from the farm it was nice to have that connection. He was a good guy." Her voice broke on the last word, and she rose from her seat. "I'm going to call Andrea." Brenna left the room.

Jake watched her go, the concern evident on his face. Scott got up to help Nikki bring mugs to the table for everyone. Nikki went to the fridge and got creamer and put out the bowl of raw sugar Stan kept for guests. Then she sat and looked at Stan.

"I'm so sorry this happened," she said. "I feel even worse because I know you didn't want the stupid party in the first place."

Stan shot her a warning look as Patricia's ears perked up. "What do you mean, you didn't want the party?" her mother asked.

Stan sighed. "Mom, it's fine. Not really the time to talk about all that, right?"

Patricia didn't look like she agreed — in her mind it was always time to talk about things like that — but she stayed respectfully quiet as Brenna returned to the room.

"I told Andrea she could come here for a while. I hope it's okay," Brenna said to her brother. "Sydney is going to drop her somewhere and she doesn't want to go home."

"Of course," Stan and Jake said in unison. Selfishly, Stan hoped they could get the girl talking and maybe get some clues about who could've done this.

"Thanks." Brenna slid back into her seat, squeezing Scott's hand. "So what happens now?"

81

"Well, the shop will be closed until they're sure they have found all the evidence." This made Stan sad too. She wouldn't even have work to keep her mind off this. Then again, she wasn't sure she could face being back in the shop just yet, so it was quite the catch-22. "Then Jessie will find out who did it." Stan hoped.

"That's right," Jake agreed. "She's on it. Jessie will figure it out."

"Was Sydney able to get ahold of her mother yet?" Patricia asked.

"I don't think so," Brenna said.

Patricia looked troubled. "That's an awful thing, as a parent," she said. "To not know something has happened to your child."

CHAPTER TWELVE

Patricia left a few minutes later, after Tony called to make sure she was okay. Stan thought it was sweet. "Tony's got to call Jessie and get the details," Patricia told Stan. "He wants to keep up with what's happening."

Sydney and Jason dropped Andrea off soon after Patricia left. Andrea was crying when Brenna led her into the kitchen. She looked terrible. Her eyes were red and swollen, and what was left of her makeup was smeared down her cheeks. Someone had given her a sweatshirt that was way too big for her, and it hung on her small frame like an ill-fitting dress. Nikki, who wasn't used to handling so many emotions, went back to the coffeepot and did what she knew how to do. She gave Andrea a mug.

"Andrea. We are so, so sorry," Stan said, hugging her. "Please let us know what you need." Stan handed Andrea off to Jake, who also wrapped her in a hug.

"You're all staying here with us tonight," he said with a stern look at his sister, leaving no room for argument. "You too, Andrea. We don't want you to be alone."

"Thank you." Andrea sniffled and wiped her face on Jake's shirt. "I need the police to find out who would do this," she said, her voice thick with tears. "Perry was a good guy. He didn't deserve this. He just wanted to live his life, and everyone was always *on* him!"

"What do you mean? Who was on him?" Stan asked, catching Jake's eye.

"Just . . . everyone. His stupid parents. The people he worked with at the farm. Even me, sometimes. I thought he worked too much. He had like, three jobs. And he went to school, and he took acting classes. He so wanted to be an actor. And a dancer. He would've gone to Broadway, you know. He was that good." She swallowed. "But he never complained about any of it." She sipped her coffee, her hands shaking as they lifted the mug.

"Acting classes? Wow," Stan said. "He was busy." The dancing, she figured, he practiced during those stripper gigs, but she didn't mention it. It still seemed like a touchy subject.

"Yeah. His parents made it hard for him. They have so much money, you know? And just because he didn't want to do what they said, they cut off his tuition payments. But he still felt like he had to go to school. He really wanted to do well. So he had to work these other jobs to pay for it." She made a face. "Jerks."

Just like Patricia had suggested, although she'd refrained from opining about their parenting methods. "That must have been stressful for him. I imagine he was resentful of them?" Stan asked.

Andrea shrugged. "I think I was more than he was. He thought they were ridiculous, but he didn't spend a lot of energy dwelling on it. He did his thing. He was happy. That's it. And someone took it all away." She started to cry again. "Who could do this? It's so vicious!"

She was right about that. Every act that took another person's life was hateful and vicious, but this one seemed even more so. Maybe the setting, and Stan's fondness for it, contributed to that feeling. But the thought of stabbing someone to death in a tiny, enclosed space where he couldn't fight back, and was likely not expecting it, was unconscionable. And scary. The thought that someone who could commit that kind of violence had just waltzed into her shop was unsettling, to say the least.

"How long was he doing this, um, particular side job?" Stan asked.

"The stripping? About three months." Her tone suggested she wasn't thrilled about it.

"Which company did he work for?" Jake asked.

"It's called Party Pleasers. Their office is just outside of town."

"Did he get along with everyone there?"

"I don't know. I didn't really ask him much about that job," Andrea admitted. "I don't think he really worked with anyone, you know? I think he just got sent out on jobs. I tried to be supportive, but, you know. It's kind of weird that your boyfriend is taking off his clothes for other women. No offense," she added hastily, remembering who she was talking to. "But now I feel bad for not asking him more about it. He really didn't have anyone to confide in a lot of the time. His life was so . . . compartmentalized." She shoved the mug away. "Can I lie down somewhere?"

There were so many things Stan wanted to ask her about that, but it wasn't the time. "Of course. Come on." Stan led her upstairs to the guest room, grateful she had two guest rooms, along with her couch downstairs. She had plenty of room for Nikki, Andrea, Brenna, and Scott. "Do you want some comfortable clothes that actually fit you? I have some sweats you're welcome to."

"Yes, please. Thank you so much." Stan found some clothes, which Andrea accepted gratefully, then she impulsively gave Stan a hug. "Thank you for being so nice to me. I'm sorry your party got ruined."

"Oh my gosh, please. Don't even think twice about that. I'm devastated this happened," Stan said. "Jessie will figure it out. I know it won't bring him back, but I know she'll get him justice." She gave Andrea a hug. "Get some sleep. I have a feeling the next few days are going to be long."

CHAPTER THIRTEEN

Stan went back downstairs and found Scott sitting alone in the kitchen. "Where is everyone?" she asked.

"They all went outside for a bit," Scott said, nodding toward the back. "The dogs wanted to play."

"Ah. You want more coffee?"

Scott shook his head. He looked troubled.

"Are you okay?" Stan asked.

"I don't know. It's surreal, right? Like, this doesn't happen in real life." He hesitated a minute, then said, "Stan. There's something . . ."

The doorbell rang and he trailed off.

"Go on," she said.

"No, get the door. We'll talk later." The back door slammed, and everyone started to troop back in, the dogs galloping into the room with the humans.

Stan hurried for the front door, her curiosity piqued. Scott looked like he'd been about to tell her something. Was it about Perry? Had he seen or heard something that could help them figure out who killed him? She flung the door open to find Izzy and Liam standing with trays of food in their hands.

"Hey," Izzy said, offering a wan smile. "Wanted to bring some food over for the next couple of days. I had extra made and waiting at the café in case people ate everything in sight tonight."

Stan felt her eyes burn with tears — a combination of the night's stress and exhaustion. And love for her friends and this town.

"You doing okay?" Liam asked. "Is Jake here?"

Stan nodded and held the door wide. "Everyone's here. You can go to the kitchen."

"I can't believe this happened," Izzy said in a low voice, trailing behind with Stan as Liam headed down the hall. "Does Jessie have any idea who did it?"

"I don't know. I'm sure she's got her theories. Perry's girlfriend is here. She's upstairs. God, I feel awful for her."

"I know. The whole town has heard about it already," Izzy said. "I got a call from my cashier at the bookstore. People have been in there yapping about it. I guess since the café is closed, they figure that's the next best place to gossip." She didn't seem to know whether to look disgusted or amused. After all, it was business. "And hey, so you know, Cyril is on it. He was getting reactions from people at the bookstore."

Cyril Pierce was the publisher, editor and writer of the *Frog Ledge Holler,* the town's newspaper. He was always on it. As long as it was happening in town. Izzy's new business venture, Frog Ledge's first bookstore, had filled the gap that existed when Izzy's café closed for the day. The bookstore was a place for people who weren't pub-goers to spend their evening. The bookstore was a partnership between Izzy and Jake, who had jumped in to invest when she was having trouble affording the building and completing the renovations last year.

"I wouldn't have expected anything less from Cyril," Stan said. "I'm sure he'll show up here before too long."

"I'm surprised he hasn't been here yet. Or to the Pucks, although he probably heard they were out of town," Izzy said.

"Do you know the Pucks?" Stan asked.

"Nope," Izzy said as they entered the kitchen. "I've seen the sister in the café, but never spoken to her. Hey there," she said with a nod to the rest of the group. "Brought some eats." She set the trays down on the table. "Figured you all might need some comfort food."

The thought of food made Stan's stomach turn, but Jake helped himself to some and passed the tray to Scott. Scott declined too, but Liam joined his cousin.

"Stan. Is the shop closed indefinitely?" Liam asked.

Stan nodded. "Jessie's going to let me know when they're finished." She covered her face with her hands. "What am I going to do for the next few days? I won't be able to get this off my mind, especially if we can't work."

"You guys can still bake, right?" Jake said. "You can bake here, or use the pub's ovens. Like the old days."

Stan considered this. "You're right. And we can do some deliveries. Treat deliveries, to cheer people up." She looked at Brenna. "You in, Bren?"

Brenna nodded. "Yeah. I'll need something to occupy my mind too. I can work extra shifts after we're done baking," she told Jake.

"We'll see how you feel," he said. "You both need to get some rest, not work yourselves into oblivion."

"I'll help with that. I'm going to stick around," Nikki added. She'd been quiet during most of the conversation. "If that's okay."

"You are? Of course it's okay! That makes me happy. What about the dogs?" Stan asked. "Can everyone get along without you?"

Nikki shrugged. "Justin is home." Nikki's boyfriend Justin was home from his latest diving expedition out in California, so was on dog duty. "He can hold down the fort with some volunteers for a few days. You'll need to keep your mind occupied. And we've got some wedding stuff to do. Besides, you might need a buffer when your mother refocuses her attention on the wedding," she added.

"We definitely have wedding stuff to do," Stan said, looking at Jake. "She's still pushing for a church ceremony."

"I know, babe. We'll figure it all out. Don't worry."

The doorbell rang again. Scruffy and Duncan, the official greeters, raced down the hall. Henry and Gaston stayed behind and barked. This was the routine.

"I'll get it." Jake rose and went down the hall. He returned a moment later with Jessie.

She took in the crowd in the kitchen and

winced a little. "Sorry to disturb. Can I talk to you two?" She motioned to Stan and Brenna.

Wordlessly, Stan rose and followed Jessie down the hall, Brenna trailing behind like she was in trouble. "What's going on?" Stan asked when they reached her little den, her favorite room in the house.

"There was no sign of forced entry into your kitchen. Did you guys leave the door unlocked?" Jessie looked at her sister.

Brenna nodded miserably. "Yeah. There was so much going on, and people were coming in and out. The people bringing in the food, Jake and Scott with the bar . . ."

"I need you to think. How much of that stuff had already been delivered by the time Perry arrived?" Jessie asked.

"Jake and Scott brought the bar stuff over right after Stan left to bring the dogs home, so that was before Perry came. The food was coming nonstop. A bunch of local people brought things, all before the party started. Izzy was in charge of that. She probably has the list of who was bringing what. And then the guests were supposed to be out of sight waiting for the signal once they'd dropped off the food."

"What time did Andrea get there? Did you notice?"

Stan had known this was coming. Jessie didn't even try to soften the question. Of course Andrea would be a suspect. Her boyfriend was the stripper. Most people wouldn't be okay with that, no matter how enlightened, or how open, their relationship was. Plus, she had opportunity as a party guest. One who knew the person running the kitchen, who wouldn't blink an eye at her coming and going.

"She's upstairs," Stan said quietly. "In case you want to keep your voice down."

"I really didn't notice what time," Brenna said, defensiveness creeping into her tone. She crossed her arms. "Why are you asking? Didn't you talk to her?"

Jessie exhaled. "I did talk to her. But I need to know if you saw anything different, Bren. Was she mad at Perry? Did they have a fight? How soon before he died did she see him?"

"Why, do you think I did it?" All three of them jumped at the voice that came from behind them. They all turned.

Andrea stood there. She didn't try to hide the dismay on her face at what she'd over-heard.

CHAPTER FOURTEEN

"Can you give me a few minutes with Andrea?" Jessie asked Stan and Brenna.

"Can I stay?" Brenna responded.

"Of course not. This is a criminal investigation," Jessie said.

Stan took Scruffy and slipped out, not wanting to be part of this argument. She went back to the group in the kitchen. Jake, Liam, and Scott talked quietly. Nikki was in the sunroom on the phone. Izzy was doing dishes.

"You don't have to do that," Stan said.

Izzy shrugged. "I feel like I need to do something. This is so unsettling."

"It really is. And it feels so . . . personal." Stan shivered and wrapped her arms around herself. "Not only for poor Perry, but since it was in my shop. I'm so sad about that. And then I feel bad that I'm thinking about that when Perry is . . ."

Izzy stopped what she was doing and gave

Stan a hug. "We'll get it back to normal. I promise."

"Hope so," Stan murmured. "And I hope they find who did this. Soon."

"Jessie thinks the girlfriend had something to do with it?" Izzy dropped her voice lower and went back to drying dishes.

"Sounds like," Stan said grimly. "Or at least she has to look into it seriously."

The doorbell rang again. Stan hurried down the hall and opened the front door. As she'd expected, Frog Ledge's quirky newspaperman stood there, wearing his signature black trench coat despite the spring weather, steno pad in hand, waiting for the breaking news.

He nodded at Stan. "Hi. I'm here on official newspaper business. May I come in?"

"You know we can't comment on the murder." Stan leaned against the door, blocking his way.

Cyril smiled a little. "No, but you can comment on how you feel about it." Cyril was relentless in his pursuit of the news, and he never apologized for it. Newsprint ran in his blood. His family had started the *Frog Ledge Holler* generations ago, and they had all been one hundred percent dedicated to it. Cyril took his duties as the captain of the ship very seriously, even more so because he was likely the last Pierce in line to run the show. Cyril was quirky and he didn't date much, so the chances of him continuing the family line seemed slim.

Not that he seemed concerned about that most days. Too busy reporting.

Stan stepped out on the porch and pulled the door shut behind her. "You can ask, but I don't have much to say. And then you have to go."

Cyril looked unfazed. He poised his pen over his steno pad. "Can I get a reaction from you on what happened at your party?"

Stan took a deep breath. "I'm shocked and deeply disturbed that this happened to such a vital, happy young man," she said. "And the fact that it happened in my place of business adds another layer of concern. It's hard to believe that evil like that could live in our town."

Cyril raised his eyebrows, nodding as he scribbled. "That's a good quote."

"I'm glad it works for you," Stan said dryly.

Cyril glanced at the cars in the driveway. "You've got a full house. Is our state's finest here? I'm having a hard time tracking her down."

"Cyril, please. This has been a crap night for everyone. I can't deal with this."

He sighed and put his steno pad away. "Fine. But you know those PR people at the department," he said with a knowing look at Stan. "They say a lot of nothing."

She smiled despite herself. She used to run PR for a financial corporation in her former life. "Hey, we spend a lot of time thinking up those words that mean nothing."

He turned to go, then turned back to her. "Did I tell you I'm writing a book?"

"A book?" Stan repeated. "No, you didn't."

Cyril nodded. "I'm writing a book about murders in small towns. I'm also giving a series of talks at Izzy's bookstore leading up to the book's release. I'll make sure I get you the schedule. And maybe you'll want to be a part of it. I'll reach out when I'm ready to do interviews."

"Okay, Cyril," Stan said. "You do that." Shaking her head, she went back inside. Izzy and Liam were on their way out.

"You need anything else before we leave?" Liam asked.

"No. We're fine," Stan said. "You guys go. Thanks for bringing the food."

"Eat something," Izzy instructed, giving her a hug. "I'll see you tomorrow."

Stan went back into the kitchen. "Where's Jessie?"

"Talking to Andrea in your office," Brenna said. "Like she's a criminal."

"Bren. Take it easy on her," Jake said. "She's doing her job."

Brenna sniffed.

"Come on," Stan said. "Why don't we go get the other room ready for you and Scott?"

"I'm happy to take the couch so Andrea can have the other guest room," Nikki offered.

"Thanks, Nik." Stan led Brenna upstairs, checked to make sure the room had fresh blankets, then handed her some towels.

Brenna sank down on the bed and kicked off her shoes. "I can't believe my sister. How could she think Andrea could do this?"

"Because not looking at the significant other would be shoddy police work," Stan said. "Don't take it personally, Bren. The faster she can rule out who didn't do it, the faster she can find who did."

"I guess."

"I'll send Scott up. You need anything else?"

Brenna shook her head.

Stan went downstairs just as Andrea came out of the office, her face streaked with tears, and raced upstairs. Jessie came out a minute later.

"Everything okay?" Stan asked. It was a stupid question, but she didn't know what else to say.

"Dandy," Jessie muttered. "I'll be in touch." She left, slamming the front door on her way.

Stan sighed and locked the door behind her. Scott, Jake, and Nikki were still in the kitchen.

"Scott, you can go up whenever you want," Stan said. "Brenna's upstairs."

"Thanks," he said and left the room.

"I'm going to sleep too," Nikki said. "You okay?"

"Yeah, fine." Stan looked at Jake.

"I'm right behind you."

Stan made sure Nikki had blankets, then headed upstairs to change and call her sister. She hadn't heard from her since Kyle had picked her up at the shop once Jessie had said she could go. Stan guessed she wasn't doing so well.

Kyle answered Caitlyn's phone. "Hey Stan. She's sleeping," he said in a low voice.

"How is she?" Stan asked.

Kyle sighed. "Not good. She feels responsible. And she's having a hard time with . . . what she saw."

"Yeah," Stan said. "I know the feeling."

"I know you do. I'm so sorry this happened. Do they have any idea who did it?"

"No. Well, maybe Jessie has a theory already. I'm not sure. But she's got a lot of ground to cover. Perry was a busy guy."

"What's going to happen with your shop?"

"Closed until they're done with it. It's a crime scene, sadly."

Kyle promised to have Caitlyn call her in the morning. Stan put her phone on silent and turned to Jake, who'd come in and climbed into bed while she was talking.

"Do you think I'm cursed or something?" Stan asked. "Seriously."

Jake had the good sense not to laugh. He considered the question while Stan settled next to him, her head on his chest. "I don't think you're cursed at all," he said.

She was silent for a moment. "What are we going to do?"

"We're going to let Jessie figure this out."

"Jake." Stan propped herself on one elbow. "I can't not help if there's a way for me to do that. I mean, it happened in my shop."

Jake sighed. "I figured. Just please tell me what you're doing, okay? And don't try to go around my sister. She needs to know what you're up to."

Stan nodded, relieved that he was so

CHAPTER FIFTEEN

As usual, Stan was up before the rest of the house the next morning. She felt like she was running a B&B, given that people were crammed into all corners of her house. But unlike at Char's B&B, Stan wasn't cooking. She hoped her guests were good with coffee.

Stan went into the kitchen to get the coffee ready. After setting the coffee maker to brew, she surveyed her group of furry friends, sitting in their usual semicircle on the floor waiting for whatever treats she had in store for them today. Next to Jake, they were her world. Even on the darkest days, it helped having them there to lift her spirits.

"So what do we think, guys?" she asked, placing her hands on her hips. "Should we have some of the salmon and potatoes this morning?"

Scruffy wagged. Duncan sat straight up and barked. Nutty swished his tail in annoyance. *Stop talking and get on with it,* Stan knew he would say if he could talk. The other three, as the newer members of the family, weren't as demanding. Henry was content to sit and wait for whatever came his way. Gaston was well behaved, sitting at attention, his tail vibrating with excitement but not moving. Years of being in a kitchen with his former owner, who'd been a chef before his unfortunate demise, had taught Gaston to be on his best behavior waiting for food. And Benny hung back, watching the dogs warily. He still wasn't sure what to make of them.

Stan retrieved the food from the fridge and got busy warming it and putting it in bowls. She didn't notice Nikki had come into the room until she'd put the last bowl on the floor and turned back to see how the coffee was doing.

"Morning," Nikki said. "Is the kitchen still open?"

Stan smiled. "Yeah, although it's not as fancy for the humans. We'll probably be eating leftover food from last night." She cringed a little at the thought of last night but put a brave smile on. "Coffee's almost ready."

"I see that." Nikki pushed a stray strand

of hair out of her eyes. "How are you feeling?"

"Numb. Antsy. I want to do something, you know?" Stan pulled down two mugs from the cabinet. "And I want to stop wondering which person in town snuck into my shop and . . . did that. Did they sneak in the back way and kill Perry, then come around front and join the party? It's killing me, wondering about this." She poured coffee into both mugs and handed one to Nikki. "It feels so . . . personal."

"Of course it does. Your place of business was violated." Nikki went to the fridge and took the creamer out. She added a generous dollop to her cup and stirred. "Have you talked to Caitlyn?"

Stan shook her head. "No. I called last night but she was in bed."

The doorbell rang. Stan looked at the clock. "It's not even seven. Now what?" She went to open the door, Nikki trailing behind her, Scruffy running ahead.

Jessie stood on the other side dressed in civilian clothes, but that didn't mean she wasn't working.

Stan took a deep breath and opened the door. "Hi. What's going on? Did you arrest someone?"

"No." Jessie pushed past her into the

house, took in Nikki standing there. "Sorry. I didn't know you still had company."

"I'm not company," Nikki said. "Want coffee?"

"No thanks," Jessie said, which Stan knew meant she wanted Nikki to leave the room.

"I'll be in the kitchen, then." Nikki padded down the hall in her fluffy socks. Scruffy, torn between staying with Stan and Jessie and following Nikki to where the food was, finally gave up and raced after Nikki.

"Come in here." Stan led her into the den. "Did something happen?"

Jessie sat down on the edge of the couch. "I can't believe I'm doing this again, but I have to ask you something," she said.

"Shoot." Stan took the chair opposite her.

"Can you talk to your mother about helping me get to the Pucks?"

"My mother?" Stan frowned. "What can she do?"

"Believe me, I think the whole thing is ridiculous." Jessie got up and paced the small room. "Sydney got ahold of her parents last night. They decided not to speak to me without enlisting their lawyer."

Stan's mouth dropped. That didn't seem like normal behavior for grieving parents. "Really? But why? The parents were on a plane when he got killed. It's not like they can think you suspect them, right?"

"I have no idea why rich people do the crazy crap they do," Jessie said. "I'm sure it's because of who they are and their business and wanting to control what goes in the newspapers. I'm equally sure they're embarrassed by the way their son was found dead. A dead stripper in a fake cake is hardly something you want your friends to read about over their morning smoked salmon. But it's putting a huge monkey wrench in my life, because I kind of need the parents to get some details about this guy's life. She gave me her mother's cell, and when I called they refused to speak to me. Directed me to this lawyer. Your mother said she knows Mrs. Puck. Do you think she would help me try to convince her to talk to me? Mother to mother, or something?"

"I don't know. I can ask," Stan said. "I'm not sure how well she knows her, though."

"I'm thinking if she can get to the mother without the father, maybe that will work. He could be the one insisting on this," Jessie said, focused on her own train of thought. "They're coming back today. This afternoon was the first flight out they could get. So maybe your mother can offer to take her out for coffee when they get back. Or brunch. Wouldn't brunch be more appropriate for high-society ladies?" She focused on Stan, waiting for an answer.

Stan sighed. "I don't know, Jess. Do you want to call her and pretend to be my mother? That way you can just ask her what you want?"

"Funny. No. But seriously, can you help me? Because I need to get to her soon. I'm going to try the sister and her husband again, but I don't know if they'll be allowed to talk, either."

"Sure. I'll ask her," Stan said.

"Thank you."

They were both silent for a moment.

"What about the people at the farm? They seemed to give Perry a hard time," Stan said. "Even Wallace, and I like Wallace. I think they all thought Perry was just there for fun. Although I don't know what's fun about that job."

"I talked to the owner last night. He didn't have a lot to say. Perry hasn't been working there all that long. Roger Tate said he was a good worker, did everything he was asked to do, did it with a smile, all that happy crap employers say about dead people. I didn't get to talk to any of the other workers yet."

"Are you going to talk to the people at the other place he worked? The stripper business? Maybe he did a job and something happened, or someone got obsessed with him? I mean, I'm sure you've thought of that," Stan hastened to add at the look on Jessie's face.

"It did cross my mind," Jessie said dryly. "In any event, my point is I've talked to all these random people and I'm sure I have more to talk to — Lou is getting a list from Andrea of his friends — but the parents have the most history. They might be able to point us in a direction no one else would know about."

"Not necessarily," Stan said slowly.

"What do you mean?"

"Well, if they were disappointed in Perry, cut him off from the family funds, et cetera, maybe there was a lot they didn't know about him. He probably wouldn't be confiding in them about his life and his friends, right?"

Jessie considered this. "No, probably not."

"So if Perry ran into any trouble because of his extracurricular jobs, Mummy and Daddy wouldn't be the ones he'd run to for help."

"Then who would be?" Jessie asked. "Because Andrea seemed to think his life was hunky-dory swell too. Aside from the fact that she hated his side job, as much as she tried to convince me she was good with it."

"I don't know," Stan said. "Have you talked to Tyler Hoffman? Emmalee said they were friends. There has to be someone who knew the guy enough to know what kept him up at night if anything did."

"He's on my list too. But I didn't come here to vet my list of interviews with you." Jessie stood. "When can you talk to your mother?"

"I'll go see her this morning," Stan said.

CHAPTER SIXTEEN

Nikki waited in the kitchen with a refilled mug of coffee for Stan. "So what was that about?" she asked when Stan returned.

Stan took the mug and sipped. There wasn't enough coffee in the world to clear the fog from her head today, and it was way too early for this. "Jessie needs my help."

"Really?" Nikki asked. "What's up with that?"

"She can't get access to Perry's parents. She wants my mother to help her. So of course she wants me to ask my mother to help her."

"Why can't she get access?" Nikki asked.

"I don't know. They lawyered up." Stan smiled a little, despite the situation. "I've always wanted to say that. Maybe I did miss my calling as a police officer."

"Look at it this way. If your mother has a job to do for the police, she might be too busy to worry about your wedding for a few days. And that means we can get a lot of things done, right?" Nikki beamed, obviously proud of herself.

Now that was a thought she could get behind. "You're a genius," Stan said.

Stan waited until Jake, Duncan, and Gaston had left for the pub before heading out. She wanted to see Caitlyn before going to her mother's. And since she was going to see Caitlyn, she'd bring her along as a buffer.

She stepped right over the newspaper that Cyril had flung onto her front porch, likely from the seat of his bicycle, purposely ignoring it. Not that she didn't want to keep up with what was going on, but she didn't think she could stomach reading about the murder in bold headlines above the fold yet.

The weather was beautiful, again. It seemed surprising to her that the sun could shine so brightly after such a tragedy, when so many people were hurting. A family had lost their only son and brother. A young girl had lost her boyfriend. And from what Andrea had said, the world had lost out on someone with the potential to be an amazing actor.

Such a waste.

Stan drove slowly around the town green. Half the town was out enjoying the weather, after being cooped up by a long, cold winter and the start of a rainy spring. Humans and dogs walked the gravel path around the green. Dogs stopped to sniff each other while the humans stopped to chat — no doubt about murder. It was inevitable.

Stan crossed Main Street and continued east, stealing a look at her shop as she passed by. She'd expected her cozy little storefront to be marred by crime scene tape and police cars. Not the image she'd had in mind when she opened. But when she passed, it was strangely quiet. Unless all the activity was in the back.

Both Kyle's and Caitlyn's cars were in the driveway when she pulled up in front of their adorable Cape. Another occurrence she never could have predicted in a million years — Caitlyn moving to Frog Ledge. This house was a far cry from the estate she'd lived in back in Narragansett near their mother's house with her investment banker husband, with whom she'd been silently miserable for so many years. Then she'd met Kyle, and things changed.

After spending some time in Frog Ledge during her divorce, she and Kyle ultimately decided it would suit their lifestyle. And it was a perfect place for a vegan restaurant since there were none in the area. Kyle was a gourmet chef — that's how Stan had met him — who owned a restaurant in Miami, where he used to live. He'd been itching to find the right spot to open a restaurant. Stan had been surprised when he'd declared Frog Ledge was that place. Then again, it made sense given its recent reputation as an up-and-coming town that had started to attract different kinds of people. People who weren't just looking for the next greasy-spoon diner. They wanted high-quality, healthy food.

Kyle had run into some problems, both with the location he picked and the old-time naysayers who thought all vegans were boycotting farms. With a lot of political politeness and patience, he'd managed to convince most of that group that he was supporting all the local farms for vegetables, and that these days not everyone ate meat so why not cater to a broader group of people and bring them to town to spend their money? His approach had won him friends in town, and now he was getting ready this summer to open his restaurant, where Caitlyn planned to work full time, in addition to doing Stan's books and helping Izzy at the bookstore. Her sister was like a complete stranger: not the girl Stan had grown up with. It was scary.

Except for the whole bachelorette party thing, of course. Some old habits die hard.

Stan heaved a sigh and got out of the car, heading to the door. Cooper, their rescued golden retriever, stood up on his hind legs and placed his paws on the door when he saw her, tail wagging.

"Hi Coop!" Stan tried the door. Locked. Kyle appeared a moment later, alerted by Cooper's whining.

"Sorry," he said, unlocking the screen and opening the door wide. "Caitlyn made me promise to keep all the doors locked. I could barely get her to let me keep the front door open so we could get some air in here."

"Are you making *fun* of me?" Caitlyn wailed from the other room.

"I guess she's distraught," Stan murmured.

Kyle nodded.

"I'll talk to her," Stan said.

"Good luck," Kyle said.

Stan's niece Eva raced into the room.

"Auntie Krissie! Where are the dogs?" she demanded.

"They're home right now, sweetie. But you can come see them later. How about that? You can bring Coop so he can have a playdate," Stan said.

"Yay!" Eva launched herself at Stan for a

115

hug. She'd gotten so big. She'd also settled in nicely in her new town, despite her father's efforts to make her feel like it was inadequate. She liked her school, and she'd become good friends with Lily, Jessie's daughter.

"Where's your mom?" Stan asked.

"This way." Eva took her hand and tugged her into the kitchen. Caitlyn sat at the table, forehead in her hand, a soggy bowl of cereal in front of her. Caitlyn looked like she hadn't slept at all. She glanced up at Stan and burst into tears.

Eva looked alarmed. Kyle came in. "Come on, kiddo," he said to Eva. "Let's take Cooper for a walk."

"What's wrong with Mummy?" Stan heard Eva ask as they left.

"She's just sad right now," Kyle said. "She'll be better soon."

Once the door shut behind them, Stan turned to her sister. "I have to go to Mom's. Do you want to go with me?"

"Not really." Caitlyn shoved her bowl aside.

"Please? I need a buffer. I'll buy you a coffee on the way," Stan said.

Caitlyn sniffed. "Krissie. Why aren't you a mess?"

"I'm a mess inside," Stan said, and she

wasn't kidding. The whole situation had her feeling edgy and anxious. "But I'm antsy. And I have to ask Mom something. For Jessie."

"For Jessie?" Caitlyn's ears perked up. "About the case?"

"Yeah. About the case."

"Well, I guess I can go. Do I have to change?"

Stan eyed her striped pajama bottoms and white tank top. "Probably."

While Caitlyn went upstairs to change and call Kyle to let him know she was leaving, Stan got rid of the cereal and cleaned up the dishes, then she began straightening the counter. There was a pile of mail buried under a plethora of magazines. Most of them wedding-related. Caitlyn was way more into planning a big wedding.

Stan lingered over one particular magazine all about the perfect wedding dress. Despite herself, she began flipping through it. The dresses were gorgeous, of course. And likely all designer.

And Stan didn't think she could pick one she'd actually wear if someone held a gun to her head. As she flipped through the magazine, she felt increasingly anxious. What was wrong with her that none of these struck her fancy?

Stan slapped the magazine shut as Caitlyn returned. Her sister gave her an inquisitive look but didn't say anything.

"Ready?" Stan asked.

"Yeah. So what do we need Mom's help with? Is she a suspect or something?" Caitlyn sounded a bit more like herself.

Stan rolled her eyes and pushed her sister toward the door. "No. But she might be able to hook the police up with Perry's parents. They won't talk." Stan shut the door behind them.

"Make sure it's locked," Caitlyn said over her shoulder. "I feel like I moved into a bad neighborhood."

CHAPTER SEVENTEEN

As Stan expected, Izzy's was full this morning. And given the newspapers spread out on tables and the buzz in the air, the topic of murder was on everyone's mind. Izzy and Jana worked steadily behind the counter, making coffee, handing out pastries, refilling the case. Despite the long lines and the recent events, Izzy looked completely relaxed. She loved this place. Catching Stan's eye, she lifted her hand in a wave.

Stan sent Caitlyn to get a table and got in line, listening to the bits of conversation drifting around her. From the snippets she pieced together, Perry was definitely the topic.

"How you feeling?" Izzy asked when she stepped up to the counter.

Stan shrugged. "Like I got run over by a truck."

"I bet." Izzy shot her a sympathetic look.

"Want something yummy to take your mind off it?"

Stan nodded. "Make it two lattes and two yummies. Caitlyn's here."

Izzy glanced over at the table where Caitlyn huddled inside her sweatshirt, looking miserable. "How's she doing?"

"Not so good," Stan said.

"And Brenna?"

"I didn't see her this morning, but she feels terrible. Guilty, I think. Since she hired Perry for the party. And she's worried about Andrea."

"Ugh." Izzy poured steamed almond milk into the shape of a heart on top of both mugs and handed them over. "Let me know how I can help."

Stan took the coffees and carried them to the table, then went back for the pastries Izzy had handpicked for them. Mocha muffins with chocolate chunks and some kind of frosting dribbled on top. Nice and unhealthy. Stan presented them to Caitlyn with a flourish.

Caitlyn eyed them suspiciously. "I don't think I'm hungry."

"Well, you better be eating yours. I don't need two but I'll eat it if you don't." Stan bit into hers and sighed. It was no wonder Izzy's place had gained such a following.

Her food was amazing.

"Did you see this?" Caitlyn shoved a stained copy of the *Frog Ledge Holler* across the table at her sister.

Stan read the headline and wanted to thunk her head down on the table.

STRIPPER STABBED!

Local bachelorette party turns deadly, the subhead added.

Stan scanned the article, cringing when she saw her name and her shop's name clearly articulated as being at the center of the crime, as well as the standard quote she'd given Cyril last night. As was typical of the day after something like this, there wasn't a lot of information other than the crime and the usual party line about the police investigating and that they were sure to have a resolution soon.

And there was a recent picture of Perry smiling at the camera in some formal photo. As a sidebar, a shot of his sister and her husband leaving the hospital.

Stan flipped the paper over and pushed it aside. "Eat," she said to her sister.

Caitlyn took a bite and raised her eyebrows. "Wow. This is good."

"Told you."

"So what does Mom have to do with this guy's parents?"

"I guess she's friendly with Perry's mother from some charity organization," Stan said.

"Oh yeah, I vaguely remember hearing that last night," Caitlyn said. "Isn't it the domestic violence place?"

Stan frowned. "I think that's what I heard. I didn't know Mom was interested in that cause."

Caitlyn shrugged. "She told me she got involved on the board of a place. I guess it's something Tony suggested?"

"Interesting. I had no idea." She'd have to ask her mom about it sometime. Stan turned her attention back to her muffin and coffee, but her appetite took a dive when Cyril walked in the café and, spotting her and Caitlyn, headed straight toward them.

"Morning, ladies," he said, sliding into the free chair at their table uninvited.

"Hi, Cyril," Stan said.

Caitlyn eyed him suspiciously. Stan had to smile. As a former PR person, she should've been the one wary of the newsman.

Cyril nodded at the paper on the table. "Did you read today's edition yet?"

"Skimmed it," Stan said.

Cyril nodded. "I'd hoped to have some more information from Connecticut's finest, but they're still hot on the trail, I guess."

"Most likely," Stan agreed.

"So." Cyril leaned forward conspiratorially. "I need to talk to the family. And the girlfriend. Can you hook me up?"

"Me?" Stan asked. "Why are you asking me?"

Cyril shrugged. "You and Brenna McGee are tight. She's best friends with the girlfriend. They both stayed at your house last night. And I'm sure the girlfriend has an in with the family. You seemed like the perfect conduit."

"Well, I'm not," Stan said. "They all probably want to be left alone, Cyril."

"Yeah, clearly the police can't even get to the family if they want our mother to broker the conversation," Caitlyn added.

Stan kicked her sister under the table. At least she tried to.

"Hey," Cyril protested. "Why are you kicking me?"

"Sorry. I meant to kick her." Stan glared at her sister. "You have a big mouth."

"What?" Caitlyn asked defensively.

"She thinks you shouldn't have told me that because now I'll probably start following your mother around," Cyril said. "She hasn't been around the media much, huh?" he asked Stan.

"Nope," Stan said. "A couple of Rhode Island social-page interviews about her divorce. Which she actually handled very well."

"I'm right here," Caitlyn said. "In case you forgot. But thanks, I didn't know you even read those interviews."

"Of course I did," Stan said. "You have to be ready for damage control. Old PR habits die hard."

"Anyway," Cyril interrupted. "Your mother?"

"What about her? Leave our mother alone. You don't really want to mess with her, Cyril," Stan said. "She's been known to chew people up and spit them out."

"Including us," Caitlyn muttered.

Cyril lifted his chin. "I have First Amendment rights."

"Sure," Stan said. "And she has the right to make your life miserable. Trust me, she won't hesitate to use it."

Cyril frowned, drumming his fingers against the table as he pondered this predicament. "Well. I'm sure there's a solution available. I just have to find it." He rose and nodded at them. "Nice to see you both. Thanks for the chat." Cyril left the café, his long black trench coat flapping behind him.

Stan watched him go. When Cyril got

something in his head, she knew it wasn't easy for him to let it go. But taking on Patricia Connor . . .

She drained her coffee mug and popped the last bite of muffin into her mouth. "Let's go," she told her sister, standing up. "At least if we get to Mom's before Cyril we can run interference."

Chapter Eighteen

"Mom's going to be all over me about going out like this," Caitlyn said. She'd gone from pajama bottoms to sweats. At least they were stylish.

Stan shrugged. "You're a grown woman. You can dress like you just rolled out of bed if you want to. Plus, you don't live in Narragansett anymore where people would actually care."

"True story," Caitlyn agreed. "It is kind of nice."

Stan turned onto Main Street and headed east, where her mother and Tony lived in Tony's giant house up on a hill overlooking the town. He'd moved in when he decided to run for mayor last year on a platform supporting farms, and his win was a surprise to most people in town — especially the reigning mayor, Mona Galveston. Mona had counted on the progressive folks of Frog Ledge to keep her in office, where she could push for new development and embracing the future while still supporting the agricultural history of the community, as well as the residents who still made their living that way. But a core group of people who believed in farming and wanted to see the town stay the same had banded together and elected Tony.

Stan hadn't liked him at first. She especially hadn't liked him when her mother started dating him. Turns out they'd been college sweethearts, before Patricia had met Stan's dad, and running into each other in town had been fate.

But over time, Stan and Tony had arrived at a grudging respect, which had actually turned into a decent relationship. It had been a pleasant surprise to find out that Tony wasn't here to quash development, much to some of his supporters' chagrin. He'd actually been very vocal in his support of the new businesses in town, such as Izzy's bookstore and Stan's shop. And he genuinely loved her mother. Since they'd been together, Patricia's edges had softened just a little, which was a huge deal.

Stan turned onto the long road leading up to her mom's driveway and pulled to a stop at the top of the hill. There were no cars in the driveway, but they were most likely in the three-car garage. No sign of Cyril, which surprised her a bit. Maybe he would try calling first. They went to the front door and Stan rang the bell.

Tony answered with a genuine smile for both. "Hi, Stan. Hi, Caitlyn." He leaned down and gave Stan a kiss on the cheek, then ushered her inside, pausing to give Caitlyn the same treatment as she passed through the door. Stan felt it was a win, too, that she'd gotten him to start using her preferred nickname. Her mother and sister couldn't come to terms with her preference to be called Stan rather than something more . . . feminine.

"How are you doing?" Stan asked him.

He brushed aside her concern. "I'm fine. The real question is, how are you?" He regarded her seriously. "I don't even know what to say about what happened."

"I'm okay," she lied. "Thank you for asking. Is my mother here?"

"Of course. Darling!" he called. "The girls are here! Come on in the living room," he said. "She'll be right there. Can I get you coffee? Tea?"

"Tea," Stan decided. She'd already ingested enough coffee to give herself an ulcer. Caitlyn asked for water.

"Coming right up." Tony went to the

kitchen. Stan took a seat on one of the comfy chairs in the living room. Caitlyn chose the couch. Probably so their mother would sit next to her and it would be harder for Patricia to see her outfit.

Despite being a huge, fancy house, Tony had managed to keep some of his own touches. Stan could see her mother in a lot of the decor — well, most — but the chair she was sitting in had to be Tony's, whereas the stiff couch was definitely more up her mother's alley.

Patricia came in a few minutes later. "This is a surprise. Both my girls visiting me on a Saturday? Good morning." She air-kissed both, her gaze only lingering for an extra moment on Caitlyn's outfit. "What brings you here this early?" She took a seat on the couch next to Caitlyn. "Are you both doing all right? I know as the shock wears off it's harder to wrap our minds around what happened." She looked expectantly at Caitlyn.

"I'm okay," Caitlyn said. "It's so sad and scary, though."

"It certainly is," Patricia said.

"Mom, I hope we're not interrupting your morning too much, but I have a favor to ask you. Well, it's not really my favor. Jessie asked me if you might be able to help her." Stan glanced up as Tony came in, delivered two cups of tea and a glass of water, blew his wife a kiss, and left the room.

"Thank you, darling," Patricia called after him. She turned back to Stan. "Is this related to Perry?"

Stan nodded. "I guess his parents got some fancy lawyer and they won't even talk to her. She really needs to get some insights from the family. Especially given the circumstances." She picked up her cup and sipped her tea. Peppermint. It was soothing.

Patricia thought about this. "That's surprising. I understand not wanting this to be splashed all over the press, but it seems like they would be more willing to find a way to help."

"Yeah. Cyril's all over that," Stan said. "He might even try to talk to you about it."

Patricia, mid-sip, smiled a little. Stan thought her mother had actually become fond of their quirky newsman. Cyril did grow on you. Unless he was stalking you for a quote. Then he was relentless. As Patricia would soon find out once he formulated his plan of attack.

"Why would he talk to me?" she asked.

"He sort of heard you had an in with the Pucks," Stan said.

Caitlyn slouched down against the sofa and said nothing.

"Well," Patricia said. "I can't guarantee you anything, Kristan. It's really none of our business. But," she added, "this is our community, and since it did happen at your place of business, I suppose we're already involved. It wouldn't hurt for me to voice my opinion to Gabrielle. I don't know when the Pucks will be back, but I can certainly call to offer my condolences and try to go see them."

"Thanks. I heard they're coming back today." She hesitated. "What is Mr. Puck like?"

"Frederick? I only met him once. Gabrielle attends a lot of the functions alone."

"Do you think he's the one insisting they don't talk to anyone? Maybe if you talked to her without him she'd be open to meeting with Jessie," Stan said.

"It's possible. But Gabrielle doesn't seem the type to be silenced by anyone. Then again, I don't know the husband well enough to say. I'll do my best, though."

"Thanks, Mom." Stan finished her tea and, catching Caitlyn's eye, started to rise. "We should go. Nikki's at the house, and Brenna and I have to do some baking. Even though we're closed until Jessie says we can open, we're going to bake and make some deliveries."

"That's lovely, dear. Let me know if I can help. Oh, but before I talk to Gabrielle, there's one condition," Patricia said.

Stan sank back down into the chair. She'd known it was too good to be true. "Condition?"

"Yes. You have to do me a favor too."

"Mom. This is hardly a favor. It's helping solve the murder of a young man who was very special in the community."

"I know that, Kristan," Patricia said, waving her concern away. "And of course I'll do what I can. But it seems a good opportunity to discuss some things related to the wedding."

"I really can't today —"

"There are a number of your cousins out in California who really want to come. I did explain that you wanted to keep this a small — er — town affair. But they insist. So given that, it makes more sense to look at a venue larger than Jake's lovely . . . bar. Continuing our discussions from last week."

"We talked about this," Stan said, dismayed. "I'm flattered that Dad's side of the family would make the trip, but I really don't want a big thing. And for the last time, I don't want to do it anywhere else. And Mom, we're three weeks away. Everything is planned."

"I've spoken with Pastor Ellis," Patricia said, as if Stan hadn't spoken. Pastor Ellis was the lovely man who ran the Congregational church in town where Patricia and Tony had gotten married. "I really think his church would be best. And, I'm going to ask Char if she can put the family up in her inn. We can figure out the logistical details about the party from there."

"I don't want a church wedding," Stan said through gritted teeth. She stood, remembering one of her tricks when she worked in corporate America and needed to come off as more forceful than she felt. "Mom. We are *not* changing everything —"

"And we have to set up some time to go dress shopping," Patricia added, getting up also. Stan might as well have been speaking to the beautifully decorated wall. She narrowed her eyes at her daughter. "I'm presuming you haven't gotten your dress yet? Which I really can't believe. I mean, what if you need to have alterations made? Honestly, Kristan. If I wasn't here to help you get this wedding moving, you'd show up in shorts and an apron."

Remember how badly you want to be married to Jake, Stan chanted in her mind. "Dress shopping. Yes. No, I haven't gotten my dress. It's been on my list. I've been so

133

busy. That I can do. We should do that soon, huh?"

"Yes, we should. Maybe while Nikki's here. I'm sure she'd love to be part of it, as your oldest friend. Of course, your sister will come too. Won't you, Caitlyn?" Patricia slipped her arm through Stan's as she walked her to the door. "Let's go Monday. I have a luncheon, but after that I'm completely free."

"Oh — I'm not sure, Mom. I have to see what's going on at the shop."

"I trust you'll figure it out, given how important it is you actually have a dress to get married in. I'll call you later to confirm." Patricia smiled. "It will be such fun. So, I'll let you know when I speak to Gabrielle. I'll call her in the morning."

"Okay. Thanks, Mom." Stan and Caitlyn hurried back to her car.

"Aren't you glad you asked?" Caitlyn said as Stan buckled her seat belt and started the car.

"Oh, hush." Stan kept the smile pasted on her face as she drove away while her mother waved them off. When she reached the bottom of the driveway, she stopped and dropped her head to the steering wheel, not sure whether to laugh or cry.

CHAPTER NINETEEN

Stan dropped Caitlyn off with a promise to call her later, then headed home. Scruffy and Nutty greeted her at the door. Just like the old days — her first two babies.

Brenna was at the kitchen counter, already with two mixing bowls and ingredients spread out everywhere. Jake and Nikki sat at the table, drinking coffee. Scott and Andrea were nowhere in sight.

"Morning," Stan said, dropping her bag and going over to give Jake a kiss.

"Hey," Brenna said. "I was up early so I figured I'd get a head start."

"Thank you. Reminds me of the early days, right?" Stan smiled and perched on Jake's knee, leaning back against him. "Did Scott leave?"

Jake nodded. "Went over to the pub."

"Are you going too?" she asked him.

"Not until later, around lunchtime. I have a full crew on." Jake slipped his arm around her waist. "Where've you been?"

"I went to my mother's. Your sister was here earlier. She needed me to ask my mother to talk to Perry Puck's mother."

"Why?" Jake asked.

"They won't talk to the police. Their lawyer is dragging his feet. She thought maybe a mother-to-mother appeal would help." Stan shrugged. "Anyway. I'm not sure I ever told you, but I have cousins in California."

"Okay," Jake said. "That's nice."

"Yeah. A bunch of them. My dad was one of four kids. So, I have two aunts and an uncle out there. Each with a few kids, who have apparently taken a sudden interest in me even though we haven't been in touch in about ten years."

"Is there going to be a quiz?" Jake asked.

Stan lifted her head and looked at him. He was so gorgeous, she thought, reaching up to touch the scruff along his chin. And she was so lucky she was going to marry him in a couple weeks, meddling mother or not.

"My mother told me today that they all want to come to the wedding. She reached out to them and told them about it. If I know my mother, she manipulated the situation and made them feel like they should come. So, they're coming. Which prompted my mother to reiterate that the pub won't be big enough. I figure it's her way of getting us to cave and not have it there. I have to hand it to her," Stan said with some admiration. "Patricia Connor pulls out all the stops to get things to go in her favor."

"I'll say." Jake thought about this. "So how do you feel about it?"

"How do I feel? Like I wish she would just leave it alone." Frustrated, Stan rose and paced the kitchen. "Like she should understand this isn't about what she wants, it's about what we want."

Jake nodded. "I know, sweetie. Unfortunately, my mother is kind of echoing the refrain too."

Stan looked at him in dismay, then at Brenna, who busied herself stirring batter for a batch of cookies, and finally at Nikki. "So we're just going to let everyone tell us what to do? Nik. Help me out here."

Nikki lifted her shoulders, palms up. "Happy to jump in and be on your side. Not sure I'll get anywhere, but I'll try my best."

"Listen, babe." Jake tugged her back onto his lap. "If we have to do the wedding ceremony somewhere else, it's okay. We're still having the reception at the pub. Liam got us a band he knows in New York. An Irish band. They're supposed to be amazing. This is going to be a helluva party, mark my words." Jake hugged her. "Don't worry about the rest of it. Let your mother have her fun. Let both have their fun. They're excited. Give them that. In the end, none of that stuff matters."

As usual, he was right. Stan rested her head against his chest. "I said I wasn't doing this, you know. That I wasn't going to be that bride who got stressed out about everything and was cranky and angry. And here I am doing it." She felt tears sting her eyes, but she knew they weren't solely related to her changing wedding plans. Perry Puck's murder had left her feeling helpless and out of control — and angry — and she could barely think of anything else.

"You're not. You're fine. Really." Jake tipped her head back and found her lips with his. "There's a lot going on. I get it. I wish you could focus on the wedding."

But Stan knew she wouldn't rest easy until this killer was caught. And if she could help with that, she had to. It had happened in her shop. And she owed it to Perry, who had died trying to help her have fun. If his death was connected in any way to the stripper job, she felt responsible.

There was also the possibility that it wasn't related at all, and that someone else saw an opportunity and took it. But who would be that angry with a young man who, by all accounts, didn't bother anyone?

"Where's Andrea?" Stan asked. "How is she today?"

"She feels awful," Brenna said. "She can't believe Jessie actually thinks she did it."

"I don't know if Jessie thinks she did it," Stan said carefully. "I think she's trying to make sure she covers all her bases."

"Well, she should know better," Brenna said stubbornly. She started plopping mounds of batter on her cookie sheet, taking the time to shape them into perfect circles. "Andrea's almost part of our family too."

"She's trying, Bren," Jake said. "She wants to solve it as much as we want it solved."

"Well then she should focus on the people who actually hated him enough to kill him!" Brenna said angrily. "Not the person who loved him." She dropped her spoon and rushed out of the room.

Stan watched her go. She didn't think it was the best time to point out that sometimes the people who loved someone the most were the ones who lost control and did the unthinkable.

Chapter Twenty

"So where are we bringing our cookies?" Brenna asked once they had half a dozen batches in various stages of cooling on the counter.

Brenna had finally come back downstairs, but it was clear she'd been crying. She didn't bring up her sister again.

Between batches, they'd had leftover food from the party for lunch, then Nikki went out for a walk and Jake left for the pub. The dogs had decided not to accompany him, as they knew treats were in the oven. Stan had promised to bring at least Duncan over later. The customers looked forward to hanging with him.

"I think we should bring some to Izzy's. A lot of people who come to us also go to her café. Then we can bring some to the general store. Abby will love that. She's been trying to get me to stock treats with her for months. I guess she doesn't get that it would be counterintuitive to me actually getting customers into my shop." Stan smiled. Abby had been running that store for about forty years, and she was an acquired taste.

"Maybe the bookstore too," Brenna suggested. "And the pub."

"Perfect," Stan said. "I'd say the library too, but it's Saturday and they close early. That should be plenty. Want me to do the drop-offs?"

"We can split them if you want," Brenna said. "I'll hit the general store and the bookstore. I figure you'll want coffee soon, and I know you told Jake you'd bring the dogs."

"Sounds good. I'm going to shower first." Stan hadn't bothered to do that this morning after Jessie's visit had gotten her out the door so early. She hesitated. "Have you talked to Andrea? How is she?"

Brenna shook her head. "She won't answer her phone. I'm going to go by once I do my drop-offs. I think I'll try to get her to come stay with me. Her roommates might be a little much right now. And I know she's not going to go to her parents'. They didn't really approve of her dating Perry once they found out he was a stripper."

"Not a popular line of work," Stan said. "He must've made good money at it, though."

Brenna nodded. "He didn't talk about it much, but I would guess so. Plus, I have to admit he was kind of vain. It suited him." She looked horrified as soon as the words came out, and she clapped her hand over her mouth. "Oh my God. I didn't mean that in a bad way. I swear. Don't tell Andrea I said that!"

"Of course I won't. And I don't think that's a judgment. I think it's a fact. Anyone could tell Perry knew he was good-looking. And likely used it to his advantage." Stan shrugged. "Human nature. You can't fault him for it."

"I know. But Andrea's sensitive right now. She really loved him."

Stan felt sad for the girl. That had to be so tough, especially at such a young age. "Where did they meet?"

"In class. Before he stopped going." She froze. "Shoot. I wasn't supposed to mention that."

"He stopped going? To college?"

"Yes and no. He enrolled in some local drama classes and dropped his college classes down to one a semester. Given how much it cost and all, and since he wasn't getting any help. He didn't love college. At least not the classes he was taking."

"Which were?" Stan prompted.

"The usual business classes. His parents were fixated on him getting his business degree and moving right into a leadership role in the company. I'm just telling you what I heard from Andrea," Brenna cautioned. "But he didn't want to be CEO of an organic market. I mean, he knows it's a good mission and all, and he cares about it, but he didn't want to do it. His sister wanted to do it, though."

"Really," Stan said. "So the parents wanted him to do it why? Because he's the son? Is it a name thing? Like, as the boy he needs to carry the name on and have his kids take over?"

"Who knows," Brenna said, shrugging. "Again, I'm hearing this from Andrea. Who heard it from Perry, who probably had his own perspective. But he really wanted to be an actor. That was his passion."

And he surely would've been good at it. He had a presence just doing meat and vegetable deliveries. Why did parents have to operate that way? If every parent accepted their child for who he or she was, Stan was convinced the world would be a less messed-up place. Now his talent had been silenced, and no one would ever know what a difference Perry Puck could've made.

The whole thing stank.

But if what Brenna said was true, a picture was emerging of this family that didn't sit well with Stan. What if his parents had been so angry about his life choices that they'd set this in motion? It was shocking to consider that his parents could actually want him killed, but what if? The thought made Stan shiver. It also made her want to see for herself what Gabrielle Puck was like.

She called her mother as soon as she left the room. "When you make plans with Mrs. Puck, can you either invite me or tell me where you're going to be?" Stan asked. "I'd really like to meet her."

Patricia didn't sound like she thought that was the best idea. "I'm not sure, Kristan. She might be less likely to speak in front of you. Especially if she realized you hired him to strip at that party."

She had a good point. "Technically, I didn't hire him," she said. "I see what you mean, though. I'll give you a chance to talk to her before I show up, but I really want to see what she's like."

It took some coaxing, but Patricia agreed to let Stan know what the plan was when she reached her friend. In the meantime, Stan thought a visit to Perry's coworkers at the farm might be helpful. too. Just to get a sense of what else was going on over there.

CHAPTER TWENTY-ONE

"Want to run some errands with me?" Stan asked Nikki when she got back. Brenna had packed up her share of the treats and headed out.

"Sure. Where we going? Somewhere fun?"

"I need to deliver these treats to Izzy's and the pub. And then I need to stop by the farm," Stan said casually.

"Which farm?"

"The farm where I get my meat and veggie deliveries from."

"Ah. The farm where Perry worked?"

"Yeah. So? It's the farm I get my food from."

"What are we going to the farm for? Didn't you just get a delivery?"

"Because I have to adjust my delivery since I don't know how long I'm going to be closed," Stan said. "Because I want some more organic spinach and they have the best. And because I *like* going to the farm."

She crossed her arms over her chest and gave her friend her best defiant look.

"I see," Nikki said seriously. "And while you're there are you planning on asking them anything about Perry?" A smile twitched at her lips.

"Maybe," Stan said, lifting her chin.

"Ha. Well, at least you're honest." Nikki got up and grabbed her cowboy boots. "Let's go."

After Stan had delivered all the treats, plus Duncan for his pub dog duties, to Izzy and Jake, they drove out to the farm. It had been a while since Stan had actually been there. After her first couple visits to assess whether it was the farm she wanted to use, she basically ordered the same amount every week. If she needed to change anything, it was a quick phone call to Roger or Wallace.

Roger was out front talking to a young woman when they pulled up. She definitely didn't look like she belonged on the farm given the expensive jeans, white tank top, and high wedge sandals she wore. Their discussion seemed heated. He leaned forward as he talked, waving his hands, while she stood sullenly, hands shoved in her back pockets and a defiant look on her face. They both glanced up when they realized they had an audience.

Roger's face changed and he waved when he recognized Stan. "Hello there," he called as she and Nikki got out of the car and made their way over. "What brings you here this morning?" He offered his hand to Nikki. "I'm Roger Tate."

"Nikki Manning," she said, shaking it.

"Hi, Roger," Stan said. "I wanted some vegetables. And to talk about my next delivery."

His face fell a bit. "Yes. Sure. Come on into the barn." He turned to the young woman, who'd been standing silently since they arrived, shooting daggers at him with her eyes. "Lucy, honey, I'll be inside in a bit. Ladies, this is my daughter Lucy," he said.

"Nice to meet you, Lucy," Stan said.

"You too." Lucy turned to Stan and smiled, showing perfect white teeth — a completely different look than what she was giving her dad. She was a pretty girl, probably early twenties, with thick brown hair that fell halfway down her back.

Lucy sauntered back toward the house. Roger watched her go for a moment, his face unreadable, then ushered them inside.

"Roger, I'm so sorry about Perry," Stan said.

He nodded. "Me too. He was a good worker. Good kid overall. I don't think he saw this as a long-term job, but he wasn't one of those kids who took something on then complained about it the whole time. He jumped in and did what he had to do. He had a good attitude. Something some of my other guys could use," he added. "And Stan, I'm so sorry that . . . what happened had a direct effect on you."

"Thanks. But none of that is as important as finding out who did this," Stan said.

"I agree. Luckily we have our trusty police on the case. So what can I do for you with your delivery?"

"Well, Jessie closed the patisserie until she feels she's gathered all the evidence. So I'll be a little behind on my cooking and baking, and can probably cut my order to a third of the usual. The meat, at least. Since I just got a delivery and all."

"Sure thing." Roger pulled a book out of a drawer behind the counter and made a note. "You still want the full veggie order?"

"Sure, why not. If all else fails, I'll make a lot of juices."

Nikki came over, her arms full of kale. "I see what you mean about this place," she said. "This kale is gorgeous!"

Roger laughed. "Glad you think so. We

take a lot of pride in our farm."

"I need some spinach too," Stan said.

"You ladies take your time. I'll be around," Roger said. "Yell when you need me, or just leave a note about what you bought and I'll add it to your next order."

"Thanks," Stan said.

Wallace came into the barn. "Boss, you want me to start the deliveries or give you a hand with the harvesting?" he asked, then noticed Stan and Nikki. "Oh, good morning, ladies."

"Hi Wallace," Stan said.

"You run out of goods already?" He jammed his hands into the pockets of his dirty jeans.

"No, but I did need some spinach." Stan held up a bunch as proof.

"I'll handle the harvest," Roger said. "You go ahead. Want help?"

Wallace shook his head. "Nah. I'll be fine."

Roger left the barn, patting Wallace on the back before he went. Stan, torn between wanting to browse veggies and do some detective work, decided to take advantage of Wallace's presence.

"How are you, Wallace? With, you know, everything going on."

"Yeah. I'm okay, I'm okay," he said, scuffing at the dirt with his toe.

"It's so sad about Perry," she said casually, watching him closely.

Something — not sadness, for sure — passed across Wallace's face. "Yeah. But when you live a life like he did, you probably can't be surprised something like this would happen."

His response caught Stan off guard. She hadn't expected him to be so callous about it. Maybe in his own head, but in front of other people? "What do you mean, a life like he did?" she asked.

Wallace flushed a little and scuffed the toe of his boot against the floor. "You know. Wearing his underwear for all the different ladies. Thumbing his nose at his parents, who wanted him to have a good, steady career. Boys like that, they don't got the good sense God gave the cows out there to appreciate a life like that. He was happy to have all the girls falling all over him. Like Lucy." He jerked his thumb behind him, probably gesturing toward the main house where Roger Tate's daughter had headed.

Stan raised an eyebrow. Had Perry and his boss's daughter had something going?

And did Andrea know?

"Perry and Lucy were close?" she asked.

Wallace scoffed. "She wanted to be, for some crazy reason. And he just liked to lead

151

girls on. Typical for guys like that."

Stan could feel the jealousy almost vibrating off the other man. Nikki felt it too — Stan could tell by the way she'd stopped browsing the bins of veggies and was also watching Wallace curiously. She wasn't sure how old Wallace was, but reckoned he was probably younger than he looked. Hard physical labor and a lot of time in the sun could drastically age a person. And unlike Perry Puck, he'd probably had to work hard jobs and do a lot of physical labor throughout his life to get anywhere. And also unlike Perry, he didn't have the dashing good looks. He wasn't unattractive, just . . . plain. And next to a guy like Perry, probably invisible.

But maybe he thought Lucy Tate shouldn't be looking at Perry if he wanted her to look at him.

"Did you work with him long?" Stan asked to keep him talking. "He always seemed like he carried his weight. At least when you guys came to my place."

"Worked with him since he started. Roger asked me to break him in, get him up to speed. Sure, he did his job. But aren't you supposed to do your job when you have one?"

Wallace Ames was clearly not a fan of his

dead colleague. But if Roger liked him, and there was something going on with Lucy, that changed things. Had Wallace felt so threatened by his younger charge that he could've wanted to get rid of him that badly? The thought made Stan's heart heavy. She liked Wallace. He was polite, he cared about organic farming, and he took the time to talk to her about the products, how they were grown, all the details. He knew his stuff, and she'd never gotten the vibe from him that he could hurt even a fly.

But had some kind of jealousy for Perry pushed him over the edge? Or had Perry done something that Wallace thought inappropriate, maybe to — or with — Lucy, and it got him killed?

"Of course," she said, but Wallace's attention had drifted away from her. She turned to see Cyril Pierce getting out of a car she'd never seen before. A black Honda sedan. Great. Just when Wallace had started talking.

Cyril lifted his hand in a wave as he made his way over. "Stan. Buying some vegetables?" he asked.

"I was trying," Stan muttered. "Nice car. Where's your bike?"

"It's my dad's," Cyril said. "Not getting any use given his condition, so I use it when my stops are too far to bike."

Cyril's dad was in an assisted living facility. His health had recently taken a turn for the worse.

Wallace regarded Cyril with a suspicious look. "Aren't you the newspaper guy?"

Cyril nodded modestly. "That's me. Cyril Pierce." He offered a hand, realizing too late his notebook was still in it. Wallace didn't remove his hand from his pocket anyway. "I'd like to speak with a few of you about Perry Puck."

Wallace spat on the ground. "We don't talk to reporters," he said. "And we got nothing to say about that guy." He turned and walked away, across the field.

Stan looked at Cyril. "You show up at the worst moments, you know that?"

"Why, were you getting something?" Cyril asked. "I'll pay you fifty bucks to write a story."

Stan turned and walked to her car.

"Is that a no?" Cyril called after her.

CHAPTER TWENTY-TWO

"That was kind of weird," Nikki said when they were back in the car, the kale and spinach packed safely in the backseat.

"You noticed it too?" Stan watched the farm fade in her rearview mirror as she drove slowly out of the lot. Wallace and Roger stood just outside the barn, talking. Stan wondered if Perry was the topic of conversation.

"Of course. That Wallace guy didn't like the dead guy. It's obvious. Like, so obvious that if I were the police and I heard him talking like that, I'd be hauling his behind down to the station." She turned toward Stan. "Is that what Jessie does? Hauls them into the station?"

"I guess. If she's serious about a suspect, she'll take them in for formal interviews."

"Then you should call her and tell her to get on it," Nikki said.

"Yeah. I don't know if she spoke to Wallace

yet. I know she talked to Roger, though." Stan instructed her Bluetooth to call Jessie. After a few false starts, it finally found the right number and connected her to Jessie's cell.

"Pasquale," she answered, sounding distracted.

"It's Stan."

"Hey. What's up?"

"A tip for you," Stan said. "I just left Roger Tate's farm. Perry's coworker Wallace had a lot to say about his dead colleague. And none of it is suitable for his obit, if you get my drift."

Silence on the other end as Jessie contemplated this. "Explain."

"Well, I think Wallace was either jealous of Perry or just plain hated him. And I got a vibe that it had something to do with the farmer's daughter. It sounded like she liked Perry, and Wallace didn't like that."

"Really," Jessie said. Stan could hear her brain ticking through the possibilities.

"Yeah. I feel bad saying this about Wallace. I like him. But he really had some animosity toward Perry. I mean, I picked up on it when they were at the shop together and figured Perry just annoyed him. It has to go deeper than that for him to be talking about a dead man with so much contempt,

156

though. He was clearly judging him for the stripper job. He made a comment about dancing in his underwear for all the different ladies."

"The farmer's daughter," Jessie said thoughtfully. "Was he seeing her on the side maybe?"

"I don't know," Stan said slowly.

"Okay. Thanks for the tip," Jessie said.

"What about the stripper place?" Stan asked before she could hang up.

"You know I can't talk about this with you."

"I was just curious what it's like there," Stan said.

"I haven't actually been able to get in," Jessie said. Her tone indicated she was less than pleased about that.

"Really. There's a lot of stonewalling going on, eh?" Stan said.

Jessie grunted on the other end of the line.

"You never know," Stan said. "Maybe it's a front for an escort service or something and they're panicking."

"Yeah," Jessie said noncommittally. "I gotta run, Stan. Thanks for the tip."

"Wait. Before you go. Any word on how long I'm going to be closed?"

"I need to do a few more things today, but we should be out of there by tonight."

Stan took a deep breath. It was what she wanted to hear, and it wasn't. Now she had to face the shop.

"I'll let you know for sure when we're out," Jessie said, then hung up.

Stan rolled to a stop at a red light and glanced over at Nikki. "You think there's something weird about the stripper place?"

"I'd say there's a strong possibility that they're going to be looking hard into the stripper place," Nikki said. "You could totally be right, Stan. I mean, maybe they were doing something illegal and Perry found out and was going to blow it up. Or maybe he was blackmailing them about it." She bounced in her seat, excited now. "Maybe it involved really high-profile people."

Stan laughed. "Okay, you've been watching way too much *CSI*. I doubt a little place in Frog Ledge would be the underground headquarters for some multimillion-dollar escort service or drug-running operation or something." But even as she said the words, she knew that was a poor assumption to make. If there was one thing she'd learned, it's that anything was possible. And money was still one of the most powerful motivators for murder.

"You know as well as I do that it's not

impossible," Nikki said. "I wonder if the girlfriend knows more than she's telling. Ooh, this is exciting." She clapped her hands together. "And I didn't hear the cop telling you to stay away. You two have come a long way."

"We really have," Stan said. "The best part is, I actually like her. Which I think relieves Jake to no end."

"Yeah, if she was always threatening to arrest you, that could've driven a real wedge into family dinners," Nikki said. "And hey, don't worry about the shop. I'll help you get it back in shape. If she's out tonight, you should stay closed tomorrow and Monday. Take tomorrow off and just regroup a bit. Then Monday we can use the time to fix it all up."

Stan nodded. "That sounds good. I think I need a little more time before I go back, even though I really want to get back up and running."

"We'll get a contingency plan together," Nikki said.

Stan's phone rang as they pulled into her driveway. She glanced at the screen and winced. "My mother."

Nikki held out her hand. "I'll field this one. I'll tell her you're concentrating on the road and can't talk."

"Bless you." Stan handed her the phone.

"Hello? Stan's phone," Nikki answered. "Hi there, Mrs. Connor. Or wait. Isn't it Mrs. Falco now?" She winked at Stan. "Yes, I know I should call you Patricia. I'm teasing. She's here but she's driving. What can I do for you?" She paused and listened. "You're confirming Monday evening. And I'm invited? Well thank you, I appreciate that. You'll pick us up at five. Okay, we'll be ready. Thanks." She disconnected and handed Stan the phone back.

"Let me guess. Dress shopping." Stan shoved the car into park, rested her head against her seat back and closed her eyes. "I knew she wouldn't forget."

"Hey, at least I'm invited too. It can be two against one," Nikki said.

"I'm sure Caitlyn is coming too. So it'll be a tie. I really don't want to go with her."

"I can't believe you haven't gotten your dress yet," Nikki said. "Why not?"

"Because I feel guilty not going with my mother," Stan said.

Nikki frowned. "But if you weren't planning on going with her, you see what kind of a pickle that leaves you in, right?"

"Of course I see," Stan grumbled. "But I know how this is gonna go." She pushed her car door open and stepped out.

"Maybe it'll go really well," Nikki said, slinging an arm around her friend's shoulder as they walked up to the porch. "Stranger things have happened, right?"

CHAPTER TWENTY-THREE

Nikki's words flooded back to Stan when she woke Sunday morning. Maybe dress shopping — and everything else wedding related — would go well, she thought, as she kicked off her covers and got out of bed. After all, there'd been a point in her life when she'd figured that her mother would have no interest at all in her wedding. Unless she was marrying one of her high-society friends' sons. They'd come a long way for her to be so engaged in the whole process. And that wasn't a bad thing.

It helped that Stan had gotten a decent night's sleep. Probably because she'd been exhausted after having not slept at all the previous night. It helped her face the day with a positive attitude. Maybe if she did some of those tricks such as saying positive affirmations and sending love to her family this whole situation would fall into place and be perfect. Starting with her dress. She was even getting excited to get it. Maybe she'd tell her mother about the place she'd found on her own, and the dress she'd seen there that she liked.

Buoyed by that attitude, she leaned over and gave her still-sleeping fiancé a kiss on the cheek and went downstairs to bake a couple batches of treats to deliver around the neighborhood today. People would be missing their Sunday-morning visit to the patisserie with their pups, and even though she couldn't re-create the casual, friendly, yummy-smelling atmosphere without her shop, she could at least make sure the neighborhood pups could have treats.

Stan put on some jazz music, pulled out her mixing bowls and ingredients, and began measuring. The rest of the house was just beginning to stir. Scruffy, her little shadow, had followed her downstairs, and Nutty was already camped out in the kitchen, nose in the air, waiting impatiently.

She'd gotten into the thick of her mixture when the doorbell rang. Of course, her hands were covered in flour and it sounded like Jake had gotten in the shower. Nikki hadn't shown any signs of being up, either. Stan rinsed her hands at the sink as the dogs charged down the hall, barking loudly to announce their guest's arrival. Stan wiped her hands hurriedly and followed them. She wasn't expecting anyone, but that didn't mean much around here. It could be Cyril with a new angle on the murder story.

But when she pulled open the front door, Stan didn't recognize the woman on her porch. For an early Sunday morning, she looked like she'd just come from a photo shoot. Her skin looked perfectly tanned, without the sun damage. A bottle, Stan figured. Her sleeveless red dress fluffed out at the bottom, enhanced by the nude platform heels she wore. Short blond hair was highlighted with chestnut streaks.

She didn't look like someone selling religion or anything, nor did she have a TV camera with her. Both good signs. Stan cracked the screen door so the dogs wouldn't charge her. "Yes?"

"Kristan Connor?"

Warily, Stan nodded.

"Excellent!" The woman beamed and stuck a hand with a perfect French manicure through the narrow door opening. "I'm Chelsea Saunders. Your wedding planner."

"My . . . I'm sorry, there's been a mistake," Stan said, raising her voice over the barking dogs. "I didn't hire a wedding planner. My wedding is planned."

Chelsea smiled. "No, but your mother did.

164

And she knows how much work you've done. She simply wants to . . . enhance it a bit."

Stan narrowed her eyes. "Isn't it kind of early on a Sunday for a wedding planner to be working?"

Chelsea beamed. "We work around the clock when there's a pending event. Besides, your mother is very generous. It was an offer I couldn't refuse, despite my very busy schedule."

Stan resisted the urge to thunk her head against the door. The dogs were still losing their minds — well, Duncan was — and she couldn't think. "Can you hold on a second? Let me put the dogs outside," she said. Closing the door in Chelsea's perfect face, Stan leaned against it for a minute and closed her eyes. She felt a paw on her leg and looked down. Scruffy stared up at her adoringly, pawing her leg.

Stan reached down and picked her up, giving her a hug. "I know, little girl," she said. "I have to deal with it, don't I?"

Jake came down the stairs, his hair still wet. He paused when he saw her and the dogs all frozen at the door. "What's wrong?"

"Can you put the dogs outside? I have a visitor." She grimaced. "A wedding planner."

Jake raised an eyebrow. "You hired a wedding planner?"

"No. But I guess my mother did."

"Ah." Jake grinned. "Well, you don't want to keep her waiting. Come on, guys."

Obediently, Duncan bounded over, followed by Gaston. Henry, never one to be rushed, lumbered behind. Stan put Scruffy down, but she opted to stay behind with Stan. Once the other three were outside, Stan pulled the door open again. "Sorry about that," she said.

"No problem." Chelsea stepped daintily into the house, bending down to pat Scruffy. "What a cutie."

Scruffy preened and batted her long eyelashes. Traitor.

"Come on in," Stan said, leading her down the hall to the kitchen. "Can I get you anything? Water? Coffee?"

"Water would be great," Chelsea said, pulling a giant planner out of her gleaming black Coach bag.

Stan motioned to the table. "Have a seat." She went to the cabinet and got a glass, added ice, and grabbed a bottle of water from the fridge.

Chelsea sat, glancing up when Jake came in. She looked him up and down and smiled. "Hi there," she said in a voice that could only be described as a purr. Nutty, sprawled on the floor in the middle of the room, looked disgusted. She rose and offered her hand. "I'm Chelsea. I'll be helping plan — well, reshape — your wedding."

"Reshape it, huh? Well, nice to meet you," Jake said, shaking Chelsea's hand. Stan could tell he was trying not to laugh — not simply at Chelsea, she presumed, but at the whole thing.

"So. Are you going to stay for our discussion?" Chelsea asked.

"I think I'm going to leave this in my beautiful fiancée's trusted hands," Jake said. "I have to head out and do a couple things." He went over and gave Stan a hug and a kiss, whispering in her ear, "Be nice." With a wave, he disappeared.

CHAPTER TWENTY-FOUR

Stan watched him go, dismayed. Her one chance at being rescued and he'd thrown her to the wolves. She thunked the glass and the bottle down on the table in front of Chelsea a bit harder than necessary. "I have to get back to my baking. I have a tight schedule today. So what are we talking about? I do have to leave in about . . ." she checked her watch, "an hour. Does that work?"

"Plenty of time!" Chelsea flashed that smile again. "So. Sit. Let's get to work."

Stan reluctantly perched on the edge of a chair, poised to flee at the first chance she got. Chelsea pretended not to notice.

"Your mother gave me a list of things that you still have to do. And my goodness, time is flying by!" She pretended to consult the calendar page in her book, although Stan could guarantee that the wedding date had been drilled into the woman's head permanently. She looked up, feigning shock. "Your wedding is in less than three weeks! We need flowers, a photographer, music . . ."

"Hold on," Stan said. "Flowers, sure. Haven't thought about that yet. But I have a photographer." She'd asked Tyler Hoffman, who worked for Cyril at the newspaper, to take the photos. He was fresh out of college, passionate about his camera, and a good kid who could use the money. Emmalee, his mother, had been over the moon when Stan had asked him.

"Your mom told me you'd asked one of the neighborhood kids to help out." Chelsea pursed her lips and patted Stan's hand. "That's lovely of you. But you really should have a backup. A *professional.*" She enunciated the word carefully in case Stan didn't understand its meaning.

So much for this going well. Stan cursed herself for letting her guard down this morning. "I appreciate your input, but Tyler is a professional. He's a photojournalist, and he'll do a great job. As far as the music," she said, forging on even though Chelsea opened her mouth again to argue the point, "we're having the party at Jake's pub. He's got live music coming in. So we're good there too. I guess all we need is flowers, then, right? I like purple. Well, that was fun."

She started to rise from the table, hoping to end the meeting fifty minutes early, but Chelsea reached over and clamped a hand on Stan's wrist.

"Oh, no, Kristan, hold on a minute," she said. "According to my notes, your mother wants to have the reception on her property. Outdoors. Not in a . . . bar." She grimaced a little. "So we'll have to discuss decorations, a DJ, food, the toast . . . how many people are in your wedding party again?" She uncapped a red felt-tip pen and held it poised over her notebook, looking expectantly at Stan, who was still frozen halfway between sitting and standing, not quite believing what she was hearing.

She was going to have Jessie arrest her mother. Or at the very least make her leave town until the wedding was over. How could she even *think* she was getting her way on this? Bad enough she was pressing the point about the church, but there was *no way* she was moving the party from the pub to her mother's house.

"My mother said what?" she asked, her voice dangerously low. Even not knowing her for more than ten minutes, Chelsea seemed to sense that a line had been crossed. She licked her gleaming, glossed lips nervously.

"Well, she said there was still some debate over where everything was going to be held," Chelsea said.

"My invitations went out months ago," Stan said. "There's no debate."

"Well, that's debatable," Chelsea said, still smiling. "Good thing this is a small town," she added with a forced chuckle. "You can easily spread the word about a change of plans. Do you want to confer with your mother and I can come back?"

Stan was simultaneously counting to ten and trying to come up with three good reasons not to toss this woman out on her sculpted tush without further conversation when Nikki breezed in. She'd clearly overheard the last bit, and she took one look at Stan's face and jumped in.

"That probably won't be necessary," she said. "We've got everything under control here. But thank you so much for your time. I can walk you out." Nikki smiled, poised above Chelsea's chair.

Chelsea looked from Stan to Nikki and back again, then shoved her notebook into her bag. "Well then. I'll be sure to let your mother know you're making your own plans," she said stiffly. "It was lovely meeting you. I hope you have a . . . successful wedding."

"I'd rather have a successful marriage," Stan said. "But thanks."

Nikki hustled the wayward wedding planner down the hall before Stan could get another dig in. Nikki was back a minute later, shaking her head. "Man, your mother is *persistent.*"

"Right? I'm going to call her right now and give her a piece of my mind." Stan looked at Nikki. "You came down at the perfect time. Thank you."

"I'd love to take credit for having bestie ESP, but Jake called me. Evidently he was worried that there might be another murder in town."

"Ah, yes. He ran out of here like a scared little boy, though." Stan grinned. "Oh well. I guess we both looked scary enough to get her out of here. You should've heard this chick! She says my mother is moving the reception to her house. Is she *kidding* me? I'm about to uninvite her. Maybe I should do that. Where's my phone?" She grabbed her purse and rifled through it.

"Whoa, hang on." Nikki grabbed her arm. "Don't do that. Let's calm down first and then we can figure out how to approach your mom and tell her she's not running this show. Man, doesn't she have enough to do with Caitlyn's wedding? I would figure she would be in her glory there. I'm sure Caitlyn wants the whole shebang."

"Yeah, I don't know why she's not focused on that. Although maybe because it's Caitlyn's second wedding. Maybe she's thinking she already paid for one big shebang. Who knows. Who cares? Really. I'm going to elope. Let's just get on a plane and go to a beach somewhere. You, Izzy, Brenna, Jessie, Liam. Shoot, Amara and Char would want to come too. And Jake's side of the wedding party." She sighed. "Probably not realistic, huh?"

Nikki shook her head. "Nope. Especially since I can't give Justin that many days off from manning the fort at home." She grinned. "He only gets a day's furlough, and I would kind of want him to be my date."

CHAPTER TWENTY-FIVE

"She really sent a wedding planner to your house." Izzy grimaced at the thought. "Poor girl. She probably had no idea what hit her."

It was Sunday night, and Stan, Nikki, Amara, and Izzy huddled around a table at the pub, commiserating about the latest in Stan's wedding saga. They'd decided on an impromptu girls' night out, figuring they all needed to blow off some steam.

"She almost got tossed off the porch," Nikki said with a grin. "I interceded just in time."

"I thought about sending her to Caitlyn's and just telling her there was a mistake with the address, but . . ." Stan sighed. "Really, it's impressive that my mother has such a one-track mind, even in the midst of murder."

"It's kind of nice, though, no?" Amara said, a little wistfully.

All heads swiveled in her direction.

"What?" she said defensively. "My family doesn't care about my wedding."

"Girl, when *is* your wedding?" Izzy demanded. "You've been engaged, like, forever."

"I know," Amara sighed. "Vince wanted to finish his classes first. And he's almost done, so I think it might actually be this summer. And it will definitely be a small affair," she added. "No wedding planners."

Amara and her fiancé Vincent owned the town's only veterinary practice. It was a combination of holistic and traditional medicine. Amara was the holistic practitioner and Vincent did the traditional, although he'd decided that he wanted to practice with Chinese herbs and acupuncture. So he'd been studying for those certifications in recent months.

"That's great!" Stan exclaimed. "This is going to be the summer of weddings, I guess." She eyed Izzy. "What about you?"

"What about me?" Izzy asked.

"Oh come on! You and Liam are perfect. Of course you should get married," Stan said, poking her.

"Of course we're perfect," Izzy said. "But we haven't talked about that yet."

"Well, why not?" Amara said. "You guys waited a long time to really be together. Why waste time?"

"Jeez, the peer pressure," Izzy said. "We'll get there, don't worry. I promise you guys will be the first to know. Now, when's your shop opening up again?"

Stan's smile faltered. "Tuesday. If I can ever face going back in again," which she needed to do tomorrow.

Izzy put an arm around Stan's shoulder and gave her a one-armed hug. "You will. We'll get in there tomorrow and get it all cleaned up."

"And sage it," Amara added.

"Yes. Definitely sage it." Nikki nodded emphatically.

Stan looked at her. "Since when are you into saging?"

Nikki shrugged. "I can be Zen too."

Stan giggled. She'd never thought of her intense friend as being Zen. Nikki was driven, passionate, and downright fierce about her life's work and her animals, but she wasn't the first person who would come to mind as Zen.

"Stop laughing at me. It's true."

"I'm not laughing. Really, I'm so grateful to all of you for being here for me." Stan had only had one drink, but she was feeling extra weepy tonight.

"Of course we're all here for you." Nikki

squeezed her hand.

"Do you think I should've done the wedding planner thing?" Stan asked.

"Did you want to?" Izzy asked.

"No," Stan admitted. "But I bet my mother's mad."

"You have everything planned," Nikki pointed out. "It seems silly. But I guess from your mother's point of view . . ." she sighed. "Did you talk to her?"

Stan shook her head. "I turned my ringer off. She's called twice so far. I know, I'm a wuss. I just don't have the energy to fight her right now."

Nikki hid a smile. "That's one way to do it. Look, Stan. I know you guys have had your differences. I know she drives you crazy. And I know you're totally different. But I think this might actually be her way of getting engaged and showing you she cares." She squeezed Stan's arm. "So maybe go easy on her with the wedding stuff."

Nikki was right, Stan reflected as she took another sip of the fresh martini Jake had put in front of her. If she'd learned one thing from being here in Frog Ledge, it was that family was more important than anything else. And family came in many different incarnations.

Like the family she'd found here, in this

very place.

She felt a rush of love for McSwigg's, and what Jake had created here. And for what it meant to the two of them. The moment she'd stepped inside the pub it had felt right. Jake had a hand-carved sign in Gaelic over the bar, which, translated, read *Your feet will take you to where your heart is.* It had never been truer for her than when she'd been led here.

As if she'd summoned him, Jake appeared at their side. "You girls need anything else right now?" he asked.

"I'll have another," Amara said, holding up her empty wineglass.

"You got it. Where's my cousin tonight?" Jake asked Izzy.

"He had to go into the city for a thing. He should be on his way back soon."

"A thing?" Jake repeated.

"You know. A writing thing. He's meeting that monthly group of his. I bet he'll stop by when he gets back."

Stan noticed Scott wiping down tables across the room, seemingly lost in thought. She still hadn't managed to catch up with him about whatever he'd been about to tell her Friday night. Maybe he'd be more in the mood to talk now if she took him outside on his break or something.

178

Or maybe he wouldn't, but she still had to give it a shot. If he knew something — anything at all — it could help point them in the right direction.

CHAPTER TWENTY-SIX

Excusing herself, Stan went over to him. "Hey," she said.

"Hi, Stan. What are you up to?"

"Girls' night." She waved at the bar, where Amara, Nikki, and Izzy sat. Jake had gone back to waiting on customers, and Brenna appeared behind the bar, tying on an apron and getting ready to mix some mad drinks.

"Nice," Scott said.

"Yeah. Hey, do you have a break coming up?"

Scott glanced at his watch. "I can, yeah. Why?"

"Can we talk outside?"

"Sure. Let me just tell Jake." He went behind the bar and deposited the empty glasses he'd collected, said something to Jake, then motioned to Stan. She followed him out back. She could feel Jake's curious gaze on her as she went. She'd explain later.

"So what's up?" Scott asked, holding the

door for her. They stepped out into the pub's back parking lot.

Stan waited until the door had closed completely, then she spoke. "Friday night. When we were all at my house. You seemed like you were going to say something — I thought about Perry — but then someone came in and you changed your mind."

Scott looked away, his eyes roving over the parking lot. Stan couldn't tell if he was looking for an answer to her question, or to see if anyone was around.

"I was," he said finally. "But I didn't want to say anything in front of a bunch of people. I didn't want to freak Brenna out, for one thing."

Stan's antennae were on high alert. "If you know something that might help figure out who killed Perry, you have to tell someone, Scott. You don't have to tell me. You can talk to Jessie."

He winced a bit. "She scares me."

Stan smiled. Jessie had that effect on people. It had taken her a long time to not fear Jake's no-nonsense sister too. But over time, she'd figured out how to crack that hard shell and understand the person behind it. "I get that. You can tell me. We'll figure it out." She glanced at her phone when it rang in her hand and grimaced. Her mother. Again. She declined the call. There was no way Stan could deal with her right now. She needed some distance after the wedding planner debacle.

"You're going to have to tell Jessie and she'll want to talk to me anyway," he said.

"Huh?" Distracted, she glanced back at Scott.

"Jessie? You're going to tell her," he repeated.

"Yes. But it's the right thing to do, Scott."

"Yeah." He sighed. "I get it. Okay. So Perry told me he had a stalker."

"A stalker?" Stan frowned. Her phone beeped in her hand, signaling a voice mail. She shoved it in her pocket and refocused. "Wait. I didn't know you were friends with Perry. That seems like something heavy to confide to just anyone."

Scott shrugged. "The girls hang out all the time, so we kind of got thrown together by default. He was a good guy. Not really my typical friend, but he was cool. We were out one night and the girls were huddling talking about something. He'd had a couple drinks and he confided in me." His eyes clouded over at the memory. "He was under the impression that I was a shrink of some sort. He didn't really get the whole addiction counselor thing."

Prior to moving to Frog Ledge, Scott had worked with addicts and recovering addicts, until he'd lost one of his clients and decided he needed a break. Now he worked at McSwigg's.

"So what kind of stalker?"

Scott stared at her. "I didn't know there were categories."

"You know, a dangerous one? A lovesick one? Why did he think that? What did the person do? Was it a girl or a guy?" Stan prompted. "Was he afraid?"

"He didn't really know the gender. I think at first he thought it was funny. A joke or something. Maybe he was even a little flattered. Perry was a good guy, but he did have an ego. But after a while he got a little freaked out."

"Did he tell anyone? Did Andrea know?"

Scott raised an eyebrow. "You think if she did, Brenna wouldn't have known?" he asked.

"Good point. So did he give you any examples of what happened? Did they leave him things? Call him and do the heavy-breathing thing?"

"Jeez. You've done your research on stalkers, huh?" He shook his head. "He told me there was someone who'd been sending him letters. Telling him they loved watching him,

183

stuff like that. Innocent enough, I guess. But then it got weird. I think he started to feel threatened by it. He thought . . . someone had been in his apartment once. That some of his things were moved around."

"Did he ever report it?"

"Not that he told me."

Stan closed her eyes. Jessie was going to freak out that he'd taken so long to tell her this. "Scott. We have to tell Jessie. This could be the lead that breaks the case open. Did he think it had to do with his stripper job?" It had to. Then again, who knew? Sometimes the obvious answers were completely wrong.

Scott shrugged. "I think that's what he assumed. But he didn't know for sure. The person didn't reference it specifically in the notes. I don't know, it would've seemed creepy to me right from the start, but I'm different." He sighed and leaned against the wall, fiddling with the keys on his belt. "Jessie's going to be mad that I didn't tell her right away, isn't she?"

"Probably," Stan said bluntly. There was no time to sugarcoat matters. "So why didn't you?"

"I don't know. I just froze, I guess." Scott shoved his hands in his pockets. "I guess I didn't want to think that it was real, that it was the reason for this."

"It was a pretty violent crime," Stan said quietly. "Did the notes outwardly threaten him?"

"Not in so many words. But it was the only time we talked about it. The girls came back and he stopped talking. He didn't want Andrea to know. She was already giving him grief for doing that job."

Andrea again. "When did he tell you this?" Stan asked. "About the stalker?"

"This was a month or so ago."

"Did he say how long it had been going on before he told you?"

Scott thought about that. "I can't remember for sure. Maybe a month or two?"

So it had been going on for a while. Stan wondered if it had escalated beyond a few notes and into something a lot darker. "Okay. Let me talk to Jessie first. That way I can smooth the path for you. But she'll want to talk to you herself."

"I know. Thanks, Stan." He checked his watch. "I gotta get back inside."

He held the door for her and followed her back into the pub. She slipped back onto her stool, watching him walk back to wiping his tables, shoulders slumped, head down.

A stalker. This changed everything. She had to call Jessie. Now. If she left this for even a few more hours, her sister-in-law-to-be might kill her.

"Hey Bren?" she called over to where Brenna mixed some kind of pretty rum drink.

"Yeah?"

"Can I run upstairs for a minute? I have to make a call." Brenna and Scott lived in Jake's old apartment above the pub. They kind of took it for granted that Jake, and by default Stan, would use it as needed when they were in the pub, given the time they spent there.

"Of course. It's open."

"Be right back, guys," she said to her friends, slipping out before they could ask her what she was up to now. She took the narrow stairs two at a time, slipped into the apartment, and pulled out her cell phone.

Jessie answered on the first ring. She was working, Stan could hear it in her voice. She always had an air of no-nonsense about her, but when she was working it was amplified by a thousand. She might be working in her home office, or in a room Marty had turned into an office in his house for her, or maybe she was over in the town hall.

"It's me. I have a possible lead for you," Stan said.

"Another one? You've been busy. Do tell."

"Perry had a stalker."

Silence. Then, "A stalker."

"Yeah. For a couple months at least."

"How did you find this out?"

Stan hesitated. "Scott told me. Just now."

"Scott? Brenna's Scott?"

"Yes. Go easy on him, Jess," she said before Jessie could explode. "He's still afraid of you."

"If he was afraid of me he should know that this wouldn't go over well. He should've been in my face telling me this on Friday night. What is *wrong* with him?" She was pacing, Stan could tell. She could hear Jessie's shoes slapping against the floor.

"I know. But I'm telling you now."

"Great. I've been chasing my tail with family and farmers in the meantime." Jessie sounded disgusted. "What kind of stalker? A scary one or a lovesick one?"

"Ha. That's exactly what I asked," Stan said. "It sounded like he wasn't scared at first, but then it changed. You really should talk to Scott."

"Is he working?"

"Yeah. I'm here at the pub. I pulled him aside because when everyone was back at our place Friday, he looked like he was about to tell me something, but then someone came in and he stopped. I finally got to ask him about it and he caved. I guess he and Perry had gotten somewhat friendly because the four of them were out together quite a bit. And hey, Jess." Stan took a breath. "I keep hearing how Andrea was not a fan of Perry's side gig."

"I've been sensing that too. And that makes my life hard. I can't rule her out as a suspect, and it's really driving my sister over the edge."

"I know. This whole thing . . . what a mess."

"Yeah."

They were both silent for a minute.

"Well, I guess I better come over there and talk to him," Jessie said. "You want to give him a heads-up so he doesn't pass out when he sees me?"

Stan smiled despite herself. "I'll make sure there's a couch or something in the vicinity when I tell him."

Chapter Twenty-Seven

Stan headed downstairs and found Scott in the kitchen picking up some food orders. "Jessie's on her way," she said.

He winced visibly. "Is she mad?"

"No," Stan lied. "She just wants to solve the case. As we all do."

"Okay. I'll let Jake know I need to disappear for a bit." He sighed. "I guess Brenna will find out."

"Most likely," Stan agreed.

"Great," Scott muttered. "She'll be mad at me too."

"Scott." Stan put her hands on his shoulders. "Listen. Brenna will be fine. She understands the whole concept of guy talk. There was no way to know . . . what would happen. Okay?"

He looked at her for a long moment, then nodded. "Okay. Thanks for helping me out, Stan."

"Of course. Now no running out the back

door," she warned.

He smiled, a little. "I'll try."

Stan went back to the bar and joined her friends.

Nikki surveyed her. "What's going on? You have that look."

"What look?"

"The look like you're either doing something on the down-low, or you're in trouble and trying to hide it."

Stan laughed. "I'm not in trouble. At the moment, anyway." She trailed off as Scott came out and pulled Jake aside, leaning in to say something.

Jake raised his eyebrows, then nodded. When Scott walked away, he looked at Stan. She offered a weak smile.

Brenna was watching all of this with one eye as she chatted up customers, poured and served drinks, and wiped down the bar. When she was finally able to take a second, she came over to Stan. "Is something going on?" she asked.

Shoot. She didn't really know how to answer this. "Scott has to talk to Jessie about something, that's all," she said.

"About what? Something to do with Perry?" Brenna went on alert. "Something new? What's going on?"

Stan reached out and squeezed her hand.

"I'm going to let him tell you, Bren. Okay?"

Without a word, Brenna dropped her towel, eyes searching the bar for her boyfriend. When she found him, she marched over and tapped him on the shoulder. Stan watched Brenna bend her head close and say something to him, and the two of them went out the door leading to the apartment.

Looks like Scott would be telling the story a few times tonight.

"What was that about?" Izzy asked, watching the scene with morbid fascination.

"Scott remembered something that might help Jessie," Stan said.

"And clearly he didn't tell his girlfriend about it, either," Izzy said.

Jake came over and tapped her on the shoulder. "Babe," he said. "What's going on that half my staff is vanishing on me?"

Stan feigned innocence. "Why do you think I would know this?"

He arched an eyebrow. "Really? You're always involved when there's trouble. No offense. That's just a fact. So why is my sister coming to talk to Scott? And why did Brenna freak out and drag him upstairs?"

"Can we talk about this out back?" Stan said, acutely aware of the other bar patrons. Not that anyone was outright listening to them, but she didn't want more rumors circulating around town. Especially with Perry's family so sensitive about the whole thing. That would create more problems for Jessie's investigation.

"Sure," Jake said. "As soon as I find someone to cover the bar. Meantime, you wanna help me clear tables? My guess is, Scott'll be tied up for a bit." He nodded over Stan's shoulder at Jessie, who was making her way toward them, ignoring offers of drinks as she passed. Jessie didn't drink. The one time Stan had seen her take a few sips of beer, she'd been spiraling into a depression about possibly losing one of her cases to higher-ups in the department. Once she'd stopped wallowing, she'd put the beer down and gotten right back to work.

Jessie barely paused as she reached their table. "Is he upstairs?" she asked, her gaze roving from face to face until Jake nodded. She marched over to the door leading upstairs. It slammed behind her.

Jake looked at Stan. She got up from her seat. "Do I at least get a McSwigg's T-shirt if you're putting me to work?" she asked.

Jake had been kidding — he didn't really expect her to clean tables. But Stan didn't mind. She was feeling antsy and really wanted to go upstairs and listen to the conversation between Jessie and Scott. But she knew Jessie would toss her out, as she had Brenna, so she figured she'd do something else to keep her mind occupied. She loved this place, and anything she did here to help didn't feel like work. Just like when she worked at her own shop. So she left her friends laughing and chatting together, and set about doing some chores.

It was Sunday, so it wasn't as packed as the rest of the weekend, but there was still a good crowd. And Perry's death was still the hot news in town. Stan could feel the eyes on her as she moved around, saying hello to people, picking up glasses and empty dishes, and stopping to chitchat with certain people. She hadn't realized Jake's Uncle Seamus and his longtime companion, the endearing Miss Viv, were snuggled together at a table way in the back until she was nearly on top of them.

Seamus brightened when he saw her. "Hello there, little lady!" he boomed in that deep, Irish voice. "That nephew of mine putting you to work? I'll go tell him a thing or two!"

Stan laughed and allowed Seamus to pull her over for a kiss on the cheek. "I volunteered. Hi, Uncle Seamus. Miss Viv. How are you both?"

"We're terribly upset," Miss Viv said. "Aren't we, Seamus?"

Seamus didn't look terribly upset to Stan, but she focused on Miss Viv. "I'm sorry to hear. What about?"

"Why, the murder, of course!" Miss Viv lowered her voice on the dastardly word, glancing around to see if anyone was listening.

"Right. Yes, it was very upsetting," Stan said.

"I bet that was quite a moment," Seamus said, shaking his head. "A poor sucker like that, getting knifed in a cake. It's a bit like the whole Santa fiasco, no?"

Stan sighed inwardly at the mention of the excitement over the winter involving an imposter Santa, a murder, and a failed heist. Seamus wasn't the most politically correct or socially savvy guy she'd ever met. Granted, he'd improved a lot when faced with his own mortality during the "Santa fiasco" of last winter, and Stan had grudgingly changed her mind about him. But he still had his moments where he could use some coaching.

"It was quite a moment," Stan said, picking up his empty beer bottle and a plate with one sad-looking French fry left on it. "But Jessie will solve it." She started to walk away, but Seamus called her back.

"You know, that newspaper friend of yours is doing some research. For a book," he said.

Stan paused. "How do you know that?"

Seamus shrugged. "He interviewed me. Said I was top of the list." He puffed out his chest, looking proud of himself.

"Yeah, he's going to be famous," Miss Viv chimed in. "I'm so proud of him." She pulled her pashmina around her shoulders and gazed up at him adoringly.

"Oh, boy," Stan muttered. "Congrats, Uncle Seamus." She hurried back to the bar.

Jake raised his eyebrows when he saw the look on her face. "What?"

"Apparently, your uncle is going to be prominently featured in Cyril's upcoming book," Stan said.

"You're kidding."

"Wish I was. Can I get another martini?"

An hour and a half later, Jessie came down, followed by Scott. He looked a little pale, but at least he was still standing. Jessie didn't stop to talk to anyone, and headed straight for the door. Stan followed her outside and caught up with her as she was about to get into her car.

"Hey," she said. "You're just going to leave?"

Jessie turned. "Yeah, well, I have to start figuring out who was stalking my murder victim, since I'm now behind the eight ball with that information." She rubbed her temples. "A freakin' stalker. Kill me now," she said, then winced. "Bad joke."

"Right. But, yes, a stalker. That changes things, doesn't it?"

"Everything about this case changes on a moment-by-moment basis. God, this is one of those times I actually wished I drank. Between my sister's best friend possibly being involved and all the roadblocks around this guy, it's really frustrating."

Stan nodded. "I get it. And it's tough because Brenna is feeling protective of Andrea."

"She's barely talking to me," Jessie said bluntly. "And it stinks."

Stan was silent. Jessie had never been one to share her feelings, and she wasn't quite sure what to do with this. "She'll come around," Stan said finally.

"Yeah." Jessie shrugged and looked away. "I should go. Marty has Lily and Eva. And I have to tell him I'm going to be working all night now."

"Eva? My niece?"

Jessie nodded.

"Wow, those two have really hit it off,"

Stan said. "I'm so glad Eva found a friend right away."

"Are you kidding? She's like the most popular kid in the class, according to Lily. She just walked in the door and acclimated. It's pretty amazing."

"Caitlyn was always that way too. Doesn't surprise me."

Stan watched Jessie drive away, in no hurry to get back inside. It was a beautiful night out, another clear sky with stars as far as she could see. She pulled out her phone to take a picture, and saw the icon indicating she had a voice mail.

She sighed. Her mother. She had to deal with this situation. Ignoring it and letting it fester was the wrong way to handle it, but there was still a part of her that retreated into teenager mode when facing a conflict with her mother. Old habits die hard.

She played the message. But it wasn't what she expected. Her mother wasn't calling to give her yet another mandate about her impending nuptials. Instead, she wanted to tell her she was having coffee with Gabrielle Puck the next morning at Izzy's.

"I expect you'll make an appearance," Patricia said. "Please make sure you don't incriminate me. And Kristan? I'm not pleased about what happened with Chelsea.

We're going to revisit this."

"Sure, Mom," Stan muttered. "After we deal with finding a killer."

CHAPTER TWENTY-EIGHT

Monday morning. Stan woke earlier than normal, her stomach churning with butterflies. Between the meeting with her mother and Gabrielle Puck, having to face her shop, and an evening of wedding dress shopping, she wasn't sure how to think about the day ahead. Kill it with positivity? Prepare for the worst? It seemed so daunting.

"Babe?" Jake murmured next to her. "What's wrong?"

"I'm sorry. I didn't mean to wake you." Stan leaned over and gave him a quick kiss. "I'm getting up."

"Where you going so early?"

"I . . . have to meet my mother."

He seemed to accept that and dozed off again. Stan got up and showered, fed the dogs and cats, and slipped out the door.

Stan jumped a foot when she saw Caitlyn standing next to her car in the driveway.

"God, you scared me," Stan said. "What are you doing here?"

"I heard through the grapevine that Mom was meeting the Puck lady today," she said. "I wanted to come with you."

"Through what grapevine?" Stan beeped her car open and slid into it. "What kind of grapevine knows that?"

Caitlyn climbed in the passenger side. She looked a bit more put together this morning, if also tired. "Mom told me. She also said we're going dress shopping tonight. Were you going to tell me?" she demanded. "Or try to go without me?"

The now-familiar headache began to throb above Stan's eyebrows. She needed coffee. She backed out of the driveway and headed toward Izzy's. "Yes, I was going to tell you. It's been a little crazy around town, if you hadn't noticed."

Caitlyn sniffed. "You didn't even invite me out last night. Was that a substitute bachelorette party?"

Stan felt a twinge of guilt. She probably should've made it a point to call her sister. "Caitlyn. No. We were just hanging out and decided to get a drink. I'm sorry I didn't call. It happened last minute."

"Hmmmph," Caitlyn said.

"I heard Eva and Lily were hanging out

last night," Stan said.

"How did you hear that?"

"Through the grapevine," Stan teased. "Jessie told me."

"*Jessie* even came out for drinks with you?" Caitlyn exclaimed.

"No. God. She stopped by the pub to talk to someone." Stan decided to keep her mouth shut from here on out. Luckily, they arrived at Izzy's. She parked and opened her door. "Remember, this is a chance meeting."

"I know," Caitlyn said. "I can do the detective thing too. Jeez."

Stan gritted her teeth and got out of the car. She took a minute to reset a pleasant expression on her face, and breezed into Izzy's as if she'd been passing by on a whim and needed an iced coffee to get her through the next part of her day.

She spotted her mother sitting in the back and feigned surprise, pushing Caitlyn in her direction. "Mom! What a nice surprise," Stan said, hurrying over and bending to give her a kiss.

"Girls! What are you doing out this early?" Patricia squeezed both their hands.

"Caitlyn's helping me with some deliveries," Stan said. "But we need to fuel up first." She turned her attention to Gabrielle

Puck, offering what she hoped was a polite but questioning smile.

Patricia took her cue nicely. "Girls, have you met Gabrielle Puck? We serve on the board of Safe Harbor together. She's become quite a dear friend. Gabrielle, these are my daughters, Kristan and Caitlyn."

"Hello," Caitlyn said.

"Pleasure." Gabrielle Puck held out a hand to Stan, who was closer. Stan used the hand-shaking time to take a closer look at her.

She wasn't quite what Stan had expected. Younger, although Stan wasn't sure why she'd pictured her as older. Perry was young, and his sister couldn't have been more than a few years older than him. Stan pegged Gabrielle in her early fifties. She could see why her mother had bonded with her. They looked very similar, dressed to the nines to go out for a neighborhood coffee on a Monday morning.

And for someone who'd lost her son three days ago, she looked very put together.

"Nice to meet you," Stan said. "I'm so sorry for your loss."

Gabrielle's pasted-on smile flickered, and she looked down at the table, where a cappuccino was getting cold. "Thank you," she said. "I understand you knew my son."

Stan nodded and slid into the seat next to her mother. Caitlyn grabbed a chair from the next table and pulled it over for herself. "He delivered my orders from the Tate farm. He was lovely."

Gabrielle nodded. "Thank you. He was."

The four of them lapsed into an awkward silence for a minute or two. Stan risked a glance at her mother. Patricia raised an eyebrow to say, *What do you want from me?*

Aww, screw it. "Mrs. Puck. Everyone in town is so upset about this. We all want to help the police find out who did this. As I'm sure you do as well."

Gabrielle inclined her chin a notch, a subtle agreement, but she said nothing.

Stan pushed on. "I know you have an attorney representing your family, but it would really help our sergeant in charge of the investigation if you talked to her. You know, to give her some information. You're the only one who's known Perry, well, all his life." She offered a smile that she hoped was charming, yet properly subdued given the nature of the conversation.

Gabrielle tensed across the table, her fingers clutching the handle of her coffee cup so tightly Stan worried it would break off. "My husband has reasons for doing things this way," she said. "Given the . . .

circumstances of my son's death and our public lives, we didn't want any of that unnecessarily promoted in the media." Her voice had dropped to nearly a whisper, even though everyone around them was engaged in their own conversations and not paying the least bit of attention.

Stan nodded earnestly. "I understand that completely," she said, although the words stuck in her throat. This woman's son was dead and she was worried about her public reputation? "But Sergeant Pasquale has no interest in the media, either."

Gabrielle considered this. "I suppose she wouldn't," she said, with a glance at Patricia. Looking for input.

"Of course not," Patricia said emphatically. "That's the last thing she wants. All she's hoping to do is find the path to solving this case for your family. Sergeant Pasquale is very dedicated, you know. She's going to be Stan's sister-in-law soon, so we can personally vouch for her as well as professionally."

Patricia leaned forward and covered Gabrielle's hand with her own. "I can't imagine being in your shoes right now. Losing a child, grieving, and having to deal with advice and the public on top of it. But truly, Gabrielle, anything you can offer to the police so they can track this maniac down would be so helpful."

Stan held her breath. She thought it had worked, especially when she saw a glint of tears in the other woman's eyes. But then Gabrielle took a deep breath and withdrew her hand.

"I really don't have anything else that might help them," she said stiffly. "Perry wasn't as . . . close with the family as some would imagine. He had his own life. I'm sorry. Thank you for your kindness, Patricia, and the coffee. Nice meeting you girls." She picked up her purse and hurried out of the café, nearly knocking over a woman trying to enter.

Stan watched her go, then turned to her mother. "It was a good effort," she said.

Patricia's tight lips and the set of her jaw told Stan she wasn't pleased. Stan figured she'd get a good talking-to about how this could hurt her mother's social standing in town, make a powerful enemy for Tony, and so on. It would probably result in some other indignity being forced on her at her wedding. She slouched in her chair, waiting for it. Across the table, Caitlyn held her breath too.

It never came.

"There's something very strange about

that family's attitude," Patricia said. "If something happened to one of you girls, I don't care how much public ridicule it could cause me. I'd be doing whatever I could to help the experts find out what happened. Unless, of course, I had something to hide." She looked at Stan. "Now I want to get to the bottom of this. You must be rubbing off on me." With a wink, Patricia brushed Stan's cheek with her lips, picked up her own purse, and walked out, leaving Stan staring after her in amazement.

CHAPTER TWENTY-NINE

"Not even a word about Chelsea," Stan said in wonderment to Nikki after she dropped Caitlyn off and went home. "I mean, it was kind of surreal."

"I can imagine. I figured you'd be walking into some kind of trap," Nikki said.

Stan nodded emphatically. "Me too! I mean, I'm sure she's planning it for next time. That's not the point. The point is that she stopped fixating on it long enough to actually have a reaction to someone else being a horrible mother!"

"That is notable," Nikki said, stifling a yawn and pulling two mugs out of the cabinet. "Coffee?"

"Of course," Stan said.

"How are you so chipper, anyway?" Nikki filled the mugs and placed one in front of Stan, then sat across from her.

"I had a giant latte with two extra shots at Izzy's. But it's wearing off." Stan sank down into a chair. "I have to go see Jessie and tell her about this. You know, I have my differences with my mother, clearly, but Perry Puck's mother . . ." Stan shook her head. "It sounded like her son wasn't as important as her reputation. Or at least that's what her husband thinks. It made me really sad for Perry. And my mother was mortified. I mean, she actually got mad on Perry's behalf. What do you make of that?"

"Well —" Nikki began.

"Then she turns around and does this stuff she's doing with my wedding and it makes me crazy," Stan went on, without even noticing Nikki had started talking. "Sorry," she said, realizing she had cut her friend off.

Nikki waved her off. "If you really want my opinion, I think your mother will always be Patricia Connor, socialite, rich lady, a bit snobby. No offense."

"None taken."

"But," Nikki continued, "I think she's realized a lot of things. Maybe it's because of Tony, maybe it's because she moved here and sees the life you created, maybe it's just mellowing with age. Regardless, people grow, you know? And I think your mother has done some growing."

Stan sipped her coffee, her eyes meeting

her friend's over the coffee cup. "Yeah. I think you're right. She has, hasn't she?"

"She has. Which is why I said the other day, maybe you might want to go a little easy on her about the wedding stuff."

Stan sighed. "I hear you."

Nikki's eyes widened. "You do?"

Stan nodded. "I do. I mean, seriously, I had no problem with her getting involved. But I don't want it to be all her way. You know? I don't want her changing everything. I wanted her help in planning what *I* wanted. And I hate that this is bringing out the sixteen-year-old in me."

Nikki laughed. "I think it's inevitable with some mothers and daughters. Especially in your case."

"So maybe we can compromise," Stan said. "Maybe if we do the church thing, we can still do the party at McSwigg's. Sounds fair, right?"

"Sounds fair to me," Nikki said with a shrug. "We'll have to see what Chelsea thinks."

"Now," Stan said, "you're pushing your luck."

"It was weird. And my mother even thought so," Stan said, pacing the little kitchen at Jessie's boyfriend Marty's house. She'd

managed to track Jessie down there. Sometimes when Jessie was in the middle of a big
case she avoided the office, just to eliminate
the steady stream of townspeople who
wanted to come in and offer their help —
or talk about it. "That was weird too. But
she definitely was displeased with the way
the Pucks are handling this. It was like she
took it as a personal affront that they were
not putting their son first."

"It sounds like the way a good mother
would react," Marty said.

He was always so reasonable. And so . . .
chill. Marty Thompson would not have been
someone Stan would've guessed could
capture Jessie's heart. He wore his blond
hair messy and a bit long. The laugh lines
around his brown eyes attested to his sense
of humor and showed that he enjoyed his
life immensely. He was laid back where she
was intense, found the humor in everything
when she tended to go to the dark side, and
was satisfied where she was overly ambi-
tious. Marty owned his own moving company and was perfectly happy to serve the
surrounding community and then come
home every night to watch whatever sport-
ing event was on television. He didn't need
to get bigger, or expand, or travel all over
New England. He was happy with what he

had. He'd definitely helped Jessie strike more of a balance in her own life, and maybe even lighten up a bit.

"Exactly," Stan said. "I just didn't expect *my* mother to react like that. Not to say she's not a good mother," she hastened to add. "You know what I mean. Ugh. This is all coming out wrong. I'm a terrible person."

"You're exaggerating, Stan," he said affectionately. "She's a nice lady."

"She can be," Stan corrected. "She can also be the quintessential dragon lady. You haven't seen it." She shook a finger at Marty. "Come back and talk to me when that side of her makes an appearance in front of you."

"So Mrs. Puck won't budge, eh?" Jessie sat at the table, both legs drawn under her so she was cross-legged. Clearly, she wasn't interested in dissecting Patricia's personality adjustments. An abandoned piece of toast and pages of notes sat in front of her. She wore leggings and one of Marty's old UConn sweatshirts. Her long red hair was pulled back in a ponytail and she wore no makeup.

But Jessie never wore makeup, and she looked better than most twentysomethings who spent hours at the mirror with the latest products. She was one of those redheads with clear, smooth skin, not the million-freckles kind of redhead. Worst part was, Stan knew half the time she didn't bother to pay attention to her looks. It killed Jessie to even wear eyeliner.

"Nope." Stan slid into the seat across from her. "For a second I thought she was going to. My mother laid it on pretty thick. But she chickened out. I wonder if her husband is crazy mean, or if they really have something they're trying to hide."

"That's a really good question," Jessie said. "I'm bringing them — and their lawyer — in tomorrow. The sister and husband too. They finally deigned to fit me into their schedule. They wanted to get all my questions in at once, they said. They've apparently been tied up with making arrangements for Perry and alerting family of the tragedy since they've been home." She rolled her eyes at that. "I don't get people."

"My mother said the same thing. She usually would be the one to pipe up and say she understood the concerns about status, etc. I'm not saying that judgmentally," Stan said when Marty looked like he was about to interject again. "I get that my mother is who she is, and I'm *not* who she is. It's a different way of thinking, you know? But she seems to have . . . adjusted her thinking a bit."

"That's a good thing, then," Marty said. "Want a drink, Stan?"

"Sure, I'll have some water," she said. Marty rose to get her a glass.

"So, how's the other thing going?" Stan asked, turning back to Jessie.

Jessie lifted her head and gave her a blank stare. "What thing?"

"The *other* thing." Stan raised her eyebrows suggestively, inclining her head in Marty's direction, not sure if she'd told him.

Jessie continued to stare at her.

"For the love of God. The thing Scott told you about."

"The stalker?"

Stan sighed. "I was trying to be discreet."

"That's never been your strong suit." Jessie dropped her head back to her papers.

"Well?" Stan asked.

"Oh. You want me to give you an update," Jessie said.

Stan blew out an impatient breath. "I just wondered if you had any news."

"Not really. But that was another excellent reveal, wasn't it? Nothing like withholding information."

"Ah, Jess. Go easy on the guy," Marty said. "Regular people don't think like you, remember."

"Regular people? What does that mean? And how exactly do I think?"

"Like everything's a conspiracy," Marty explained patiently. "It's not a criticism, hon. Scott probably didn't make the connection at first."

"Someone has a stalker and then they're killed," Jessie said. "I don't have to be a mathematician to add that up."

"So you have no leads?" Stan asked, trying to interject before Marty said something else and got his head taken right off.

Jessie kept her cop face in place. "We're looking into all possibilities."

Stan frowned. "That's it?"

"That's it for you," Jessie said.

"Why?"

"Because this is a police investigation," Jessie said. "Not a sharing circle."

Stan didn't know whether to laugh or get annoyed with her. She chose a different topic. "When's the funeral?"

"Friday. They're not doing a viewing. Just a church thing and a reception here in town."

"Well, what about Wallace at the farm?"

Jessie shrugged. "He *says* he was working late Friday night. Not that I can find anyone to confirm that."

It was a big farm. Easy to say you were there, somewhere out in the fields, but really be someplace else. Stan felt terrible even thinking it, but she'd be kidding herself if she said it wasn't a possibility.

"And the stripper place? Come on, Jessie. You have to have a list of viable suspects."

"Of course I have a list of suspects. But that doesn't mean I'm discussing it with anyone. Plus, the stripper place is as hard to get info from as the parents. They've been stalling too."

Stan's ears perked up. "Really? Like they won't talk to you?"

"It's been hard to get the owner," Jessie said. "It's a little frustrating, honestly."

"You want me to have my mother call them too?" Stan was kidding, but Jessie sat up, immediately on guard.

"No. Listen. I know I asked for help once, but she already did what I asked. I don't need a bunch of cowboys — that includes you — running around town conducting independent investigations."

Too late, Stan thought, but she kept her mouth shut.

Marty looked at Stan. "She sounds serious."

"She always sounds serious," Stan said. "I'm used to it."

CHAPTER THIRTY

Stan left Marty's and climbed back into her car, checking her clock. She wasn't supposed to meet the crew at her shop until two. Amara had appointments at the clinic until then, and Char had a special lunch she was cooking for some of her guests. So Stan had some time to kill.

And she had a few ideas on how to do it, all of which directly contradicted Jessie's instructions to not conduct her own investigation. But she'd gotten really curious about this stripper business. Maybe there was something odd going on over there. And maybe they were scrambling to make sure the police didn't know about it. On the other hand, if a potential customer came in and poked around —

On impulse, she pulled out her phone and called her sister. "Free?" she asked.

Caitlyn hesitated. "Depends. I'm coming to help you clean the shop in a bit."

"I know. But are you free now?"

"Why?"

"Because I have an errand to run. One that has to do with Perry Puck."

"Pick me up," Caitlyn said, her tone changing. "I'll be ready."

"Where the heck is this place?" Caitlyn held the phone, watching the GPS as Stan tried to keep up with the turns the robotic voice barked at her, as well as Caitlyn's commentary. "This shouldn't be this hard."

"Maybe they don't want anyone to know where they are." Stan paused, thankful for a red light, and took in her surroundings. They were still in Frog Ledge, according to the GPS, but way over on the western side, heading north. Or so her phone told her. Personally, she couldn't figure out the north/south/east/west thing if there was a gun pointed at her head. But this place was kind of in the middle of nowhere. Stan didn't get out this way much.

The towns around Frog Ledge were a study in contrasts. There was the college town on the eastern border, with an "urban area" of about four miles that didn't have the best reputation. Then there was the elite, wealthy town on the west side full of giant homes and upscale boutiques. Frog Ledge was the agricultural center that was gaining its own reputation as an up-and-comer, with its combination of rural farmland and evolving downtown. She didn't know much about this northeast border town, but given the size of the houses over here, they seemed on the more expensive end of the spectrum. It suggested to Stan that this outfit had its foot in both types of communities. She could easily see Perry Puck performing for socialites. Which brought an image of their mother to mind, making her cringe.

"Stan?" Caitlyn pointed out the windshield. "Green light."

"Where am I going? You're the navigator."

"Right. Sorry." Caitlyn picked up her phone again. "Turn left."

Stan made the turn. The guy behind her made a nasty hand gesture at her apparent confusion. She blew him a kiss, enjoying his puzzled look. "Then what? We're kind of in the middle of nowhere."

"I know. Oh wait." Caitlyn pointed. "That must be it. There's a tiny sign."

The two-story Cape didn't look much like a business. It was in the middle of an area that wasn't only residential but fancy residential. The house was modest compared to its neighbors, which dwarfed the smaller structure. The only indication that a business was in operation here was the small purple sign at the mailbox with its name in script.

Stan pulled slowly into the driveway and parked. She and Caitlyn sat for a minute. They'd gotten this far but hadn't really concocted a plan. Did they go in and ask about Perry? They probably wouldn't get anywhere if they did. Especially if these people were up to no good. But if they went in and asked for the cute blond who'd provided services for them in the past, maybe that would give them a clue. If the people sidestepped Perry and offered them someone else, it was possible they'd talk freely about past services without making them clarify what they actually were.

"This is weird," Caitlyn said finally. "I didn't expect it to be in a house."

"It kind of is," Stan agreed. "But I guess it's not that far-fetched. I mean, Izzy's café used to be a house."

"Yeah, but a downtown house they converted. This is in someone's backyard. How do you suppose the neighbors feel about this place being here? Aren't people kind of snooty and conservative here? It looks snooty and conservative," Caitlyn said doubtfully.

"That's what I heard. But there's a hodgepodge of communities in this area. It's kind of random. Plus, they're not stripping *here,*" Stan pointed out. "They're just booking parties and stuff." *Unless they're doing something else too.* She grabbed her purse. "Let me do the talking."

Caitlyn frowned at her. "Why?"

"Because." Stan didn't know why, really. Her sister might get emotional and where would that get them? They needed answers, not to draw attention to themselves.

"Whatever." Caitlyn shoved her car door open and walked to the house's front door without waiting for Stan.

Stan rolled her eyes, locked the car, and followed her sister. Caitlyn pushed the door open and they stepped into a foyer that reminded Stan of her mother's house in Narrangasett. Gleaming hardwood floors, an expensive-looking rug, a table with a sculpture on it. Just beyond the foyer was a large, circular front desk that could've been straight from the lobby of a fancy building in New York.

The girl at the front desk had a nose, chin, and eyebrow piercing. The bottom half of her hair was blue. Her eyeliner reminded Stan of the Goth girls in high school. She lifted her gaze from her phone but didn't smile. "What can I do for you?"

Stan offered her friendliest smile. "Hi there. I'm looking to rebook a guy we had. I don't know his name but he was *awesome.*" She swooned a little for effect. "He was blond, with a sweepy piece of hair over his eye. And young. Pretty hot. Green eyes."

"We've got a lotta guys like that." With a barely concealed sigh she opened a book and flipped the pages. "This one?" She held up the book opened to a page with guy who looked like Fabio.

Stan shook her head. "No. He was much younger."

She flipped another couple pages, pondered, then held the book up again.

Stan shook her head again.

"What'd you hire him for?" Clearly the girl was losing patience and wanted to get back to Facebooking or Snapchatting or whatever she was doing.

Shoot. This wasn't working well at all.

Caitlyn took her pause as an opportunity to jump in. "What services do you have available?" she asked. "We're really open. We want to have a good time." She winked at the girl. "You know?"

Stan wanted to strangle her sister.

The girl gave Caitlyn a strange look. "We do birthday parties, bachelorette parties, private events . . ." she recited in a monotone. Stan would've thought a college student or someone in that age-group might enjoy this job a bit more, but she looked like it was painful to be here. Stan was trying to figure out her next move when the sound of high heels clacking on the floor approached.

A woman with long, gleaming black hair came into the reception area. Unlike the front desk girl, she oozed class. Her suit looked like something Stan would've worn to her old job on a particularly important day of meeting with the media. Her heels were not cheap, and if her makeup wasn't professionally done, Stan would've lost a bet.

The girl at the desk sat up straighter, self-consciously pushing her hair behind her ears. The woman looked at Stan and Caitlyn, then smiled and came over.

"Good afternoon. I'm Miriam Sherman. Is Jewel helping you?" She cast a sidelong glance at the girl.

Stan felt Caitlyn snicker beside her. "She's trying," she said, casting an apologetic look at Jewel. "We're hoping to book a gentleman for my sister's party, someone who . . . performed for me before."

"I see. Do you know his name?"

Stan shook her head. "Which is why we're

driving poor Jewel crazy here, making her look at pictures. Kind of like a mug shot exercise." She immediately wanted to suck the words back in even as they exited her lips, but it was too late.

Miriam cocked her head slightly, as if they made her very curious, but she took the book from Jewel. "Where was your party?"

"Frog Ledge," Caitlyn blurted out.

Stan toe-heeled her foot closer to her sister's and not-so-subtly stepped on it.

But Miriam didn't blink an eye. She flipped pages. "And when is your event?"

"Uh, we haven't picked a date yet. We wanted to see if we could get the guy we wanted."

"Okay." Miriam slapped the book shut and looked up at then, offering them a smile that didn't quite reach her eyes. "If you'd like to leave your name and number, we can give you a call back with some options. And we'll follow up with an email with photos. Does that sound okay?"

"Yes," Stan said. "Yes, it does." There was nothing else to possibly say to this woman other than to agree with her. Then she had a moment of panic. She couldn't leave her real name. Miriam would figure out who she was, if Caitlyn had booked everything using their real names.

"Well then." Miriam pushed a notepad over the counter and tapped a pen against it. "I'll be in touch."

"Great." With a flash of inspiration, she wrote *Kristan McGee* on the pad, scrawled her phone number, then hustled Caitlyn out the door.

CHAPTER THIRTY-ONE

Stan followed Caitlyn outside. They silently got back in Stan's car. She slowly buckled her seat belt, eyes on the house in front of her. "That was . . . odd," she said finally into the silence.

"It was," Caitlyn agreed.

Stan pondered the house in front of her, wondering if there really was something else going on there. Not that she'd ever been to the home office of a stripping business, but this one didn't feel like she'd expected it would. Aside from Jewel, the millennial with attitude, the place had a different vibe to it.

"I thought it would be cheesier in there," Caitlyn said, almost as if she'd read her big sister's mind.

"Me too," Stan said. "Have you ever been in a place like that before?"

Caitlyn shook her head. "I set up my friend Erin's bachelorette party with strippers. She was much more grateful than you,

by the way. But I did it over the phone."
She shrugged. "Maybe these places are
classier nowadays. Maybe they don't have
fake cakes and cardboard cutouts of men
all over the office."

Stan turned and stared at her. "That's
what they usually have?"

"I have no idea. I just told you I've never
been in one."

Stan shook her head to clear it and started
the car. "Okay. Let's cruise down the street
and see if any neighbors are around. Maybe
we can see if anyone has seen anything
weird going on here."

She put the car in reverse, waiting as
another vehicle approached the driveway.
Then realized with a sinking heart that the
car was turning in.

And it was Jessie. She was in her car, not
the police car, probably so she didn't freak
anyone on the street out. Or maybe so she
didn't alert the people inside.

Either way, she pulled her car right up to
Stan's bumper so she couldn't move, got
out, and walked over to the driver's side
window.

"Shoot," Caitlyn muttered.

Stan rolled the window down and smiled
at her almost sister-in-law. "Hey."

"Hey," Jessie responded, her tone dripping with sarcasm. "Fancy meeting you here."

"Yeah, well." Stan shrugged. "We were in the neighborhood."

"And what? You decided to rebook your party with a new guy?" Jessie leaned into the window. "Why are you here?"

"We wanted to help you," Caitlyn blurted out. "Stan said you guys were getting stonewalled here, and we thought if we went in and asked about Perry — innocently, of course — that maybe we'd find something out to help you."

Stan shot her sister a deadly look.

Jessie's gaze lingered on Caitlyn, then slid back to Stan. Stan held her breath, waiting for the tongue-lashing that was sure to come. Sure, Jessie had asked for her help — but only with one specific piece of this puzzle. The Pucks. As she'd pointed out just this morning. She'd specifically said she didn't want them traipsing around conducting their own investigations into a business that may or may not have had something to do with Perry's death. It probably was a stupid idea. And she deserved the scolding she'd get.

But it didn't come.

"So what did you find out?" Jessie asked.

Stan swallowed her shock. "We met the

woman who seems like she runs the place. She seems way too classy to be running a small-time strip show in the middle of nowhere. She was practically dripping money."

"Miriam?" Jessie asked.

Stan nodded.

"Yeah, she's the owner. The one I can't seem to get through to," Jessie said.

"The receptionist, Jewel, was pretty stereotypical. But when the boss was around, she was practically shaking in her boots," San said. "I gather this woman runs a tight ship. I don't know what these places are like normally, but this doesn't seem like a cheesy operation."

Jessie looked at the house, then back at Stan. "You should go," she said finally. "I don't want them to see me talking to you."

"Okay. Will you let me know what you find out?"

"Now you're pushing your luck." She headed toward the front door.

Stan backed out of the driveway and headed down the street. "I'm going to park down here a bit and then we can knock on a couple doors," she said. "I want to know if people know anything about this place. If there's something weird going on here." She drummed her fingers on the steering wheel.

"I wonder what the story is."

Caitlyn sniffed. "Why did you give me a dirty look when I told Jessie what we were doing?"

"Because sometimes you have to figure out the right way to handle her," Stan said. "I thought she'd be upset we were there. She isn't, which makes me wonder."

Caitlyn turned her head to look out her window. "I don't know why you brought me. You didn't want me to say anything inside, either. If I'm such an embarrassment I would've stayed home."

"Caitlyn. No. I'm sorry. Listen, that was a good effort, asking Jewel about their services. I thought she'd definitely spill it if something was . . . on a different menu. She didn't seem like she was that concerned about her company's reputation. Not like the boss. I wasn't trying to shut you out. I'm sorry."

"Thanks." Caitlyn sat up straighter. "I thought so, too, about Jewel not caring so much. But then again, I wouldn't mess with Miriam, especially if I worked for her. She looked kind of scary. Maybe it's been repeatedly drilled into Jewel's head that she can only talk about the basics. Maybe the boss lady handles the other stuff."

"We don't know for sure there's other

stuff," Stan reminded her.

"Well, we need to find that out." Caitlyn pointed out the window. "Look. Here's a neighbor. Let's stop and ask her."

"We should figure out what exactly we're going to ask her," Stan said.

Caitlyn shrugged. "We'll ask if they've noticed anything weird at the stripper house."

"This woman is about seventy," Stan said, watching the neighbor slowly maneuver flowers into a pot. "You really think she'd notice even if there was something?"

"You'd be surprised what people notice," Caitlyn said. "Although you shouldn't be, given where you live."

"You live there too," Stan pointed out.

"Exactly. Which is why I know that everyone notices everything. Especially if they don't have better things to do. Pull over."

Reluctantly, Stan did. Caitlyn rolled down her window. "Excuse me," she called.

The woman looked up, immediately wary. "Yes?"

"Hi," Caitlyn said, getting out and going over to shake her hand. Stan followed reluctantly. "We were wondering about the business down the street." Caitlyn pointed to the nondescript house with the purple sign.

The woman's gaze followed Caitlyn's finger. She pursed her lips. "Why are you asking? What do you want to know?"

"We, ah." Caitlyn looked at Stan, who'd joined her on the sidewalk.

"We're curious about its reputation," Stan said. "I want to have a classy party for a friend of ours, and this place was recommended."

"I have no idea, about its reputation," the woman said indignantly. "Do I look like the type of woman who would use those services?" With a huff, she turned and walked back to her house, slamming her front door behind her.

Stan and Caitlyn looked at each other. "Guess that was a bad idea," Stan muttered.

"Nah, she's just uptight," Caitlyn said with a shrug. They headed back to the car. But before they could get inside, Stan heard someone call out from across the street.

"Hey!"

CHAPTER THIRTY-TWO

They both turned, shielding their eyes from the sun. A young woman pushing a baby stroller waved at them. She wore baggy sweatpants and an old Fleetwood Mac concert T-shirt. Stan didn't think she looked old enough to even know who Fleetwood Mac was.

"Hi," Stan said, not sure if they were about to be yelled at, or if the woman maybe thought they were someone else.

The woman looked around for cars, then pushed her stroller across the street. "I saw you talking to Mrs. Gallo and had to laugh. If you're asking for directions, she's the last person you want to ask. She can be cranky." She smiled, pushing frizzy hair out of her eyes. "Can I help you find something?"

Stan and Caitlyn glanced at each other. "Yes, actually," Caitlyn cut in. "We're looking for Party Pleasers. I thought my map app must be malfunctioning because, well, this doesn't really look like I would find that here." She indicated the cozy houses tucked along the street.

The woman raised her eyebrows and glanced around. "Actually," she said, dropping her voice even though the street was completely empty of life. Not even a squirrel or chipmunk disturbed the quiet. Then she stopped. "Come over here," she said, motioning for them to follow her, and hurried back across the street.

Caitlyn looked at Stan. She shrugged. They followed her across the street where she stopped on the sidewalk. "I just didn't want to talk in front of that nosy old bat's house," she said apologetically. "I'm Judy, by the way."

"I'm Sta— Stacy," Stan said. "This is Crystal."

Caitlyn sent Stan a confused look, then smiled at Judy. "Yes. Crystal. That's me."

"Nice to meet you both," she said. "Now. The place you're looking for is *right there.*" She stage-whispered the words while pointing in what Stan guessed she thought was a discreet manner. "But you look like nice gals. Why do you want to go there?"

"Um. Well, we're planning a bachelorette party," Stan began, praying that they hadn't stumbled onto a block of religious fanatics who were going to hold them hostage all day while lecturing them on the devil's practices. "And we're new to the area so we looked up places to rent . . . entertainment, and they looked reputable."

Judy sniffed. "Of course they *look* that way. But they're not."

"No? Tell us more," Caitlyn said eagerly.

Judy looked at her oddly. "Actually, it's a really weird place. And no one on the street will talk about it. I'm not sure how they even got permission to operate out of here." She smiled. "My father is a zoning board officer in another town. I was telling him about it."

"It happens, though," Stan said, trying to play devil's advocate. "The place could have been grandfathered in as commercial. But what do you mean by weird?"

Judy bit her lip, clearly trying to work out if she should be talking about this. "I don't know," she said finally. "I walk a lot with my daughter. It's the only way she'll go to sleep. Like, ever. So I'm out at night sometimes, pushing her up and down the street. There are always cars coming and going there. And I see a lot of women come in and out. But I thought it was only a place that offered men." She blushed as she said it. "That sounded weird, right? You know what I mean, though."

"Yeah," Stan said thoughtfully. "I do. What are the women like?"

"I don't really know," Judy said. "And I guess I wondered, if they were placing women strippers too, why do all the women need to come here? I hardly ever see men here. I guess they wouldn't have any reason to come except when they get checked out, right?"

"Checked out?" Caitlyn repeated.

"Well, yeah. Like when they're applying for the job? I'm sure someone has to assess if they look good enough." She sighed. "I know it happens to women all the time, but it still seems wrong when it's done to anyone. Like they're looking at a car to buy or something."

She was right. The whole business was degrading, for men and women. Stan had always thought so. But right now she didn't want to get into a debate about that. She wanted to know who these women were.

"So the women," she said, nudging Judy back to the topic at hand. "Are they dressed up? Like they're auditioning?"

"Not really. Some of the ones I saw looked like they'd just rolled out of bed, honestly. I know that's kind of the look these days, though." She hesitated. "And a couple of times, I saw kids."

"Kids?" Caitlyn asked, looking at Stan with a horrified expression.

Judy nodded. "Not sure if they were coming with their moms for something, or what. I didn't see anything that made me feel icky," she hurried to add. "I mean, my best friend runs a vape shop and he brings his daughter there all the time."

Stan didn't really know how to respond to that one, so she let it go. "How are they getting here? Is someone bringing them?" she asked.

Judy thought about that. "I've seen people arrive in like an Uber or a Lyft. A couple times there were a bunch of people getting here at once. I don't know. I didn't really start paying attention until the day the police were here."

"The police? Recently?" Stan asked, thinking of Jessie and Lou.

"No, this was a month or so ago," Judy said. "There were a lot of police cars, too. And after they left, a black car came and picked someone up and left, too. It was all very *24*."

Stan suppressed a smile at that. Nothing about Party Pleasers reminded her of Jack Bauer's high-stress efforts to save the world. Whatever was going on in there, she felt sure it wasn't related to counterterrorism efforts. Although . . . one never knew, she supposed.

"And you never heard anything about what happened?" Stan asked.

Judy shook her head. "The people who work there don't socialize. They drive in, hurry inside, then leave at the end of the day."

"Does anyone live there? Upstairs maybe?" Stan thought of Miriam and her expensive outfit. She couldn't necessarily picture her living here, but if she wanted to keep a close eye on her business . . .

"I don't know," Judy said. "I guess I'm not much help at all."

"No, you've been great," Stan said. "Really. We appreciate your time."

"No worries." Judy looked at them curiously. "That was a lot of questions for your party though. Are you guys sure you aren't undercover with some CIA unit?"

CHAPTER THIRTY-THREE

"What do you make of all that?" Caitlyn asked Stan as they drove back to Frog Ledge to meet the neighborhood cleaning crew, dubbed by Amara as the "pet patisserie energy cleansers." They were going to clean, sage, and basically try to wipe any traces of murder and evil out of the patisserie.

Stan prayed it would work, because right now she was dreading even going back inside.

"Aside from the fact that Judy is a conspiracy theorist who watches a lot of TV? I don't know," she answered. "It seems weird, right? I was kidding when I said maybe the place was a front for something, but jeez. It sounds like they're definitely operating a second business out of there, at the very least."

Caitlyn snorted. "I think business is the wrong term."

"How do you know that? We can't assume it's something bad," Stan said. "I mean, clearly our friend Judy likes conspiracy theories. But I'm not convinced Miriam is the female Jack Bauer."

"No, but she's got to have money from somewhere, and renting out pretty boys to jump out of cakes isn't necessarily going to earn you that kind of cash," Caitlyn said.

"So what do *you* think she's doing?"

Caitlyn chewed on her lip, then blurted out, "What if she's doing sex trafficking? Or child porn?"

"Caitlyn! Seriously?" Stan shook her head. "Maybe I'm completely naive, but I highly doubt that place is a front for . . . those awful things. Maybe she's running a female escort service."

"That's kind of awful too," Caitlyn said.

"Right, but at least the people involved would be doing it of their own free will," Stan pointed out. "I don't know. I think we're trying too hard to make that place bad."

"Well, what if Perry found out what they were up to and he wasn't supposed to? Maybe this Miriam chick had him killed. She certainly didn't seem broken up about his death. She didn't even mention it."

"I doubt that she would start an interaction with a new customer with, 'Have you heard about one of my strippers being murdered?' I'm sure she wouldn't be open to discussing it with us anyway. But maybe we should try coming back sometime at night," Stan said with a sideways glance at her sister. "Maybe we'd see something for ourselves."

"That's one way to find out," Caitlyn said. Then she brightened. "Maybe we can go ask about being escorts! What do you think?"

"I think," Stan said, "I'd rather snoop around outside."

They drove back to Stan's house to pick up Nikki. "Jake's doing a few things at the pub and says he'll be over soon to help," Nikki said, sliding into the backseat. "And your weirdo newspaper guy stopped by earlier. He wanted to know when the shop was reopening."

"Did you tell him?" Stan asked.

Nikki nodded. "I figured he'd find out anyway."

"Maybe he'll come over and help us clean," Stan said.

"Any news after this morning's events?" Nikki asked.

Stan shook her head. "Jessie has the Pucks

coming to the station with their lawyer tomorrow."

Nikki whistled. "You'd think that would be a worse thing to have publicized. Getting dragged to the station."

"Right?" Stan pulled into the shop parking lot and gazed doubtfully at her pretty little patisserie. For any innocent passersby, the place still looked adorable and inviting, with the polka-dot curtains in the windows and her custom-made patisserie sign. It still seemed surreal that such a terrible thing had happened inside it.

Char's gray SUV careened into the lot like she was making a pit stop at the Daytona 500. A minute later, she erupted from the driver's side, waving a mop. "What are y'all waiting for, Christmas?" she demanded, reaching back into the truck and pulling out a bag of materials.

"You," Stan admitted. "Not sure any of us want to even go in."

"Oh, nonsense." Char waved Stan inside. "Unlock that door and let's get to work."

Stan obliged, taking a tentative step inside. Caitlyn nearly bumped into her, she moved so slowly. But Stan needed to take a minute and *feel* the place.

Which made her think she'd been hanging around Char and Amara too long. The air felt stale, and there was a certain emptiness to the shop that wasn't usually there. But that could've been because no one had been in it for nearly three days, and it hadn't gone without human or canine interaction since it opened in December.

She stepped all the way in, Caitlyn and Nikki fanning out next to her, making room for Char to sweep in, holding her mop high like it was her dance partner. Thankfully, it wasn't as bad as she'd feared. Jessie's team had made some effort to remove as much evidence of the murder as possible, and had even thrown away a lot of the party plates and cups abandoned by guests in the mayhem. The food had been removed. All that remained were the decorations and the bar, which Jake would take care of now that they could get back inside.

Whether she'd sent a cleaning crew or done it herself, Stan was grateful.

Char surveyed the room too, then nodded. "Okay. Not too bad," she said. "Don't worry, honey." She shoved the cleaning materials at Caitlyn and hugged Stan to her generous bosom. "We'll get it all back to rights."

"Thanks, Char." Stan hugged her back and stepped away, frustrated to find tears welling up in her eyes. Not only because she was sad, but because she was so happy she had such good friends. "So what magic did you bring with you?"

"Ah. Wait'll you see." Char took the bag back from Caitlyn and brought it over to the counter, unraveling her bright red silk scarf from around her neck. For the first time, Stan took in the rest of her outfit. Char's flowy orange pantsuit didn't scream *cleaning day,* but that was Char — she did everything in style. Her New Orleans up-bringing wouldn't allow for anything less.

It also didn't allow for her to apply traditional solutions to nontraditional problems. So Stan wasn't even surprised when, along with some lavender Dr. Bronner's soap "just in case any blood got on the floor," Char pulled a bunch of candles out of her giant bag and set them on the counter, along with a small, black voodoo doll with creepy button-like eyes.

Nikki, however, looked horrified. "A voodoo doll?" she said. "Isn't that just as bad as physically killing someone?"

"Oh, baby doll," Char said sympathetically, shaking her head. "Honey, you need to brush up on your magic. This little guy here is to dispel negative energy."

Nikki didn't look convinced.

"You can't believe every crackpot thing

you read about voodoo," Char said, exasperated. "Voodoo is a sacred tradition! And we might even be able to get a message from Perry."

"Okay, okay," Nikki muttered. "I get it. I'm just going to mop." She grabbed the bucket and went to the bathroom to get water.

"You think we'll get a message?" Stan asked. "For real? Like, he'll tell you who killed him?"

"You never know, honey. Stranger things have happened." Char arranged the candles carefully, then took out a lighter. "We have to do some special cleansing," she said.

"I thought we were saging?" Stan said.

"We're definitely saging," Amara said, appearing at the door waving a sage stick.

"Of course we're saging," Char said. "This is just an extra ritual to get rid of bad juju. Lord knows we need some extra help," she said, glancing around. "That was certainly some negative energy that made its way in here."

"Do you have to remind me?" Stan muttered.

"Don't worry, honey. Between George here" — she waved her doll — "and our other rituals, we'll be up and running in no time."

When Jake showed up with Brenna a few minutes later, the place smelled like a yoga studio and vaguely resembled a séance. The lights were off, candles were lit, and Char presided over them with her eyes closed. Amara was walking the room waving her sage stick in every corner. Nikki tried to ignore all of it by scrubbing the floor in the dark, and Caitlyn had excused herself to go clean the kitchen.

"Don't ask," Stan whispered, as Jake opened his mouth.

"You're right. Better off not knowing." He went over to start removing the makeshift bar.

Three hours later, when the sage had burned out and the candles were puddles of wax, George still hadn't told them who'd done it, at least that Stan had heard. And when Jessie showed up a few minutes later, she didn't look like she had any more answers than George did.

But the store almost felt right again. Stan felt like she had more room to breathe.

"There's our superhero crime fighter," Char said fondly. "Did you find our killer yet, honey?"

"I wish," Jessie said. "I'm taking a break and thought I'd come help. Sorry I'm late."

"Any developments?" Char asked. "Cyril

hasn't been printing much."

"We're following all the leads," Jessie said, following her usual script.

"Well, I hope those parents are coming around," Char said, moving to the counter to scrub off some wax from one of her candles. "I did wonder if they were dragging their feet because of the conditions the granddad put around the business. And all that money that was on the table for Perry."

They all turned to stare at her.

"The money?" Jessie said finally.

"Yes, the elder Mr. Puck set the business up so everything was in Perry's hands, instead of his son's." She stopped scrubbing and looked at Jessie. "Oh, you didn't know about that?"

Jessie looked like the top of her head was about to blow off. "No, Char, I can't say that I did. Do tell."

"I'm not sure of all the details, but Mr. Puck's parents used to live here in Frog Ledge. His mama Marge was good friends with Ray's cousin. Marge got shipped off to the nursing home a few years ago," she said. "Her husband couldn't care for her. Anyway, I heard all about this back in the day. Through the grapevine." She turned and offered Jessie a smile. "It's the best way to get information, usually."

"So I've heard," Jessie muttered.

"The elder Mr. Puck wanted to hold on to control of the Greenery markets even after he couldn't physically run them anymore," Char said. "I heard it was because he didn't have a lot of faith in his own son. He wanted Perry to run the business. Apparently, he saw something in his grandson that reminded him of himself. Anyway, he set everything up so Perry is the one who actually controls the money he's designated for the business. The only way it would revert to Frederick is . . ." she paused, "if something happened to Perry that rendered him unable to do it any longer."

"Like if he was killed," Jessie finished.

"Well, yes, I suppose that would be the reason." Char put down her sponge. "Now that I say this out loud, it sounds a bit incriminating, doesn't it?"

They all sat in silence, digesting this news. "How much money are we talking?" Stan asked finally.

Char swept her candles back into her bag. "I'm not sure, but the markets are worth a few million, at least, given the expansions."

Stan and Jessie looked at each other. Stan thought her future sister-in-law might actually have a stroke.

"I have to go," Jessie said, and she left the

shop, letting the door slam behind her.

Stan wondered what she was going to do. Threaten to arrest Perry's father if he didn't talk, now that she had this information?

Char looked troubled. "I can't believe I didn't put that together sooner. I hope she's not upset."

"She'll be fine," Jake assured her. "You know how my sister gets during an investigation."

Char smiled. "I do. And she also knows how I get with my voodoo dolls, so she better be careful." She winked at Jake, but Stan wasn't totally sure she was kidding.

CHAPTER THIRTY-FOUR

They locked up the shop a few minutes later so Stan, Nikki, and Caitlyn could go get ready for the dress shopping excursion. Patricia picked them up at Stan's house exactly at five, as she'd promised, and they set off.

The Royal Bridal Shop just outside of Frog Ledge was a small, boutique store, the likes of which could be found in a very exclusive downtown. Stan thought this downtown wanted to be exclusive, but it wasn't totally there yet. It was a good effort, though, and they did have some nice dresses. None of which called Stan's name.

"These are all kind of old lady-ish," Nikki muttered, holding a dress with more lace and tulle than Stan had ever seen out for a closer look.

"They're awful. I don't see anything I'd even try on, much less wear." Stan looked over at where her mother and Caitlyn were

249

oohing and aahing over gaudy, beaded creations. "Maybe she can buy Caitlyn's dress here."

"Seriously, what are you wearing? I can't believe you have no dress yet," Nikki said.

"Not you too. Jeez, I know." Stan sighed. "Thing is, I know what I want to wear. I saw it in a little shop about an hour from here."

Nikki gasped. "You went dress shopping on your own?"

"I was running an errand and drove by," Stan said defensively. "I saw something pretty in the window and stopped."

"So why didn't you get it?"

"I don't know. Because I felt guilty. And because I'm crazy."

"Guilty because you didn't bring anyone with you?"

"Pretty much."

"There's no law that says you need a dress committee." Nikki glanced over at Patricia and Caitlyn, who were stroking some fabric with looks of awe on their faces. "Especially not that one."

The saleswoman, who'd been watching them with an eagle eye, couldn't stand it any longer. She needed a sale. "So who's the beautiful bride?" she asked brightly, sidling up to Caitlyn and Patricia.

They both turned and pointed at Stan. Nikki stepped slightly back so there'd be no confusion about whom they were pointing at. Stan's face turned red.

"She's a bride too," Stan said, pointing back at Caitlyn.

Caitlyn frowned, then fluffed her hair. "Technically I am," she said modestly. "And I really love this dress." She pulled one off the rack and held it up in front of her.

Patricia glared at her. "You'll have your turn, dear," she said through gritted teeth.

Caitlyn frowned and reluctantly put the dress back, her sulk apparent.

The saleswoman zeroed in on Stan. "What a lovely shape you have!" She came over and put her hands on Stan's waist, smiling and nodding. "Tiny waist. I have just the thing." She marched over to a wall with some of the frillier dresses and perused them, tapping one long, pink fingernail against her chin. Then she smiled and used some contraption Stan swore had miraculously appeared in her hand to reach up and pull the dress down. "Yes, this is wonderful. You must try this one. Lucy!" she called. "Please set up a fitting room for this lovely bride."

Stan's eyes widened when she saw the young woman the salesperson had beckoned. Lucy Tate. Roger Tate's daughter. Maybe this outing was fate, after all. Lucy hurried over, pasting a smile on her face. Recognition flashed in her eyes when she saw Stan, but she didn't say anything.

Lucy took the dress. "Follow me," she said. Stan did, already planning what she could ask Lucy without drawing attention to the fact that she was interrogating the dress gal.

"I'll keep looking for the next perfect one," the saleswoman sang after them.

"Great," Stan said. "Thank you."

She followed Lucy behind a curtained-off area with five dressing rooms in a circular design. When you stepped out of any dressing room, you were face-to-face with giant, angled mirrors so you'd have no choice but to see yourself in all your lacy, frilly glory.

"Hi," Stan said, once they were behind the curtain. "Not sure if you remember me, but I'm one of your dad's customers? Stan Connor?"

"Sure," Lucy said, glancing curiously at her. "Nice to see you." She used her key to open one of the rooms and hung the dress carefully on a hook inside. "Take your time. I'll be right out here if you need a different size. And it sounds like Rose will be bringing you some other choices." She smiled and stepped aside so Stan could enter, already pulling out her cell phone.

"Thanks," Stan said. "Hey Lucy? Can I ask you something?"

Lucy glanced up from her phone. "Sure. But Rose probably knows the material better."

"It's not about the dress." Stan took a breath. "Did you know Perry Puck well?"

Lucy sucked in a breath. "The guy who worked for my dad?" she asked casually, although Stan could tell she was expending some effort to be casual.

"Yes."

Lucy nodded. "A little bit."

"A bit? So were you guys friendly?"

Lucy didn't seem to know what to do with her hands. "Sure. We talked some."

"Did he get along okay with everyone at the farm?"

Lucy's glance slid away. "I guess. I didn't hang out much on the farm. Why are you asking?"

"I just wondered," Stan said. "Perry did all my deliveries and he seemed like such a nice guy. I feel sad that he's gone."

"Yeah," Lucy said softly. "He was a really nice guy." She smiled a little. "He used to pick wildflowers from the grounds and leave them for me."

"Really," Stan said, trying to hide her surprise.

Lucy nodded. "He was just being friendly. He had a girlfriend and stuff." Her tone dipped ever so slightly on the word *girlfriend.*

"Did you ever meet his girlfriend?" Stan asked.

Lucy narrowed her eyes. "Why?"

Stan wasn't expecting that for an answer. "Curious."

"Once," Lucy said. "She came to the farm." She crossed her arms defensively. "Look, Perry was fun to talk to. We both like movies a lot." She looked away, blinking rapidly. "He tried to help me out when that other creepy guy kept asking me out and I totally didn't want to go. He finally told him to leave me alone. That was it. And I told his stupid girlfriend that when she came and threatened me if I didn't stop talking to him, but she's nuts and she wouldn't listen!"

"Wait. What guy? And Andrea threatened you?" Stan asked. She was having trouble keeping up with all this.

Lucy brushed angry tears away. "Yes, she threatened me. And it was one of the other farm guys. I wasn't interested but he wouldn't stop trying to get me to go out with him. Perry finally told him to knock it off and leave me alone."

"Wallace?" Stan asked, trying to keep from sounding too excited.

"Yeah," Lucy said suspiciously. "How did you know that?"

Her head snapped around at the sound of her name being called out on the floor. Rose, no doubt with some other horrid creation she wanted to stuff Stan into. "I have to go. Let me know if you need help with the dress." She pocketed her phone and hurried out through the curtain.

Stan went into her dressing room and absently worked her way into the dress, her mind running through all the possibilities behind what Lucy Tate had just said. If Wallace didn't like Perry anyway, his defense of Lucy surely would've been the nail in the coffin — no pun intended. And it was probably exacerbated by the fact that Wallace knew Perry had a girlfriend already, so what did he need Lucy's affections for?

She finished adjusting herself and gazed into the mirror, not really seeing her reflection staring back at her. Instead, she kept seeing Perry's face, so full of life as he laughed with her and Brenna that last morning in her shop kitchen, as Wallace watched him with barely concealed disgust.

Had something gone that terribly wrong

between those two after they left the shop that morning that Wallace had followed him back to his side job that night and killed him?

CHAPTER THIRTY-FIVE

"I think it's lovely," her mother said when Stan stepped out of the dressing room a few minutes later.

Stan looked dubiously down at herself. She couldn't even see her feet under all that lace. "I don't know, Mom. It's not really me," she said. "Where's Nikki?"

"She's over there with your sister." Patricia waved behind her without looking. "Now, what's wrong with this dress?" she demanded. "I think it's gorgeous. The lacework alone is brilliant." She fingered one sleeve with reverence. "Excuse me, Rose," she called.

The saleswoman materialized as if Patricia had summoned with her wand. "Yes? Oh, my goodness!" she exclaimed, clasping her hands together and pressing them to her lips with excitement. "That is *fabulous* on you."

"Isn't it?" Patricia nodded with satisfaction. "Is it a Vera Wang?"

"You do have the eye." Rose nodded. "Yes, it is. It's brand new, actually. I love it on her."

Nikki and Caitlyn, hearing the squeals, made their way over. The look on Nikki's face alone told Stan her initial feeling was right. This was not the dress for her.

Caitlyn walked around her in a slow circle, making her assessment. "I don't know," she said. "I don't think it's her."

Stan wanted to hug her. "No?"

Caitlyn shook her head slowly. "You need something without all the flounce. More understated."

"I totally agree," Stan said with relief. "Don't you, Nikki?"

Nikki froze, looking at Patricia, who sent her a look that said, *Disagree with me and regret it forever.* Nikki's mouth snapped shut.

Patricia's head whipped back around to Stan, her lips thinning in that way they did when she was very displeased. "It's your wedding day," she said. "Why on earth would you want to be understated?"

Blessedly, Stan's phone rang from inside the dressing room. She hurried in to grab it. Brenna.

"Hey," Stan said, trying to shut the dressing room door. Unfortunately the ten miles of lace on the dress's skirt kept catching in the door. "Everything okay?"

"Not really," Brenna said, and Stan could hear the touch of hysteria in her voice. "Andrea just called me. I thought she was overreacting, or had made some mistake. But she hasn't."

"Bren. Slow down. Mistake about what? What happened?"

"My sister," Brenna wailed. "She just brought Andrea down to the station to talk to her. Like she would've killed her own boyfriend! Jessie's known her since we were kids. How could she?" Stan could hear the tears as Brenna's voice simultaneously shook and rose a notch or two. Hysteria was about to set in.

Stan closed her eyes briefly. Jessie must be trying to get to the bottom of the money thing, and she probably anticipated Mr. Puck wouldn't be straight with her, so she had to question Andrea about it. "Listen. It's her job, okay? She has to do what she has to do to get answers. She's probably just trying to see what else Andrea might remember that could help her."

"I told her I'd go get her, but I'm freaking out. Can you please take me to pick her up? I'm so sorry, I know you're looking for your dress, but . . ." she trailed off, her voice fading into sniffles.

"Of course. I'm coming now." Stan disconnected, already reaching behind her to unzip the dress. As she wrestled with it, she stuck her head out the door. "I have to go. Brenna needs help with something."

She thought her mother was going to lose her mind. "Excuse us, please," she said to Rose, and the saleswoman disappeared as quietly as she'd come. "Are you trying to destroy your own special day?" she demanded, keeping her voice low. Which required her to come nose to nose with Stan through the crack in the dressing room door.

"No. But I have to help her," Stan said. "It's important. And I don't like this dress anyway, Mom."

"Well, there's a whole store here to choose from," Patricia said. "Or is it just that you are so dead set on me not being involved in your day that you're willing to go to any length to keep me out of this? First Chelsea, now this. What, are you going to order your dress online with two-day shipping next weekend?"

Stan pondered that idea. It actually wasn't bad. Then she saw the steam nearly coming out of Patricia's ears. "Of course not. We can come back as soon as you have time. I actually wanted to tell you about this other place I found that has really beautiful dresses . . ." she trailed off as Patricia turned and simply walked away from her.

Well then. Biting back the surprising sting of tears, Stan finally got the door shut and the dress off. Relieved, she pulled on her jeans and T-shirt, jamming her feet back into her flats.

Rose waited at the door as she hurried out, thrusting a card at Stan. "Please let me know when you're coming back," she sang. "I'll have our best selection waiting! And I'll hold this one for you."

Stan mumbled a thank-you and pocketed the card. Patricia marched out behind her and opened the driver's side door of her car. She got in, barely waiting as the three of them piled in, and drove to Stan's house without a word.

"Thanks, Mom," Stan tried again as she got out of the car. "I'll call you later and we can pick another day?"

Patricia stared straight ahead, not answering. Caitlyn shot her a sympathetic look from the front seat.

Stan stifled a sigh and shut the door. She and Nikki watched as the car backed out of the driveway and headed up the street to Caitlyn's house. They looked at each other.

"Thank God," Nikki finally said. "That dress was awful."

Stan looked at her for a moment, then they both burst out laughing. Stan laughed so hard tears streamed down her face. It took her a few minutes to regain her composure. "Shoot. I have to go. But thank you for that laugh. I needed it."

"What happened with Brenna anyway? Or did you make that up?"

"I did not make it up!" Stan unlocked the door and greeted the dogs, who all clamored around her feet. "Jessie brought Andrea to the station. Brenna needs me to drive her to pick Andrea up."

"Wow," Nikki said.

"Yeah. Did you see who the assistant was at the dress shop?"

Nikki shook her head. "Who?"

"Lucy Tate. And I tried to talk to her about Perry a little bit. I think they were friendly. Actually, I think she liked him. And she said Andrea threatened her."

"Threatened her?" Nikki repeated.

"Yeah." Stan ran upstairs, grabbed a sweatshirt and ran back down. "See you in a bit."

Nikki saluted. "Have fun."

She hurried out to her car. As she slid into the driver's seat, she noticed a piece of paper folded under her windshield wiper. Frowning, she leaned out of the car and yanked it loose. "Who leaves notes around here?" she muttered to herself. "People usually just barge right in and tell you what they want."

But as she unfolded the piece of paper, she felt the blood drain from her face. The note was on a blank piece of paper that looked like it had been neatly cut from a larger piece. She could see where the scissors had left a slightly crooked edge along one side. Large capital letters, printed in neat block handwriting, spelled out, I SEE YOU.

Gasping, Stan slammed her door shut and hit the lock button, looking around wildly. She half expected to see some crazed, knife-wielding maniac jump out from behind her neatly trimmed shrubbery and try to attack her. But the yard was quiet. The street was quiet. There was activity on the green across the street, the sounds of the town ushering in the warm weather as people stayed out later walking, basking in the glow of no jackets, calling out greetings to each other. She watched in her rear view mirror as people power-walked the gravel path around the green, searching for anyone who lingered too long in front of her house, or looked in her direction, but no one seemed to be paying attention to her.

So what was this about? Who had left it? It had to be related to Perry Puck's murder. The people at Party Pleasers? Lucy Tate? Perry's stalker, coming to make her pay for what had happened to Perry? She shivered at the thought.

How did these things happen to her?

CHAPTER THIRTY-SIX

She picked Brenna up in front of the pub, hoping she looked somewhat normal and not completely freaked. She'd tucked the note into her wallet with shaking fingers, grateful she was on her way to see Jessie. She had to tell her about this.

Brenna wouldn't have noticed her distress anyway. She was too upset about Andrea. Brenna slid into the car and alternated between crying and ranting the whole way. When they arrived at the state police barracks, about twenty minutes outside of town, Stan turned to her before she could get out of the car.

"I think you should wait here," she said.

Brenna stared at her. "Why? She's my friend!"

"I know. But you're really upset right now. Why don't you let me go in and get her?"

Brenna looked like she was about to protest, then slumped back against her seat.

"Fine. I don't want to see my sister anyway."

"I understand." Stan grabbed her purse and hurried inside the barracks, stepping into the small, bland waiting area with plastic chairs and some magazines probably from ten years ago. The walls were gray, or perhaps just dirty, and the whole place depressed her.

She stepped up to the counter. The trooper behind the bulletproof window gazed at her, expressionless. "Sergeant Pasquale?" she said, trying to aim her voice at the holes in the glass meant to allow the cop to hear her.

He nodded, held up a finger, pressed a button, and spoke into his phone.

Stan waited at the counter, not wanting to sit on the chairs. Jessie came out a minute later.

"I thought my sister was coming," she said.

"She's outside. She called me."

Jessie shrugged. "Saves me an uncomfortable trip back with Andrea." As much as she tried to keep her tone flip, Stan could tell this was taking its toll on her.

"Can I talk to you before you get her?" Stan asked.

"Sure. What's up?"

"Two things. One, Lucy Tate said Andrea

came to the farm and threatened her."

Jessie's eyes widened. "When?"

"Sometime over the last few weeks, it sounded like. I didn't tell Brenna," she added. "But I thought you should know."

"Okay. What's the second thing?"

Stan reached into her purse and pulled the note out of her wallet. Wordlessly, she handed it to Jessie.

Jessie read it, then looked up at Stan. "What is this?"

"It was under my windshield wiper when I left to come here."

Jessie's eyes narrowed. "Where was your car?"

"At home. I dropped it off before we went dress shopping with my mother. Do you think this is Perry's stalker?"

Jessie didn't answer. She took the note and disappeared back through the door leading into the inner sanctum.

Resigned, Stan leaned against the counter again. Jessie wasn't the best communicator. When she returned, she had the note in a plastic bag. "Can you come with me so I can take an official statement?" she asked.

Stan followed her through the door and into a room. It gave her flashbacks of the other time she'd been here, and she started to feel antsy. She wasn't a fan of police stations.

"Write down how you found this, where your car was, how long it was in your driveway with no one around," Jessie instructed, handing her a notebook and pen.

Stan did, then signed it and handed to Jessie. "You guys really need iPads or something," she said, pushing her chair back. "Can I go now before Brenna busts in here?"

"Yeah. I'll get Andrea." Jessie rose too. "Stan?"

"Yeah."

"You need to be careful," she said, and her tone was serious. "I have no idea what's going on around here, but I don't like it one bit. And make sure you tell my brother about this. No trying to hide it so he doesn't worry. Okay?"

"Okay," Stan said. Jessie sounded serious enough that she was getting more nervous. "Do you think . . ."

"I don't know what to think. I just know this is no joke," Jessie said. "Especially considering what happened to the last guy I knew who was being stalked."

CHAPTER THIRTY-SEVEN

Stan lingered longer than usual in bed Tuesday morning, despite the long list of to-dos swirling around inside her head. It was reopening day at the shop, the first day since Perry's murder. She expected there to be a full house. People who hadn't been at the party would want to come see the crime scene. Gruesome, sure, but human nature, sadly.

But she was exhausted. The trip to pick up Andrea hadn't gone as planned. Andrea had refused to go with them when Jessie told her they were there to pick her up. Apparently, she'd taken the whole police questioning thing very personally, and decided she wasn't speaking to Brenna at the moment. Which of course had made Brenna very upset. By the time she got her calmed down and brought her home, Jake was home from the pub. And then she had to tell him about the note.

Needless to say, he hadn't taken it well.

She rolled over and watched him sleep. Similar to Jessie, he wasn't taking the note lightly. He'd even proposed getting her a bodyguard. She'd declined.

But she knew he was worried. She was pretty worried herself.

She slipped out of bed and headed into the bathroom to shower and get ready. She wanted to get to the shop early and make sure everything was in order before she opened. And get some treats in the oven.

She fed everyone breakfast and loaded Scruffy into the car — Henry had gone back to bed — and drove to the shop, trying to tamp down the apprehension building in her chest. Stan parked in the back and paused before getting out of the car, grateful for their cleanup/sage/voodoo session yesterday. She knew it wouldn't have been easy to come back today if they hadn't done all that.

But still. Knowing someone with deadly intent had been in here freaked her out. It was as bad as if it had happened in her own home. And now with this note . . .

Scruffy put her paw on Stan's leg, a gentle question: *Why aren't we going in, Mom?*

"I know, baby girl. Let's go." Stan got out and held the door for her little dog. Scruffy jumped down gracefully and trotted toward the door. Stan was always grateful for her company, but even more so today.

She unlocked the back door and let them inside, locking it behind her. No more being lackadaisical with the locks around here, at least not until the little ship of their town had been righted with the capture of the murderous perpetrator.

She did a walk-through, clutching her phone in her hand — kitchen, bathroom, main room — breathing a sigh of relief when she didn't see anything out of place. Feeling better, she heated up the oven and started planning her recipes for the day. She had no idea if Brenna would even show up for work today, so she had to be ready to be out front when she opened at ten.

She spent the next couple hours baking, jazz music on in the background, and then she brought her cooled treats out front to load up the case. She arranged the doggie cupcakes in spring pinks and blues next to her version of a carrot cake for pups, complete with carrot-shaped "frosting" on top. She set the doggie "chocolates," made out of carob and designed to look like the fancy chocolates that came in boxes, on the other side.

She loved what she did.

And she nearly jumped a foot when she realized someone's face was pressed up against the front door.

Wallace.

Her heart tripled in rhythm. She wondered if he was here because he'd heard she was poking around, asking questions about him and Lucy — and Perry? Was he the note leaver?

She couldn't stare at him all day. He knew she'd seen him. Swallowing, she went to the door and unlocked it, opening it a crack. "Hey, Wallace." She forced her tone to sound normal. "I'm not open yet."

"Hey, Ms. Connor. I have the rest of your beef. You know, the back order? But your back door is locked."

"That's right," Stan said, remembering. When Wallace and Perry had come on Friday, before . . . everything, they'd only brought half the beef delivery. "I'll unlock it. You can go around back."

"Thanks." He sauntered around the side of the building.

Stan relocked the door and leaned against it, trying to slow her pounding heart. He was here to deliver beef.

She hoped.

She hurried out back to let him in just as the door swung open and Brenna stepped inside, carrying a box of coffee from Izzy's, followed by Tyler. Wallace was at the truck, unloading the box.

"Hi!" Stan was so happy to not be alone with Wallace she flung her arms around Brenna. "I wasn't sure you were coming today!"

"I wasn't, either, but I needed to get out of the apartment. I bumped into Tyler. He was looking for you." She brushed listlessly by Stan and headed into the kitchen.

"Hey, Tyler. What's going on?" Stan asked.

"My mom sent me over to see if you were open yet. One of her cats is sick and she wondered if she could get some food for him," Tyler said. "I'm sorry to bother you before you're open though. I can come back."

"Don't be silly. We're opening soon anyway. Why don't you go out front? I have to finish up with Wallace," she said, as Wallace approached with the beef. "Have Brenna show you the meat and rice selections in the freezer. Those should be your best bet."

She watched Tyler and Brenna go, then turned back to Wallace.

"Want me to put this stuff away for you?" Wallace asked.

"No, it's okay," Stan said. "I appreciate you bringing it by. It could've waited until my next delivery."

Wallace shrugged. "You paid for it. Wanted to get it to you. It's only right."

"Well. Thank you. Hey Wallace? Can I ask you something?" Buoyed by the fact that she wasn't in the shop alone any longer, she figured she might capitalize on the opportunity to ask Wallace about Lucy.

"Sure, Ms. Connor."

Stan took a breath. "I know Perry wasn't your favorite person. Did you guys have an issue because of Lucy Tate?"

Wallace's face reddened. "With all due respect, ma'am, I don't think that's any of your business."

"Look. I know Lucy liked Perry. And I know Perry's girlfriend threatened her. And I . . . got the sense that you like Lucy."

Wallace's hand balled into a fist at his side. His jaw was hard with tension. "I don't have to tell you nothin'. I already told the cops where I was that night."

"I'm not asking to interrogate you," Stan said, trying to force a reasonable tone. "I want to help you. And if you just tell me what happened with you and Perry, I can help make sure Jessie understands. So was it true? Were you and Perry fighting about Lucy?"

Wallace shifted uncomfortably from foot

to foot. Stan wasn't sure if he was going to answer her or run out the door.

"She's too good for him!" he finally burst out. "And I tried to tell her that. But . . . I think I came on too strong." He looked miserable. "I don't want her to be scared of me."

"Scared of you? Why would she be scared of you?" Stan asked.

"Because I get very intense sometimes. But it's only when I really believe in something. And I think Lucy is smart and sweet, but she always picks things that are bad for her. Her daddy tells me all the time. So I wanted to help her."

"And she didn't want to hear it," Stan said.

Wallace shook his head. "I don't know why everyone thinks he was so wonderful. I mean, I'd never wish anyone dead but . . ." Wallace trailed off, leaving the thought unfinished.

He might not wish anyone dead, but if he wanted anyone to come close, it would be Perry, Stan guessed. "Were you really working late at the farm that night, Wallace?"

Wallace looked down at the floor and scuffed it with the toe of his boot. "No," he admitted. "But it wasn't what you think."

Before Stan could ask him anything else,

Brenna came through the door. "Hey, it looks like we're out of salmon and rice. Is there any more back here?" she asked Stan, then seemed to realize she'd interrupted something.

"There might be a few in the freezer," Stan said.

"I hafta go," Wallace said, seizing the opportunity, and he fled out the door.

Stan watched him go in dismay.

"Sorry," Brenna said. "I didn't realize you guys were having a serious conversation."

"It's okay," Stan said. "Wallace just admitted he wasn't really working late Friday night."

Brenna frowned. "So what does that mean?"

"I don't know," Stan said. "But I'm guessing nothing good."

CHAPTER THIRTY-EIGHT

The store wasn't as busy as she'd expected for her first day back open after a murder. Brenna had opened the door, and she was behind the register, ringing up Miss Viv and her little Pomeranian, Daisy, when Stan emerged from the back after putting away her beef order. There were a few patrons lingering over human coffee and doggie pastries. Two young mothers sat on the window seat, talking animatedly, while their kids played with the dogs at their feet. Mr. Tully, one of her regulars, sat on the human side. Pokey, his dog, didn't really care about playing with other dogs anyway and just liked to sit at his owner's feet.

"Hi, Miss Viv," Stan said, walking over to give her a hug.

"Hi, sweetheart. We're so glad you're open again," Miss Viv said. "Daisy was very upset she couldn't come play with her friends."

Daisy didn't look all that upset. She just

wanted the treat Miss Viv waved around as she talked.

"Well, we are too," Stan said. "Thanks for coming."

She turned to Brenna after Miss Viv went to sit. "Did you happen to put on Facebook or Instagram that we're open again?"

"Shoot. I didn't. I'm sorry, Stan. I'm so distracted today." Brenna looked miserable. "I can't believe Andrea won't talk to me."

"She'll come around, hon. She's just upset," Stan said. "You can go if you want to."

"No. I need to be busy right now."

"Okay. I'm going to do some updates." Stan had neglected all her accounts over the weekend. At first she'd been skeptical of the social media aspect of her business, but recently, she'd gotten really into it. Brenna had set them up for her, insisting she needed to showcase her yummy creations. And Stan enjoyed the interaction with people who visited the pages.

She grabbed her iPad, brought the last tray of cookies out and handed them to Brenna, then sat on the stool behind the counter and pulled up the Pawsitively Organic Pet Patisserie and Café's Facebook page.

She scrolled the page. There were two

more five-star reviews, which made her happy. "My dog absolutely loves it there," one woman named Tiff gushed. "It's our new weekend hangout." The other, by Mike, declared that her carrot cake pupcakes were his dog's new favorite treat.

Not everyone was focused on murder. It was encouraging.

She noticed a post waiting for approval on her page and navigated to it. When she opened it, she had to look twice to make sure she wasn't seeing things. The comment consisted of one word: *SLUT.*

With a gasp, she hit delete. Then realized maybe she shouldn't have. She probably should've shown it to Jessie. Maybe there was a way to trace it, but now it was gone.

It had to be phase two of the note. Which made her break out in goosebumps.

"Excuse me?"

Distracted, she glanced up to see a young woman she didn't recognize waiting for her attention. She had blond, almost white hair and wore funky glasses that reminded Stan of Amara. "I'm sorry." Stan rose, slapping the cover on her iPad as if she could block out the image of that word. "How can I help you?"

"I need some treats for my dog's birthday party," she said. "Like, four mini-cakes. But your cupcakes are too small."

"When is your party?" Stan asked.

"Later today."

"Okay. How about these?" She pointed to the carrot cakes. "These are more of a mini-cake size."

"But they don't look birthday-ish." The girl pouted.

Normally, Stan would've jumped at the chance to find a solution. But right now, she felt like someone had punched her in the stomach and she couldn't focus on this woman and her cakes. "Okay," she said, mustering up all the patience she could. "How about I make you some cakes?"

"Really?" The girl beamed and clapped her hands together. "That would be great. Celeste likes peanut butter."

"What colors do you want?"

"White icing with something purple. She loves purple. Can I pick them up at one?"

Stan glanced at the clock. It was nearly eleven. That should give her enough time. "Sure," she said. "One is perfect."

After the woman left, she texted Jessie: *Need to talk to you.*

A minute passed, then Jessie texted back: *What now?*

Call me, Stan texted back.

Her phone rang half a second later. "Bren,

I'll be right back," she said, and hurried out back.

"This better be good," Jessie said.

"Someone I don't know posted the word *SLUT* on my Facebook page," Stan said.

"You're kidding."

"Nope. Think it's related to the note?"

Jessie sighed. "Probably."

"I thought so too, but I deleted it," Stan said.

"Why'd you do that?"

"Because it freaked me out."

Jessie muttered something. "Great. Well, I can't do much about a deleted comment."

"I know. Hey, Wallace was here to drop something off. Jess, he wasn't working late Friday night."

Silence on the other end. Then, "How do you know that?"

"Because he told me. But we got interrupted before he could tell me the rest, and he took off."

Jessie swore. "Are you seriously questioning my suspects?"

"I thought you said he wasn't a viable suspect anymore," Stan said defensively. "We were just having a conversation."

"Yeah. A conversation about my murder investigation. Look, I gotta go. I have the conversation with the Pucks soon. If you get any other comments, don't delete them, okay? And stay away from my suspects."

Stan didn't point out that Jessie hadn't actually articulated who her top suspects were. She made the promise and hung up, still troubled as she went back to the counter.

Just in time to see Cyril walk in, notebook in hand, black trench coat in place. "Hi, ladies," he said, coming over to them. "I'm here to celebrate your grand reopening with you. Okay if I talk to a few people?"

"Sure, Cyril," Stan said distractedly. "Just don't mention dead people."

He looked offended. "I always have a method to my questions. I don't just ask about dead people to ask about them."

"Great." Stan grabbed a mug and poured herself some coffee.

"Everything okay?" Brenna asked.

"Fine," Stan said. She hadn't told Brenna about the note, so she wasn't about to tell her about the post. She didn't think it was wise to add to her stress level right now. "All good."

The bell jangled again. Stan glanced up, then did a double take when she realized that Jason DeRoche, Perry's brother-in-law, had just walked in with his dog.

"You see who's here?" she asked Brenna quietly.

Brenna peered over Stan's shoulder, recognition hitting her face. "Yeah. Wow. Okay. I wonder what he wants?" She glanced down at her phone, which had just started vibrating on the counter. "Be right back. You'll be okay?"

"Fine." Stan pasted on a smile as they approached the counter. "Hi, Jason. Hey there, Charlie." She reached down and scratched Charlie's head.

"Hey. Charlie couldn't wait to get here to get his treats. He missed them over the weekend. We usually come in on Saturday and . . . well." He stopped and awkwardly shuffled his feet.

Stan nodded. "Of course. We just took a bunch of batches out of the oven, so most everything in this case is super fresh." She indicated the right side of the case.

"Awesome," Jason said, moving over to peruse the case. "Thanks."

Stan left him to it and started rearranging some of the pastries to fill up empty spaces.

What happened next happened so fast she barely had time to react. The door to the shop was yanked open, setting the bell off into a crazy clanging frenzy, and Andrea

CHAPTER THIRTY-NINE

"How could you even come back in here?" she demanded, her finger pointing right in his face.

Jason took a step back, flinching. Stan didn't blame him. Andrea looked insane, with her ponytail askew and her face blotchy from crying. Even Charlie looked concerned, his attention diverted from his treats to making sure his owner was okay. Everyone in the shop paused. Except for Cyril, who'd been talking to a woman watching her dog play ball, homed in on the situation like a vulture on roadkill.

"Andrea, please —" Jason began, but she cut him off.

"Is it because none of you really care about what happened? All you care about is the negative publicity from all this? Even though everything that happened to him is all your family's fault?"

"Andrea!" Stan said. "You need to calm down."

Jason held up his hands defensively. "Whoa. I'm only family by default," he said, a little desperately. "And of course we care. Everyone is devastated, Andrea. I know how you feel —"

"You have *no idea* how I feel!" The words came out with a screech, similar to nails on a chalkboard.

Stan came around the counter and took her arm. "That's enough. Let's go, or I'm going to have to call the police." She hustled her toward the door, but Andrea bucked in her grasp, jerking her arm away.

"Oh, you'd love that wouldn't you? You all want to see me locked up. Even my so-called *friend.* I'm going." She stormed to the door and pulled it open with enough force Stan winced. But before she left, she looked back at Jason. "Perry would still be alive if everyone had just left him alone." Choking back a sob, she ran out the door and vanished around the corner.

What a mess. Stan looked helplessly around for Brenna, but she was still in the back. The rest of the customers stared unabashedly, taking in the scene. "Sorry about that, folks," Stan said weakly. "Please, carry on."

As her customers started talking among themselves again, Stan came back around the counter to face Jason, who had turned white as a ghost in the aftermath of Andrea's attack.

"I'm sorry," she said. "I don't even know what happened. She must've seen you —"

Jason held up a hand. "Please. Don't apologize. It's not your fault." He hesitated. "Although she always seemed a little crazy. Very jealous of anything Perry gave attention to that wasn't her. But I understand how upset she is," he added hastily.

Jealous. There it was again.

"Yeah," Stan said. "She's pretty upset. She feels like everyone made things hard for Perry."

Jason rubbed the scruff on his chin thoughtfully. "You know, in a way she's right. Everyone did give Perry a really hard time. Wanted him to smarten up, get serious, have a plan — a real plan — for his life. He wasn't a bad kid. Just didn't like to toe the party line." He smiled a little sadly. "In a way I envied him. He didn't give a crap what anyone thought. Meanwhile, my poor wife kills herself to please her parents and they never even notice."

"Who gave him a hard time?" Stan asked. "You mean their parents?"

Cyril materialized at his side. "Hi. Cyril Pierce, *Frog Ledge Holler,*" he cut in. "Can you tell me what just happened? Did it have to do with the murder?" He peered at Jason. "Aren't you part of the Puck family?"

"I . . . I, uh —" Jason stammered, looking at Stan for help.

"Cyril," Stan hissed. "Out. Stop harassing my customers."

Cyril looked unfazed. "I'm just covering the news," he said. "I don't need a comment to write a story." He turned to go, writing in his steno pad the whole time and almost walked into someone walking in the front door.

Stan shook her head and turned back to Jason. "Sorry about that. You were saying, people gave Perry a hard time?"

Jason hesitated. "You're not going to quote me or anything, are you?" he asked.

"No! I don't work for the newspaper. Despite Cyril's numerous attempts."

He looked relieved. "Okay then. Yes, the whole family kind of gave him a hard time. Their business means a lot to them. For some reason Perry's grandfather was fixated on him running the show. Even though Syd is perfectly capable and actually wanted the responsibility. She's been hoping for years to take the reins. She has great ideas, too.

Made no sense, but whatever. Guess it's a family thing. Perry liked organic food fine, but he wasn't really into making it his life's work. He just wanted to act."

"I heard that," Stan said. "And I also heard he was very good at it."

"He was, actually," Jason said. "Syd and I went to see him at a show he did a couple months back. With the community theater group over by the college. He played a lead part."

"Jason." Stan leaned on the counter. "Was Perry worried about anything? Or . . . anyone? Did he ever mention being threatened at all?"

Wide-eyed, Jason shook his head. "No. Not to me. Or to Syd. She would've told me. Why? Was something going on?"

"Just asking," Stan said hastily. She didn't want to say anything about the stalker if he didn't know about it. She figured Jessie wouldn't want that message getting out into the world unless she was managing it.

She wasn't surprised Jason didn't know, but she figured it wouldn't hurt to ask. She doubted Perry Puck would've engaged any of his family members in his external drama, even if it was serious. He probably felt like they wouldn't care all that much. Or throw out an *I told you so. If you just focused on*

289

serious things and stopped doing crazy stuff, you wouldn't have these problems.

Lord knew she'd heard enough of those kinds of comments from her own mother for years, and it had made her stop sharing details about her life.

"I better go," Jason said finally. "I have to get back to Syd. Can I get a few treats to go?"

Stan packed up a box of goodies for Charlie while he pranced around the shop with Scruffy. Jason paid her and left right as Brenna came back down the hall, shoving her phone in her back pocket.

"Sorry about that," she said to Stan. "What did Jason have to say?"

"Bren. Andrea was here."

Brenna froze. "She was? Where is she?"

Stan hesitated. "She must've been walking by and saw Jason. She came in and . . . started yelling at him."

"What?" Brenna asked, dismayed. "Where did she go?"

"I had to escort her out. She made a huge scene, yelling at Jason, saying Perry would still be alive if everyone had just left him alone. She sounded . . . unhinged."

"Oh, man." Brenna covered her face with her hands. "I feel terrible about this. I wish I could do something to help her, but she won't even talk to me. Plus . . ." she hesitated.

"What?" Stan asked.

Brenna dropped her hands. Her eyes were bloodshot and there were dark circles under them, as if she hadn't slept in days. "I shouldn't even say this," she said.

Uh-oh. Stan felt her heart speed up but forced herself to stay calm. "Say what?"

Brenna looked around to make sure no one was listening to her. They weren't. Everyone in the shop, including the dogs, was otherwise occupied. "Andrea had a really big fight with Perry the day he died. She was upset that he was stripping here, even though she actually told me to call him for the job."

"When was the fight?" Stan asked. "Early in the day, or right before . . . the party?"

"I'm not totally sure. But, there's more. That day she told me she was going to be late. That she had something to do with her sister before coming here. But my mom saw her. Near here. Not long before the party started."

"Where exactly did she see her?" Stan asked. "What was she doing?"

Brenna shook her head. "My mom just saw her walking on one of the side streets. Talking on her phone." She looked at Stan,

291

her eyes wide with fear. "You don't think she could've really done it, do you?"

"I have no idea," Stan said, her brain whirring wildly as she tried to process this new information. Andrea had been lurking around the area before the party? Maybe while Perry had been alone in the kitchen? "I mean, she's your best friend. You've known her since . . . how long?"

"Since we were kids," Brenna said. "Kindergarten. She used to pull my hair on the playground." She smiled a little. "She said she loved it because it was so long, so she was trying to take it off me so she could wear it." Tears welled up. "My best friend couldn't be capable of that. C-could she?"

Stan couldn't answer her. She had no idea. "Does Jessie know this?"

Brenna nodded. "I told her. That's one of the reasons she brought Andrea in. She used the family questions as the lead-in, I think, but she really wanted to pin her down on that. It's why Andrea hates me now. And who can blame her? I totally betrayed her. Excuse me." Brenna fled down the hall and into the bathroom. Stan heard the door close and lock behind her.

A new customer came in and Stan automatically focused on her, but she couldn't stop thinking about Andrea.

Could she really have killed her own boyfriend?

CHAPTER FORTY

With all the talk about murder and stalkers, not to mention her own threatening note experience, Stan was back to getting barely any sleep that night. Finally, at five o'clock the next morning, she gave up and got out of bed so as not to disturb Jake with all her tossing and turning. May as well put the time to good use and get to the shop to do some baking. Her cases had been pretty empty when she'd closed up yesterday.

Wednesday. Partway through the week, and it was anything but a typical week. She felt like she was stuck in some alternate reality with no hope of escaping anytime soon. She headed for the shower, hoping it would at least wake her up some.

She crept back into the bedroom to get dressed.

"Leaving?" Jake's muffled voice came from under the covers.

Wincing, she turned to see him peeking

out from under all the blankets. "Sorry to wake you. Yeah, time to make the doughnuts." She managed a weak smile.

"You didn't wake me. Want me to come along? I can help."

He was so sweet. And still freaked out about the note. When she'd told him about the Facebook post last night, that hadn't helped, either. "No, sweetie. It's okay. Brenna will be there too. You got home late last night. You should sleep more."

He didn't look convinced, but he didn't argue. And when she went out to her car with Scruffy and found no more scary notes, it seemed like the day had gotten off on a better foot.

The entire street was silent when Stan pulled into the patisserie parking lot just before six a.m. The peace and quiet of the shop was tempting this morning. A little time alone before Brenna arrived would be good to help clear her head.

She went in the back door, flipping on lights as she entered, immediately locking the door behind her. Scruffy trotted along behind her. Stan still felt the sense of unease, but she was determined to overcome it. This was her shop and no one was going to make her feel scared about being in it.

She kept Scruffy on her leash as she did a

quick walkthrough of the store. Satisfied that all was in its place, she headed back into the kitchen to start prepping. But when she reached down to unhook Scruffy's leash, she noticed her little dog sniffing the air. Scruffy usually enjoyed a good sniff in here, but nothing was even baking yet. Even with her leash off, Scruffy didn't take off running like she usually did. She stood at attention, nose going a mile a minute.

Stan immediately felt a chill go through her. Maybe she still sensed what happened the other day, but that didn't make sense, either. She'd been fine yesterday, after all. Everything had seemed back to normal.

Stan grabbed her cell phone out of her bag.

Scruffy started barking.

Stan froze, remembering the bathroom. She hadn't peeked in there when she'd gone out to the main room. She crept out of the kitchen and approached. The door was slightly ajar. Had she left it that way? Or . . . she pushed the door open, wincing as it banged against the wall behind it, and reached for the light switch. The small room flooded with light.

Nothing. Just the flowers Brenna had arranged in there yesterday.

Stan sagged against the wall, feeling foolish. All these incidents had gotten her fired up and crazy. She needed to get a grip.

She went back into the kitchen and found her little dog pacing furiously, nose going a mile a minute. "What on earth is wrong with you?" Stan asked her.

Scruffy continued to sniff and pace.

A noise at the back door almost sent her screaming, but then she realized it was Brenna with her hands full, trying to juggle her keys. Relieved that another person would be in the shop with her — her desire to be alone had gone right out the window — she hurried over and unlocked the door. "Hi," she said, trying for casual. "You're early."

"Hi," Brenna said, handing her two bags of groceries. "So are you." She took a closer look at Stan. "What's wrong?"

"I don't know," Stan said honestly, locking the door again behind Brenna. "Scruffy's acting weird and I was starting to get wigged out."

"Weird how?" They both looked at Scruffy, who seemed fixated on one area of the kitchen. But there was nothing there, except the cabinets she'd already checked, and the stove.

"Well, for one thing, she's ignoring you," Stan said. "That's weird. She usually can't wait to see you."

"True. I think everyone's having a hard time getting back to normal." Brenna heaved her other two bags onto the counter and began unloading. "I picked up some snacks for us too. And some new peanut butter. We were running low. We've been using it a lot, have you noticed?" She stacked items on shelves and in the fridge as she talked. "But I think we have to start making some lighter treats for the summer. And the froyo. We have to start offering the froyo every day now that it's getting warm. That was a huge hit —" she trailed off.

Stan turned from where she'd been putting dishes away to see why Brenna had stopped. "What?" she asked, dropping the collection of mixing spoons she had in her hand when she registered the look on Brenna's face.

Brenna turned to her, face ashen, and held out a small sheet of paper. Stan took it. It took a second for her to comprehend what she was seeing, and when she did the urge was to crumple the paper, rip it up, stab it, shove it down the garbage disposal, anything to unsee it.

It was a crude pencil drawing of a tall cake, with a knife protruding from it and blood dripping down the side. Underneath the cake it read, *DIE.*

In the same letters as the note she'd found on her car.

"Where . . . where was this?" she asked when her voice actually decided to work again.

"On the counter. Tucked halfway under the flour canister." Brenna waved a shaking hand at the area holding Stan's canisters of flour, sugar, and other baking ingredients. A spot on the counter she totally took for granted and wouldn't have looked twice at until she needed something there. And the spot right above where Scruffy had been barking and sniffing furiously.

Her little dog had been trying to tell her something after all. Now Scruffy looked at her, tail still at attention, not sure what to do next.

Brenna looked like she might pass out, though, so that snapped Stan out of her terror. "Sit." She grabbed a chair from their little break table and shoved it under Brenna.

Brenna did. "Someone . . . was in here."

"Yeah." Stan tried to figure out if she was terrified or angry. A bit of both, she decided, with a bent toward angry. This was her happy place. She was not going to let this crazy person win.

"How the heck are you so calm right now?"

"I have no idea." Stan let out a shaky breath. "I need to call Jessie."

"Should we leave?"

"No." As she said it, Stan felt some of her strength and resolve return. "I mean, I'm not going to, but I understand if you need to. I'm not running scared out of my own shop. Again. I don't know who this crazy person thinks they are, but it's not going to work on me." She picked up her phone, scrolled to Jessie's name, and hit the button.

A sleepy-sounding Marty answered after the third ring. " 'Lo?"

"Did I call the wrong number?" Stan asked. "I meant to call Jessie's cell. Sorry, Marty."

"You did," he said. "She's in the shower, and I wanted to make sure I answered in case it was an emergency." He paused. "Is it? Are you okay, Stan?"

"I'm fine, but I need to talk to her sooner rather than later," Stan said. "Do you know if she's rushing off somewhere?"

"To work. You know, solving crimes with her superhero cape." He laughed. "I'll have her call you back."

"Can you have her stop by the patisserie

on her way?" Stan asked.

"Sure. No problem," Marty said.

Stan disconnected, then scrolled to her home number and called Jake. He sounded like he'd fallen back to sleep, like she'd encouraged him to.

"Hey," she said when he finally picked up. "Sorry to wake you, but can you come to the shop?"

He was instantly alert. "Are you okay? What happened?"

"I'll tell you when you get here. I'm fine," she hurried to assure him, even though she didn't feel fine. "Just come, okay?"

CHAPTER FORTY-ONE

Jake got there first but Jessie was right behind him, her red hair in a wet ponytail hanging down her back, dampening her shirt.

"Jeez, you could've dried your hair," Stan said.

"I was going to until my brother called and told me to get over here ASAP. Right after Marty told me you called. So I figured it was a crisis. What's going on?" Jessie asked. "It's not another note, is it?"

Wordlessly, Stan handed her the slip of paper. Jessie read it, Jake crowding over her shoulder to also get a look.

"Where was this?" Jessie asked.

"On the counter. Tucked under one of the canisters. Brenna found it."

"Does it match the other one?" Jake asked.

Stan nodded. She'd know that writing anywhere. "I didn't see anything weird when I got here. I did a walkthrough and everything was in place," she said.

"So neither door was disturbed?"

"No. Everything appeared to be locked up like I'd left it."

"Show me where on the counter."

Brenna took her over and pointed out the exact spot.

"We'll check for fingerprints." Jessie went down the hall to make a call.

"Stan. I don't like this at all," Jake said. "I know you want life to be business as usual, but I really think we need to talk about this. Until this person is caught —"

He didn't get to finish, because Jessie came back.

"Lou and Colby are on their way over," she announced. "And you're opening late today. I also have another team going back to Perry's apartment to do another search. I'm wondering if he kept anything from this stalker that we missed the first time. I'd love to compare notes. We already seized his computer, but there was nothing that helped. I'll keep you posted on what we find out."

Jake looked at Stan. "You want to stick around for this?" he asked.

"Not really," she said. "I can't take many more criminal investigations in my place of business."

"Come on," he said. "We're going to get breakfast."

"I'm not really hungry," Stan protested.

"Exactly why you're going to eat something." Jake steered her out the door.

They dropped Scruffy off at home. Stan ran in to tell Nikki what was going on, and encouraged her friend to keep the doors locked and be really careful if she went out with the dogs. Nikki, true to her personality, did not seem at all worried about herself. She told Stan that she had to go home that afternoon since Justin had to go on an overnight for work, but she would be back as soon as possible. Stan thought she didn't want to give up on her mini-vacation just yet and was using the wedding plans to keep it going.

They went to a little diner outside of Frog Ledge that Jake liked. Stan wasn't feeling super hungry, but she ordered an omelet and an orange juice to make Jake feel better. And a giant cup of coffee. The omelet was huge, and daunting. She poked at it with her fork.

"You'll feel better when you eat," Jake said. "And less coffee, more orange juice." He nudged the glass toward her.

She picked it up and drank. "I can't

believe all this is happening," she said, finally setting the glass down.

"I know. It's surreal."

"For someone trying to just do his own thing, poor Perry had a lot of people upset with him," Stan said unhappily. "Jessie must be losing her mind, between Perry's own family, all the people he worked with, his girlfriend . . ." she trailed off.

"Does she really suspect his family? That's messed up," Jake said.

"Well, the father could've felt trapped if Perry was in charge of the financials," Stan said. "And it sounds like the sister really wanted to be next in line to run the place, but the grandfather was fixated on Perry. From what her husband said. I wonder if that could've pushed her over the edge."

"The husband? When did you talk to him?"

"At the shop yesterday. He came in with Charlie to get his treats. We talked a bit. He said Sydney was ready and willing to take over. I don't think I told Jessie that." She grabbed her phone, but Jake closed his hand over hers.

"Eat. We'll fill Jessie in when we get back. She's busy right now," he said.

Reluctantly, Stan put the phone down. "I didn't get to tell you the rest of what happened yesterday. Andrea came in while Jason was there. She freaked out on him."

"Come on. Really?"

Stan nodded. "She came completely unhinged and started yelling that it was all Perry's family's fault, that he'd still be alive if they'd just let him alone."

"What was she doing there? I thought she and my sister were on the outs."

"They are. I don't know, actually. At first I chalked it up to her just walking by." But what if she'd been hanging around for another reason? Like, an opportunity to sneak in and leave a disturbing note?

Jake read her mind. "You think she had something to do with the notes?"

"I don't know what to think." Stan replayed Andrea's specific words over in her mind. "At first when she yelled at Jason it sounded like she was simply blaming the family for Perry's life taking a drastic turn. But what if the underlying message there was, *You all set this in motion, it ruined everything, and I had to kill him because of it?* God, that sounds insane, doesn't it?"

Jake pushed his coffee cup around on the table, his face troubled. "I'm taking some nights off from the pub. I don't want you to be home alone," he said finally.

"Jake. You need to run your business,"

Stan said. "I'll be fine. Really." She tried to sound braver than she felt.

Stan's phone rang. Jessie. She answered.

"No forced entry whatsoever," Jessie said. "Your bathroom window is even still locked."

"You think someone picked the lock?" Stan asked.

"Could be. Or they had a key."

Stan felt what little breakfast she'd eaten so far roil in her stomach. A key? How would some crazy stalker have a key to her shop?

CHAPTER FORTY-TWO

Stan hung up and looked at Jake. "She says there was no forced entry. And that possibly someone had a key."

Jake stared at her. "How is that possible? Did you give anyone a key besides me and Brenna?"

"Nope."

"Then who else could have one?"

"I don't know," Stan said. "I never give my whole key ring when I valet park or get service on my car. And I don't even have any extras at home. I keep meaning to get some made, just in case."

"My keys are always on me too," Jake said.

They both pondered the possibilities. Stan felt cold and tried to rub some warmth back into her arms.

"Finish your breakfast," Jake said. "I think you should close the shop today. Go home and rest. Do you want me to take tonight off?"

Stan forced down another forkful of eggs, trying not to gag. "No. Please don't do that, Jake. I'll be fine. Truly. I'll probably want to get out of the house and come over there anyway."

"Are you sure?" He didn't look convinced.

"I'm positive," she said. "And I'm going to work. Jake, I can't let this crazy person think they've won," she said, cutting off his protest. "Like I told Brenna earlier, I'm not running scared out of my own shop. I'm going back, and I'm opening, and I'm working the day." She squeezed his hand. "Thank you for being so amazing."

He regarded her solemnly. "You know I support whatever you want to do. But don't be surprised if you see some extra police patrols around the shop and the house."

"The police don't patrol around here at all," Stan pointed out. As resident state trooper, Jessie's presence was meant to counter the fact that Frog Ledge didn't have its own police department. But with her being the only one here full-time — even Trooper Lou had other assignments outside of town — she would never have time to patrol along with her other duties.

"Exactly my point," Jake said. "Given everything that's going on, I think I can convince my sister to provide some extra protection to the residents, no?"

Jake dropped her back at the shop, making her promise to call him at the first sign of anything out of the ordinary. Jessie and Brenna were still inside.

"You're not going to make me close, are you?" Stan asked.

Jessie shook her head. "We dusted for fingerprints and did what we could. I don't have a lot of hope we're going to get anything from the fingerprints, but we'll try."

Stan looked at Brenna. "I'm going to work. You can go home if you want."

"No way," Brenna said bravely. "If you're here, I'm here. Besides, I have to clean up this mess." She indicated the fingerprint dust smeared on the counter.

"Loving the solidarity," Jessie said dryly. "Call me immediately if you see anything else weird, okay?"

Stan followed her out the back door, closing it behind her. "Listen. Jake and I talked about the key. He, Brenna, and I are the only ones who have them."

"I know," Jessie said. "And that means Andrea would've had close proximity to it."

"This is so insane." Stan leaned against the door. "Hey, so what happened with Perry's parents?"

She watched the internal battle go on in Jessie's head about whether to say anything or not. "It was weird," she said finally, apparently deciding to go the saying-something-without-saying-anything route. "The mother did show emotion. At one point she went on about how wonderful her son was, how he had followed in her philanthropic footsteps and supported her charity work. The father barely said anything. They did say the daughter would be taking over the business, though."

"They did? Wait. Charity work. What charity work?" Stan asked. "I don't remember anyone else saying anything about charity work."

"I didn't, either," Jessie said. "I asked her to clarify, then she looked sorry she'd said it. She mumbled something about the board she was on — I'm guessing the one with your mother — and how Perry had supported the fund-raisers."

"Interesting," Stan said slowly.

"Yeah. Well, I'm not out for interesting," Jessie said. "I'm out for solving a murder. I have to go."

"One more thing," Stan said.

"Of course there is," Jessie muttered.

"You mentioned the sister taking over the business. I never got to tell you what happened yesterday. Jason DeRoche stopped in here. And Andrea suddenly showed up and lost her mind on him."

Jessie frowned. "You're kidding. Why didn't you call me?"

"Because I handled it and she left, but I thought you should know. She said everyone was going to pay for what happened to Perry, or something like that. But he and I did get a chance to talk, and he said that the sister really wanted to take over the business, but the grandfather wanted Perry to do it. I got the sense it didn't sit well." She hesitated. "I'm sure you had the sister in your sights anyway, but I wanted to mention it."

"Mmm. Thanks," Jessie said. "And if Andrea shows up again, call me."

Stan went back inside and heard her phone ringing in her bag. Fishing it out, she checked the number — she didn't recognize it — and answered.

"Is this Ms. McGee?" a female voice asked.

Stan frowned, confused for a second, then it registered. "Yes it is," she said.

"Hello there, Ms. McGee. This is Kyia at Party Pleasers. You stopped by looking for a performer the other day?"

"Yes, I did," she said, her heart starting to

pound. "Did you find the person we were looking for?"

Kyia, whoever she was, didn't miss a beat. "Well, sweetie, I actually found someone comparable that you're going to love! His name is Zak. With no *c*. If you give me your email I can send pictures now."

"Great." Stan recited her email.

"I'm emailing you as we speak," Kyia sang.

"That's lovely of you. Thank you so much."

"And you'll call me back to book, yes?"

"Absolutely," Stan promised.

She hung up, holding the phone against her chest. Something Jessie had said was making her rethink this Party Pleasers angle. It had to be synchronicity that Kyia had called. She was a much bigger believer in synchronicity than coincidence. And when it showed up, she'd learned not to ignore it.

CHAPTER FORTY-THREE

As soon as it started to get dark, Stan drove to her sister's house. She'd promised Jake she'd stop by the pub around nine, so she didn't have much time. But she had a theory, and given that Caitlyn had already played a part in some of this reconnaissance, she would be her best copilot.

Caitlyn waited on her front porch as promised, and Stan had to giggle. Her sister wore all black, down to a baseball cap perched over her stylish blond hair.

"Hey, Krissie. This is gonna be fun." Caitlyn jumped in the passenger seat and rubbed her hands together gleefully.

"I wouldn't exactly call it fun," Stan said. "But I have a theory, and I need to see if I'm right."

"Ooh, the intrigue. Are you going to tell me what it is?"

"I want to see what you think first. If there's anything to see," Stan cautioned.

"There may not be."

"Are we going inside?" Caitlyn asked.

"No," Stan said. "I just want to see what happens after hours."

"You mean like all those women the neighbor mentioned?"

Stan nodded.

"How do you know there'll be women coming tonight?" Caitlyn asked.

"I don't," Stan said. "But I was getting a strong gut instinct that I needed to come check it out."

"Not fair. You really should tell me what you're thinking," Caitlyn protested.

"I will. Chill."

They turned onto the street. Stan killed her lights and stopped the car a few houses down, where she had a good view of the Party Pleasers driveway, but where she wouldn't be noticeable. No neighbors were around tonight. Everything was completely silent, with the exception of a dog barking every few minutes. The night was overcast. She turned the car off, plunging them even further into silence.

They waited.

Nothing happened.

Caitlyn started to fidget after about fifteen minutes. "How long are we just gonna sit here?" she demanded.

Stan gave her a look. "You'd make a terrible undercover cop."

"So are you going to tell me your theory?" Caitlyn asked.

"Okay. But it might sound a little crazy," Stan warned.

Caitlyn made a *come-on* motion with her hand, impatient.

"Perry was apparently a big supporter of his mother's charities," Stan said. "At least that's what his mom told Jessie. It was the first I had heard about it. And the reason Mom knows Mrs. Puck is through their charity work, remember?"

"Okay," Caitlyn said. "So what?"

"Do you remember what the charity work was?"

"The domestic violence shelter, right?"

Stan nodded.

"Okay," Caitlyn said again. "And?"

Stan sighed impatiently. "What if we were all wrong about this being a bad place? What if it's really a *good* place?"

"Good how?"

"Maybe they're helping domestic violence victims," Stan said.

Caitlyn frowned. "How would they do that?"

"I don't know. A place to stay?"

"In a place where they rent out strippers?"

Caitlyn asked doubtfully.

"I know it sounds weird. And I haven't figured out exactly how it would work," Stan admitted. "But I got this feeling today after I heard Jessie talk about the mother that it has to be related."

"But she supports a different organization," Caitlyn pointed out. "I still don't see the connection with Perry stripping."

"I haven't quite figured that part out yet, either," Stan said. "But I did a little reading on domestic violence shelters and networks, and a lot of these groups work together. They could be working with Safe Harbor, somehow."

"Seems strange," Caitlyn said. "But isn't it the strangest things that always end up being the real story? I guess there's only one way to find out." She shoved her car door open.

"Wait. Where are you going?" Stan scrambled out of the car after her.

"I'm going to go pretend to be someone who needs help. I'm kind of dressed the part." Caitlyn looked down at her cat burglar outfit. "I could just say I had to be stealthy to sneak out of my house."

"I don't think that's a good idea," Stan said.

"I'm going," Caitlyn said. "Come on,

Stan! Why else did we come here? We can't waste the opportunity. If I don't come back, call Jessie."

And before Stan could stop her, she took off down the street.

Stan watched her go, mouth open, not quite sure what to do next. Her sister was crazy, and she'd enabled the crazy. She should just call Jessie now and get it over with. Surely, the police would be getting a phone call tonight either way.

Leaving her car where it was, she crept down the street after Caitlyn, hoping the cranky Mrs. Gallo wasn't holding court at her window to see her skulking around. But she should at least be within hearing distance of the house in case something went horribly wrong. She could see her sister only by the shock of blond hair visible under her hat as she went to the front door and tried it. Locked. She rapped on the door and waited.

Stan slipped into the yard of the house next to Party Pleasers. The house was dark, so hopefully no one was home. She found a thick shrub on the edge of the property and crouched behind it. From here, she had a view of the side of the house. There was a small door next to the garage.

Caitlyn left the front step and circled the

house. A motion light came on in the driveway, startling both of them and flooding the driveway with light. Caitlyn continued on, coming to a stop next to the side door. Stan could see her peering into the window, cupping her hands around her eyes. But it was dark inside, so Stan figured she couldn't see anything anyway.

Maybe no one was there. As much as she wanted to know what was going on, she only wanted to know if it was something good. Now that she thought about it, maybe daylight was better to snoop. She waited for Caitlyn to turn and head back to the car.

Instead, her sister knocked on the side door.

Stan held her breath.

Nothing happened.

She'd just let out a sigh of relief when a light on the side of the house went on. Then the garage door went up, as if someone had pressed a button. Fumbling in her pocket for her cell, Stan pulled it out and hovered her finger over the emergency call button. Just in case.

Caitlyn went over to the garage. A woman appeared in the doorway. It wasn't Miriam, and it wasn't Jewel. So at least Caitlyn wouldn't be recognized. This woman was older, with a short gray bob and an outfit that looked like she'd been out running.

"Are you Heidi?" she asked.

Caitlyn nodded. "I am."

"I thought they sent you instructions to go to the back," she said. "Sorry about that. Come in, honey."

Stan watched, fascinated, as Caitlyn stepped into the garage. At that exact moment, a car drove slowly down the street and pulled into the driveway. A minute later, a woman climbed out, holding a weekender bag. She headed for the garage, and Stan could hear her say clear as day, "Hi. I'm Heidi. Am I at the right place?"

CHAPTER FORTY-FOUR

"I can't believe you two went back there snooping." Jessie paced back and forth in Stan's sunroom as Stan and Caitlyn sat on the couch like two schoolchildren getting bawled out at the principal's office. "What were you thinking?"

"We were thinking that we were helping. You agreed that there might be something weird there," Stan said defensively.

"Sure. And as the police, it's my job to find that out!" Jessie threw up her hands and stalked back across the kitchen. "We have ways of doing this stuff. Ways that actually get us information we need to solve cases."

"Well, you hadn't mentioned you were looking into them."

"You're right. I forgot to file my report with you this week. My bad."

Stan crossed her arms over her chest. "Hey. At least we got confirmation that they're not doing bad things there. And that no one there probably killed Perry."

"That's right," Caitlyn chimed in, finally. She was still scared of Jessie, and she hadn't said a word since Jessie had arrived at Party Pleasers to escort them home, after they'd called the police on the imposter Heidi. The real Heidi had been a little traumatized about the whole thing, which Stan felt bad about. Here she was trying to slip quietly into a new life, and instead she'd bumped right into a murder investigation. "So we did you a favor, right?"

She shrank back against the couch as Jessie turned her best death glare on her.

"Great. That was pure luck. And you traumatized this poor woman who now thinks her moves will be traced. Never mind the fact that this could've turned out very differently, with bad people doing bad things," Jessie said. "You interfered with a police investigation. I *should* have arrested you! And it's not like they didn't want me to."

That was true. Miriam had not been pleased when she'd arrived on the scene and recognized them. It had taken Jessie and Colby a good hour to talk her out of pressing charges. But despite the tongue-lashing, Stan felt pretty good about what they'd found out. Party Pleasers, whatever it was doing with its strippers, had a whole other mission as well. They had living space for people who were fleeing bad situations, and they also helped them get to the next place they were going if it wasn't here.

"So did you find a lot of this stuff out already?" Stan asked. "Was Perry helping them or something? Did the strippers have anything to do with this?" She knew she was pushing her luck. Jessie wasn't in the mood to chat with her right now — and definitely not in the mood to share information — but it couldn't hurt to ask.

Before Jessie could yell at them some more, the front door opened and Jake came into the room. Kyle was right behind him.

"There you are. Jeez, Caitlyn. Call a guy when you plan on vanishing, would you?" Kyle exclaimed.

"What's going on?" Jake asked, looking from Jessie to Stan. "Are you guys okay?"

"We're fine," Stan said. "Why?"

"Well, you never showed up at the pub like you said you would, and then Kyle called looking for Caitlyn. Of course, when Jessie called to tell me she had you both with her, I figured there was a story behind it." He gave Stan that look — the one that was part amused, part frustrated, and part resigned — then turned to Jessie. "Everything okay here?"

"It's dandy," Jessie said. "By the way, she's getting an ankle bracelet until this is over." She turned back to Stan and Caitlyn and gave them one more withering stare. "Stay out of my murder."

And with that, Jessie marched down the hall and left.

Everyone was quiet for a minute. "So," Jake said finally. "Want to tell me what's going on?"

"Long story," Stan said. "But hey, it looks like the stripper place is off the suspect list."

CHAPTER FORTY-FIVE

Stan, Scruffy, and Henry headed out to the car around six-thirty on Thursday morning. Stan grabbed the *Holler* off her porch, pausing to glance at the headlines. Cyril was keeping Perry's murder in the news, above the fold, but a quick skim of the article told her there were no new developments. Nothing that had gone public, anyway.

She tossed the paper back on the porch floor. So frustrating. Stan couldn't believe it had been almost a week since Perry was killed. And they weren't one step closer to knowing who'd done it.

They got to the shop before Brenna. Despite a few minutes of sitting in the car, full of apprehension, Stan finally mustered up enough nerve to go inside. Jake had someone change the locks yesterday afternoon. She had no good reason to be worried.

Blessedly, there was nothing out of place,

no notes or other presents waiting for her, and Scruffy didn't seem fazed by anything today.

That made her feel a lot better.

She lit a couple of candles out in the main room and opened the windows, then went back to the kitchen to get the specials of the day ready. She grabbed a few recipes from her colorful recipe collector hanging on the wall — Char had made it for her when she opened the shop — and gathered ingredients. Today, for the signature treat, she planned to feature Scruffy's Simple Ginger Snaps, a local favorite. And she hadn't done her famous apple peanut butter bacon treats lately, so she put those on the menu too.

The rhythm of baking calmed her, and soon she was in the zone — mixing ingredients, spooning the batter onto a cookie sheet, using her custom cookie cutters when the recipe warranted it. As she baked, she thought about her business and where she wanted it to go. It was already doing better in a short period of time than she'd imagined, and she was so grateful. But she wanted to take it to the next level. And she needed help to get there.

By the time Brenna arrived an hour later with coffees and a bag of what smelled like heaven from Izzy's, Stan had a good head start on the day's pastry case fillers and two other trays already in the oven.

"Good morning," Brenna said, setting everything on the counter. "Sorry I'm late."

"You're not late at all. I was up early. As usual these days. Thank you for the coffee." She took a sip. She really did love coffee. "What's in the bag?"

"Danish," Brenna said. "They looked amazing."

"Just what I need." Stan pulled one out and bit into it. Maybe it was good that she hadn't bought her wedding dress yet. With all the sugar she'd been consuming, it might not fit anyway. But time was creeping up on her, and she hadn't actually spoken to her mother since the ill-fated dress trip on Monday. She knew she was avoiding the whole situation, which she could almost justify given everything else.

But she couldn't ignore it forever.

"Any progress on final wedding plans?" Brenna asked, as if reading her mind. "With all the insanity, I haven't had a chance to ask you."

Stan smiled. "Just that we're getting married."

"I can't wait," Brenna said, smiling her first real smile Stan could remember since Perry's murder. Then it faltered. "I wish we didn't have to get through this funeral first."

"I know. We all do. Hey, listen. There's been something I've been meaning to ask you."

"Sure," Brenna said. "What's up?"

"It's about the shop."

"Are you still worried about your trip? Honestly, don't be," Brenna began, but Stan shook her head.

"No. Well, of course I'm worried about the trip, but that's not it. It's about you."

"Me?" Brenna put her tray down and looked at Stan. "What about me? Did I do something wrong? I'm really sorry for being so distracted lately, but I've been having such a hard time with the Andrea thing —"

"Bren," Stan interrupted. "Would you consider being a full partner in the shop?"

Brenna stared at her for a second. "Seriously?"

Stan nodded. "I've been meaning to ask you for a while, but with everything going on, I kept tabling it. So do you — oh. Okay," she laughed as Brenna erupted into a huge smile and threw her arms around Stan, almost knocking her over.

"I would love to! Yes! Thank you, Stan." Brenna stepped back, tears shining in her eyes. "This is amazing. I have to tell Scott. And Jake! Did you already tell Jake?"

"I told him my plan, a while ago. I didn't tell him today was the day I would officially ask. Mainly because I didn't know, but I figured I'd seize a fairly quiet moment. We should talk about all the formalities we need to do to get it going, and compensation," Stan began, but Brenna waved her off.

"Yes, sure. We can do that later. I want to tell everyone first!" She grabbed her phone and her coffee and hurried out to the main room of the patisserie, already talking excitedly to Scott.

Stan smiled as she made a quick note to call her lawyer to get the formal paperwork drawn up. At least she'd done something right today.

Chapter Forty-Six

Stan left the shop a little early, leaving Brenna to finish with the last few customers and lock up. She had a meeting at her house with Tyler to talk about the photos for the wedding. She'd been putting it off because of all the uncertainty floating around thanks to her mother's proposed changes, but she couldn't put it off anymore. Plus, she wanted to give Tyler some money up front for the event.

When she pulled into the driveway, Tyler was sitting on the porch steps waiting for her. She parked and then hurried to the porch, pausing when she saw a large package leaning against the door. She didn't remember ordering anything. Maybe Jake had?

"Hey, Tyler. Sorry, were you waiting long?"

"Hi Stan. Not at all. Five minutes or so." Tyler stood. "Want me to get that for you?"

he offered, motioning to the package.

She inspected the label on the box. Addressed to her, not Jake. Then her mouth dropped when she saw the return address. Royal Bridal Shop.

"Oh, no," she muttered. "Uh, sure, Tyler. Thanks."

He picked up the box while Stan unlocked the door and stepped into the house.

"Do you mind if I just open this really quick?" she asked.

"Not at all."

She used her key to cut a hole in the packing tape, then ripped the box the rest of the way open. Her heart sank when she recognized the familiar layers of lace wrapped in plastic. A note on the top read:

It looked gorgeous on you. Love, Mom.

Using her key again to get through the plastic, she pulled the dress out, just to be sure. Yep, it was the atrocity she'd tried on the other morning. She knew she should be thankful to her mother. The dress cost a fortune. But it wasn't the dress she wanted.

And that made Stan feel worse. Then angry, because she didn't want to think of herself as a picky, high-maintenance Bridezilla. And that made her feel lousy again, because if she'd just called her mother to talk this out, be more forceful when she told her about the dress she *did* like, none of this would've happened.

"Wow," Tyler said. "That's some dress."

"Yeah," Stan muttered. "Some dress. Let's go to the kitchen." She shoved the box aside, leaving the dress in a pile on top of it. As she stood up, she suddenly realized something felt off. She'd been too distracted to notice it when she walked in. She wasn't quite sure what it was, but Scruffy felt it too. She could tell by her little dog's tense posture. Henry, by contrast, lumbered into the den and sat on his bed, obviously exhausted from the day's work.

Stan grabbed Tyler's arm to stop him from proceeding any farther. "Wait," she said, and called for the cats.

"Nutty! Benny!" Neither cat came. In Benny's case, this wasn't surprising. He usually ventured out in his own time. In Nutty's case, it was a bit more worrisome. Unless he was camped out in the kitchen, waiting for his dinner. That had to be it.

But she had to be sure. "Stay here for a second, Tyler, okay?" Stan unhooked Scruffy's leash and moved through the house, on alert. Then she heard a noise coming from the kitchen. A sound she couldn't quite identify. Picking up the pace, she rushed down the hall and into the room as the noise registered. Boiling water. Her large silver pasta pot was on the stove. This morning, it had been in its cabinet.

Had Jake been here recently and made food? Left the stove on? He wasn't usually careless.

She moved over to shut the water off, and her eyes fell on the contents of the pot. Her mouth dropped open in pure disbelief. The water in the pan was brown, and the cause of the color was made apparent by the still-bobbing head of a chocolate rabbit. Then she noticed the chocolate candy wrapping on the counter next to the stove, smoothed out neatly. To make sure she recognized it, apparently.

And she did. What had once been her prized chocolate rabbit — now a boiling brown puddle — had been a special Easter gift from Jake. An expensive chocolate. One he'd had Izzy order specially for her from Belgium. That she'd been saving. For what, she wasn't sure, but she hadn't yet had the heart to eat it.

It was . . . insane. And terrifying. Someone had snuck into her house, found it, and boiled it in a pan on her stove. And left the wrapping for her to cry over.

The double meaning wasn't lost on her. The fateful scene from the classic movie

Fatal Attraction repeated in her mind. Thank God she didn't have a real bunny in the house. But where were the cats? And was this crazy person still here?

She grabbed a knife from her butcher block on the counter and whirled around, holding it out like a sword, eyes darting in every direction. For all she knew, whoever this lunatic was could've been watching her the whole time she'd been in here. From the pantry. Or the sunroom. Or the laundry room . . .

Tyler appeared in the doorway, causing her to shriek. He jumped, holding up his hands in defense. "Whoa! What's going on? Are you okay? What are you doing with the butcher knife?" His eyes widened as he took in the scene on the stove. "What the . . ."

"Go outside," Stan instructed. "Take the dogs. Now. And wait for me to come out." She didn't want to put anyone else in danger, and she had no idea what she was dealing with here.

Tyler looked like he might protest, but he decided against it, probably given the knife. "Come on, Scruffy," he said, bending to pick her up. Before he left the room, he grabbed his phone and snapped a few photos.

"Jeez, Tyler," Stan said.

He shrugged. "You might want them later."

Either that or Cyril had taught him well.

She grabbed her phone and called Jake, her hands shaking so hard she could barely scroll to his number. Voice mail. Crying out in frustration, she dialed Jessie.

"Thank God," she said when Jessie answered. "Can you come over? Now?"

"What's wrong?" Jessie asked.

"Someone boiled my bunny," she said, her voice shaking.

"Someone . . . what?"

"Boiled my bunny," Stan repeated. "In my pasta pot. At my house. I just found it when I got home."

"You're in the house now?"

"Yeah."

"Well, go outside."

"But I have to find the cats —"

"Go outside and wait for me," Jessie repeated. Her tone told Stan in no uncertain terms she wasn't kidding. "I'll be there in five minutes. We'll find them together."

CHAPTER FORTY-SEVEN

When Jessie arrived about four and a half minutes later, Lou was with her. Stan and Tyler waited outside with Scruffy and Henry. She had left the pot on the stove but turned the heat off, so the chocolate had started to congeal in the water, the bunny's half-melted head bobbing sadly in the middle of the mess. She was kind of glad Tyler had gotten some action shots now.

But those four and a half minutes felt like a lifetime. Stan couldn't stop thinking about what she'd found in her kitchen and was torn between sobbing and laughing at the ridiculousness of it. Every time she pictured a wild-eyed blond with crazy curly hair — much like the original bunny boiler — in her kitchen with a maniacal look on her face, stirring the chocolate bunny into the pot, cackling gleefully as it melted, she felt hysterical laughter bubbling up in her throat.

She'd never been so happy to see a police car.

Jessie parked haphazardly behind Stan's car and jumped out. "Stay here," she said, heading for the front door, while Lou went around the back.

Ignoring her, Stan followed her inside. She was desperate to make sure Nutty and Benny were okay. Tyler stayed out with the dogs.

Jessie went straight to the kitchen and surveyed the mess on the stove. Then she went out to the sunroom to let Lou in. "Nothing broken or forced out here," he reported. "Windows intact. I'll check the basement."

He went downstairs.

"Can we check upstairs?" Stan asked anxiously.

"I thought I told you to stay outside," Jessie said, but she headed upstairs.

Stan followed, almost crying with relief when she saw Nutty in her bedroom doorway, tail swishing, clearly wondering what all the fuss was about. Stan sank down onto the floor, gathering him close and burying her face in his fur. Nutty didn't love public displays of affection, and she felt him tense against her, his tail swishing even more fiercely at being manhandled.

She didn't care. She was so thankful it wasn't him boiling in the pot. "Where's your brother?" she asked him. "I'm sure he's hiding. Benny!" she called, releasing Nutty. She picked up their treat jar and shook it gently. That usually brought him running.

She found her orange guy in her closet, under a scarf he'd pulled down to cover himself. She gave him lots of snuggles too.

Jessie came back into the room. "Everyone accounted for?"

Stan nodded.

"Where's Nikki?"

"She had to go home last night because Justin was traveling," Stan said. "She left yesterday. She's coming back, but she hasn't gotten here yet."

"What's Tyler doing here?"

"We were supposed to meet to talk about the wedding photos."

"He get here before you?"

Stan nodded. "He was waiting on the porch. Said he'd been here for five minutes or so."

"Hmmm. You talk to my brother?"

"I called him, but I got his voice mail," Stan said.

Jessie headed downstairs. Stan gave the cats one more hug then rose and followed her. She found Lou and Jessie conferring in the hall.

"No sign of forced entry anywhere," Jessie said. "Nothing broken. Just like at your shop."

The key insinuation again. "We changed the locks at the shop but not here," Stan murmured.

"Well, you might want to get these changed too," Jessie said grimly. "I don't like this. At all."

"It's gotta be the same whack job," Lou said. "You sure you don't want to bring the girlfriend back in?"

"I do. But I'm still trying to figure out where she was in that hour before the party," Jessie said.

"Andrea?" Tyler asked from behind them.

They all turned. He stood there with both dogs on leashes, and he looked pale.

"Tyler. What time did you get here?" Jessie asked, ignoring his question.

"Just a few minutes before Stan," he said.

"So what time was that?" Jessie pressed.

"Around four. Maybe five of?"

"And no one was around? You didn't see anything odd? No one in the neighborhood who shouldn't have been here?"

He shook his head. "Nothing."

Jessie looked at Stan. "That didn't happen long before you got here."

"I know."

"So what about Andrea?" Tyler asked again.

Jessie turned back to him. "You were friendly with Perry, right?"

Tyler nodded. He'd gone from white to red in about five seconds, Stan noticed with interest.

"Any problems you saw between him and his girlfriend?"

"No," he said, but Stan didn't quite believe him. He avoided her eyes and shoved his hands in his pockets.

Stan cleared her throat. "Hey Jess? I was thinking. My purse. I usually keep it out back at the store. And I'm not always out there when the farm deliveries come."

"Wallace?" Jessie said.

Stan nodded. "I can't stop thinking about him telling me he wasn't really working late the night Perry died."

Jessie and Lou exchanged a look.

"What?" Stan asked.

"Actually, we found out where he was," Jessie said. "We brought him in again today for questioning."

"You did?" Stan was stunned. "So, where was he?"

"At a poetry slam. At Izzy's bookstore."

Stan sank down onto the stairs, not sure

she'd heard her right. "At a what now?"

"A poetry slam," Lou repeated, grinning. "Who knew farmers wrote love poems, right? Guess this guy does. And it's not manly to admit it, so he does this whole routine of lying to everyone about where he goes one Friday night every month. He travels around to different bookstores. This time it happened to be at Izzy's place. We have a roomful of poets attesting he was there, and the sign-in sheet. He didn't kill Perry."

"A poetry slam." Despite herself, Stan laughed. "This whole thing gets crazier and crazier, right?"

"For sure," Jessie said. "But I still don't have my stalker. Or my murderer. Lou, get some fingerprints going. Not that we're going to get much. We got nothing from your shop," she told Stan. "I'll take photos of the kitchen."

"Great." Stan sighed. "What am I supposed to do about this?"

"I don't know," Jessie admitted. "But I'm doing everything I can to figure out who's doing this. I know it's small comfort right now, but I am."

"I know," Stan said. Her phone rang. Jake.

"Sorry I missed you," he said. "What's going on? Are you okay? I heard my sister is

"Tyler, you can head out. Let's catch up tomorrow on the wedding stuff," Stan told him. "I'm sorry you got tangled up in this mess." She walked him to the door.

"It's okay. I'm sorry this happened." He paused, hand on the door. "Stan. Can I —"

He broke off as the door flew open from the other side, almost knocking him into Stan. Jake stuck his head in. "Sorry. But what is going on?" he demanded. "Are you okay?"

"I'm fine. Tyler, I'll call you tomorrow." She closed the door behind him, then turned to Jake. "My Belgian chocolate rabbit that you got me for Easter," Stan said. "Someone snuck in and boiled him."

Jake frowned at her. "Want to repeat that?"

"You heard me. My bunny got boiled." She was startled to find tears in her eyes. She'd thought she was handling this okay. But apparently the stress was getting to her.

Jake glanced at his sister. She shrugged and pointed to the pot. He went over and glanced inside it, then took in the fingerprint dust all over the counter. His face darkened. "Jess. I'm losing patience with this," he said. "We need to get this resolved."

"No kidding," Jessie shot back. "You think I'm sitting around watching TV all day?"

"Jake. It's not her fault," Stan said quietly.

Jake ran his hands through his hair. "I know. I'm sorry, Jess. But I'm getting really scared by all this. And I can't imagine what Stan's feeling."

"Crappy," Stan admitted.

"Sweetie." Jake went over and hugged her tight. "Why don't you go upstairs for a while? Take a nap. Let them finish up here. Then I'll make you some dinner."

"I'm fine. I don't need a nap," Stan said. "I'll take you up on dinner, though."

When Lou and Jessie finished a few minutes later, Stan followed them down the hall. "Will you please keep me posted?" she asked in a low voice. "I know you don't like sharing with civilians, but I think I've earned it."

"I will," Jessie said. "I promise."

"Thank you." Impulsively, Stan gave her a hug. Which took Jessie a little by surprise, but she went with it.

At the door, she paused and glanced down at the dress still in a pile on top of its box. "You got a dress?"

"No," Stan said automatically. "Long story."

"Tell me another time. I don't think I can handle another long story today," Jessie said. "I'll be in touch."

Stan went back into the kitchen. Jake was cleaning up the mess the dust had left behind. Wordlessly, Stan grabbed a rag and some of Char's magic soap left over from patisserie cleaning day and joined him.

"Can you believe someone did this?" she asked abruptly, after a few minutes of silence. "I feel so . . . violated."

"I know." He put his arm around her and hugged her against him. "I'm going to have the locks changed. Tomorrow. I should've done it when I had the shop locks done. Stupid."

"How would you know?" Stan asked. "No one thought this would happen." She thought about Andrea again, appearing outside her shop on Tuesday. Why had she been there?"

She looked up at Jake. "Do *you* think this is Andrea?"

"I don't know," he said grimly. "And that bothers me most of all."

Stan put on yoga pants and a comfy T-shirt and settled in the den while Jake cooked some tuna steaks. Nikki had called to say she'd been delayed and would be back in the morning. Stan had just collapsed on the couch when the doorbell rang.

She groaned. "Now what?" Getting up, she went to the door and peered out the side window. No cars in sight. Immediately she started to get nervous, which made her angry. She was in her own house. She'd never been afraid here, and she wasn't about to start now. She yanked the door open and found Cyril on the porch.

"Cyril," Stan said. "Hey. Come on in." She was glad to see him, actually. She wanted to plant a seed in his brain.

Jake poked his head out of the kitchen. "Cyril? Can't you give her a break, man?"

"Hey, she invited me in," Cyril said, holding up his hands.

"Come on. Let's go in here." Stan led him to the kitchen. "Sit. Are you here about the rabbit?"

Cyril nodded. "Best police log I've seen in a long time," he said. "No offense," he added when Jake glared at him. "So. Are you going to give me a comment on the bunny?"

"No," Stan said. "It's a personal loss. Can't talk about it yet."

"Funny. They arrest anyone?"

"Not that I know of," Stan said.

"Well, do they at least think it's the same stalker Perry Puck had?" Cyril asked in exasperation.

"I don't know, Cyril. If they knew that, we would probably know who it is and wouldn't be having this conversation," Stan said. "Anyway, listen. I wanted to give you a story tip."

He regarded her with that frown she'd come to recognize as his deep-thought frown. He shoved his glasses farther up on his nose. "A tip, huh?"

"You sound suspicious," Stan said.

Cyril shrugged. "We were taught in J-school to question our mothers, after all."

"Lovely," Stan said. "So I heard that Sydney Puck is taking over the business officially. I thought it might make a nice local story to interview her. Kind of a best-case scenario for the family, right? The heir is gone, but the sister and her husband step in?"

"I like that," Cyril said thoughtfully, pulling out his notebook to scratch a few notes.

"When is this happening?"

"I don't know. I heard . . . thirdhand," she said, not wanting to say she'd heard about it from Jessie.

"Well. Then I'll want to get to her soon. Tomorrow's the funeral, so maybe I'll reach out over the weekend. Give her some grieving time." He nodded. "Thanks, Stan. Now let's talk about you."

"I told you I don't want to talk about the bunny —" Stan began but Cyril interrupted.

"I was going to ask how you were doing," Cyril said, putting his notebook and pen down. "As a friend. Not as a reporter."

"Oh," Stan managed, feeling tears prick her eyes again. She really needed to stop all this crying. It wasn't solving anything. "I'm okay."

Cyril nodded. "I know it's been a rough week. But I'm really looking forward to covering your wedding."

"You're — you're covering our wedding?" Stan asked, surprised.

"Of course. It's a huge deal in town," Cyril said. "Everyone will be there."

Impulsively, Stan leaned over and kissed him on the cheek. "Thank you."

"Jeez," he mumbled, blushing furiously. "It's my job. So, I better go."

"Hey Cyril, you want to stay for dinner?" Jake asked from the stove. "We have plenty."

Cyril looked at him, then back at Stan, as if he thought one of them was going to laugh and tell him, "Just kidding."

"He's serious," Stan said. "Why wouldn't he be? That's what friends do."

"Well then," Cyril said. "In that case, I'd love to."

Chapter Forty-Nine

Friday. The day of Perry Puck's funeral. The weather was gorgeous. It was a full-color send-off for a boy who'd seemed to live his life in full color, no matter what anyone else thought. Stan found it fitting. And terribly sad.

Stan opened the closet door, wincing as she saw the wedding dress, which she'd haphazardly hung without even putting it back in the safekeeping bag it had arrived in. With all the madness yesterday, she hadn't yet called her mother. Well, that and she was still in avoidance mode.

Just get through the funeral and you can deal with all of that with a clear head, she thought.

Shoving the dress aside, she chose a simple black dress and slipped it on. She smoothed her hair back into a demure ponytail, watching Jake watch her as he dressed in black pants and a gray button-down shirt.

"Not a fun way to spend the day," he said finally, as he focused on tying his tie in the mirror. "You sure you want to do this?"

It had been a long time since he'd worn a tie, Stan thought. Probably not since her mother's wedding. He didn't love them. He preferred his jeans and leather jacket, or a McSwigg's T-shirt. She didn't want him to have to wear one to their wedding if he didn't want to. It would make the experience less . . . his. The thought made her eyes well up with tears. She furiously tried to blink them away so her makeup wouldn't smudge. But Jake noticed in the mirror and turned to her.

"Hey. What's wrong?" He came over and slipped an arm around her. "You don't have to go, you know. You aren't obligated."

"No, it's not that. I'm fine." She grabbed a tissue and dabbed at her eye. "Well, not fine. You know what I mean. I feel awful about Perry. And feeling lousy in general, I guess. Everything feels . . . unsettled." She rubbed her arms, suddenly feeling cold.

"Well, it is unsettled," he said. "Listen. We'll do this, then we'll go out tonight. Are you going into the shop after the funeral?"

Stan shook her head. "I closed up for the day. I didn't want either Brenna or I to have to worry about rushing over there."

He nodded. "Good. I'm not working tonight, either. I have plenty of people on. I'll take you out."

She reached up and touched his cheek. "That's really sweet, but I'm good with just staying home too. We're going to be gone for two weeks. The babies are going to miss us."

Jake kissed her. "That's why I love you so much. Well, one of the reasons. So, hey. What are you going to do about the dress?" He nodded to the pile of lace blocking half the clothes in the closet.

"I have no idea." Stan reached over and shut the closet door, closing it out of her consciousness for the time being. "Let's get through today first, then I'll figure it out."

The funeral was at the Catholic church on the green, so they didn't have far to go. They walked across the street, joining the crowd filing into the church. When they got to the steps, Stan paused. They were supposed to wait for Brenna, who was dreading this even more than Stan was.

Brenna hurried over to them a few minutes later, Scott in tow. "Sorry I'm late," she said.

"You're not at all," Stan said.

Brenna took a deep breath. "I'm so dreading this."

Jake gave her a squeeze around the shoulders. "We all are, kiddo."

Emmalee and Tyler Hoffman walked over to them. Emmalee looked grim. "This is so tragic," she said, holding onto Tyler's arm. "So young. I can't get over it." She dabbed at her eyes with a tissue.

"It really is," Jake said.

"How is your sister doing with finding the perpetrator?" she asked Jake.

Tyler untangled himself from his mother while she was occupied with Jake and pulled Stan aside. "I have to tell you something," he said.

"Okay. What's wrong?" Stan asked.

"Andrea didn't do it."

Stan frowned. "You sound like you know that for a fact."

"I do."

"How?"

"Because that window that everyone's talking about? Where she was missing and he got killed?" Tyler took a breath. "She was with me."

Stan stared at him. "Like, *with you* with you?"

Tyler nodded. "We met up before she went to the party. She was mad at him. For

353

the stripping thing. And she gave him an ultimatum, but he wouldn't give it up. So she . . ." he swallowed, "wanted to do something to get back at him."

"Why didn't you tell anyone this before?" Stan asked.

He looked miserable. "Because she obviously didn't want anyone to know, and I promised her I wouldn't say anything."

"Oh, Tyler." Stan sighed. "Why didn't she just tell the police this? She's been freaking out about being questioned."

"She didn't want anyone to know," he repeated. "I think she felt really guilty about it. Especially given what happened. So she swore she wasn't going to tell."

"Well, you know that's not realistic, right?" Stan said. "I would strongly suggest you get her to fess up, or you'll have to do it for her."

"Stan! We're going in," Jake called over.

"Coming." She turned back to Tyler. "You understand?"

"Yeah," he mumbled. "But please don't tell anyone. We'll take care of it. I promise. I'll talk to her."

"Okay. But you need to do it ASAP, Tyler."

Stan left him scuffing at the ground with his shoe and joined Jake. "Everything okay?"

he asked.

She nodded. "Fine."

They climbed the steps and found seats in an aisle halfway to the front. Stan tried to look around without being too obvious. But she was curious about who would show up here. And what the family would be like.

Out of the corner of her eye she spotted a familiar face. Andrea walked in alone and took a seat on the opposite side of the church, a few rows from the front. Obviously she hadn't been invited to join the family. She poked Brenna. "There's Andrea."

Brenna winced. "Yeah."

"Is the family here yet?" Stan tried to peer into the front of the church.

Jake leaned over. "They're behind you," he whispered. "They just walked in."

Stan whirled around to watch as the Pucks entered the church and walked solemnly down the aisle. She tried not to be obvious. From Jake's face, she wasn't succeeding. But it was worth it. Gabrielle Puck was dressed like a true Italian widow, and Stan didn't even know if she was Italian. The only item she was missing was a veil, but she had the hat and wore all black. Her face, however, was blotchy, as if she'd truly been crying.

This was her first time seeing Perry's father. And he was everything Stan had imagined him to be. Tall and sour. The only thing that differed from the picture in her mind was that he had lighter hair. She'd expected him to be one of those dark and debonair mean people. But he was rather plain.

Behind them came Sydney and Jason. She had on a black dress similar to her mother's, but her hair was loose around her shoulders. She looked around at the crowd nervously as they walked past. Jason looked appropriately poised and solemn, in a navy blue suit, his arm around his wife's waist. They marched solemnly down the aisle to the front pew, and then the music faded.

Out of curiosity, Stan observed the rest of the crowd. Big turnout. Some faces she didn't recognize at all. Perry's parents' friends, other relatives. But her mother and Tony were there, and Roger Tate. No sign of Wallace. Or Lucy Tate. No one who looked like a stalker at first glance, either.

When the service ended, the priest urged everyone to head over to the fancy restaurant just outside of town that the Pucks had chosen for the "celebration of Perry's life." And though Stan didn't know Perry that well, from everything she'd heard and seen, it was exactly the sort of place he would've hated.

"We don't need to stay long," Jake said, when Stan hesitated at the door. "Actually, babe, we don't need to go in at all if you don't want to."

"No, it's okay. We probably should." Stan squeezed Jake's hand. "Let's get it over with."

They walked inside, into a crowd of people. Mostly Perry's parents' friends, from the looks of it, but Stan did catch a glimpse of a bunch of younger people huddled in a corner looking uncomfortable. She saw Andrea standing near them but slightly apart. When their eyes met, Andrea looked away.

Stan swallowed, thinking of the bunny in the pot on her stove. She had a hard time picturing Andrea sneaking into her house and pulling that stunt, but who knew.

"Come on," Jake said, taking her hand and leading her to the bar.

"I like how you think," she said.

He nodded. "Probably the only way we can get through the half hour we're going to stay, right?"

"Works for me. I'll have a glass of wine," Stan said. She leaned against the bar while she waited for Jake to get their drinks and saw Brenna walking through the front door.

Stan lifted her hand in a wave, just as her eye caught something behind Brenna's head. Red hair. Wild red hair, actually, framing an equally wild face, one that Stan had seen before. She realized with a start that the young woman who erupted through the door behind Brenna was Marcy, Andrea's roommate — the girl who had come to her ill-fated bachelorette party.

Her abrupt entry startled the guests gathered near the door and they stepped back, their conversations fading, to let her pass.

Stan felt her stomach clench. Whatever was about to happen wasn't good. "Jake." Stan grabbed his arm, forcing him to turn and look at what was unfolding.

"Hmmm?" He glanced down at her, still focused on placing their order.

"Look."

He finally did, and his whole body tensed. Brenna reached them and turned to see what they were staring at. Marcy had made it into the midst of the crowd at that point, standing there breathing heavily, ample chest heaving, as if she'd run miles to get here. She wore gym clothes and carried a backpack, which seemed odd at a funeral.

"Oh my God," Brenna muttered. "That's

Marcy. Andrea's roommate. What is going on?"

"She looks insane. Or scared. Where's Jessie?" Stan whispered.

"I don't know. Come on." Jake slid an arm around Stan's shoulders and started to move toward the back exit.

"No! We can't go," she protested.

"Stan," he began, but the show had already started.

Marcy scanned the crowd as the noise level in the room started to drop off — people sensing something wasn't right.

Marcy thrust her hands on her hips and shouted, "You're all a bunch of fakes and liars!" She whirled and pointed at Andrea. "Especially *you*!"

Stan watched Andrea's face change from surprise to disbelief to dread as she registered what was going on.

Then, everything seemed to happen at once. Andrea stepped forward, as if she was about to say something. Marcy slung her backpack off her shoulder and reached into it. Jake sprang into action at the same time Jessie appeared, seemingly from out of nowhere.

They both dove for her at the same time, which was a sight to see since Jessie had come to the funeral dressed as a civilian, wearing a dress. The rest of the guests either remained frozen in place or ran for the door. Stan grabbed her cell phone and called 911 in case Jessie needed backup.

And then, as fast as it had started, everything stopped. Jessie sat on top of a thrashing Marcy, trying to handcuff her while keeping her dress from flying up. Jake pulled the backpack away from her and Trooper Lou, who had apparently also been in attendance — or at least outside in case anything crazy happened — grabbed it from him like it might be radioactive and ran out the door with it. This left Jake's hands free to help his sister, and they finally got Marcy under control and cuffed.

Jessie hauled her to her feet, her face red from exertion. But before she could shove her out the door, Andrea materialized in front of them, shaking like a leaf.

"Marcy," she said, sounding like she was on the verge of hysteria. "What is going on? How could you do this?"

Marcy looked at her with pure hatred. "You're a terrible person," she spat. "You didn't love him, either. No one loved him like I did!"

"Perry?" Andrea asked, aghast. "Are you talking about Perry?"

"Let's go," Jessie said, pushing Marcy out

360

the door, leaving Andrea standing there, mouth open.

Andrea watched them go, then looked around, realized everyone was staring, and fled out the door behind them.

CHAPTER FIFTY

"Andrea's roommate was stalking Perry." Stan kicked off her heels and put her feet up on the couch, where she'd collapsed as soon as they'd walked through the door after the funeral. Nikki had returned while they were gone, and now she waited anxiously for a report of how the day had gone. She was definitely getting more than she'd bargained for.

From what they'd been able to piece together after the day's dramatic events, Andrea's roommate had developed a crush on Perry after meeting him when he'd started dating Andrea. She'd nurtured this crush throughout the relationship and used Andrea's own words against her when Andrea complained about Perry's side job. But it appeared Marcy's jealous tendencies had also extended to the women Perry stripped for.

Jessie had called to say they were "seriously considering" Marcy as a suspect in Perry's death, and she was pretty certain Marcy been terrorizing Stan. But Jessie had a lot of work to do sifting through what was real and what was part of this troubled woman's imagination.

"So this clears Andrea, then?" Nikki asked.

"It must," Jake said. "Which will be a relief for Brenna."

And Tyler, Stan thought. "How did she not see this crazy stuff was going on? I mean, didn't they live together?" Stan asked. "It sounds wild."

"Maybe she hid it well," Nikki said. "I don't know about you, but I've dated enough lunatics to know that people can hide their crazy really well when they want to."

Jake gave her a strange look but didn't say anything.

"Anyways. Wow, what a day." Nikki sat back, pulling Nutty onto her lap. "I guess it is true that the killers show up at the funerals, eh?"

"We don't know if she actually killed him yet," Stan said. "She did say she loved him. Would she want to kill him if she really thought she loved him?"

"She's definitely unstable, Stan," Jake said. "Maybe it was one of those 'If I can't have him no one can' things."

"Disturbing, but true." Stan's cell rang. She glanced down at it. Her mother. She groaned inwardly. The funeral was over, but Stan had hoped to have at least until tomorrow to deal with her mother.

On the other hand, she already had a headache. She picked up the phone and answered. "Hi, Mom."

"Kristan. May I stop by for a few minutes?"

"Right now? Mom, we just got back from the funeral —"

"That's right. I heard we missed all the excitement," Patricia said.

"It's probably good you didn't make it there in time for all that," Stan said. "It wasn't pretty."

"I can imagine. So is now a good time? Or should I come later?"

"Now is fine," she said, resigned. "See you soon."

"What's up?" Jake asked when she dropped her phone on the couch next to her.

"My mother's stopping by," Stan said.

"Did she say why?"

"No. I'm sure it's going to be to ask why I didn't call to thank her for the dress."

Jake smiled. "You could tell her no."

"I could. And guaranteed she'll show up anyway."

"Okay then. Do you mind if I run over to help at the pub for an hour or so while you're doing that? I can pick up dinner on the way back," he said.

"Of course not. Get the pub ready for its Friday night festivities." She smiled and squeezed his hand. "Can we have Thai for dinner?"

He leaned over and kissed her. "You bet. Call me with your orders. Back soon." He slipped out the front door, Duncan on his heels. Stan heard his truck start a minute later.

"He must feel better knowing that the crazy stalker is locked up," Nikki said. "You too."

"Yeah," Stan said.

"Did she actually confess to boiling your bunny?" Nikki asked, after a pause.

"Not that I've heard yet," Stan said.

"Well," Nikki said. "I bet a couple more hours with Jessie will break her."

Nikki slipped upstairs with the dogs when the doorbell rang to give Stan some privacy with her mother. Stan took a breath and opened the door, offering a hopeful smile to her mother.

"Mom. Hi."

"Kristan. Thank you for seeing me." Patricia straightened her jacket and brushed at an imaginary piece of lint on her skirt.

"That's very formal, Mom," Stan said. "No need to thank me. Can I get you coffee? Tea?"

"No, thank you."

"Well, at least come sit," Stan said, leading her into the den. Patricia perched stiffly on the couch while Stan sat across from her in her favorite chair and straightened the magazines on the coffee table. "I've been meaning to call. About the dress," she said, when the silence threatened to stretch on too long.

"Yes, the dress. It arrived, then?"

"It did. Mom —" Stan began, but her mother cut her off.

"We can talk about the dress later. I wanted to ask you something. Something important," Patricia said.

"Is it about the wedding, Mom? Because seriously, I don't know if I can handle any more questions about the wedding. At least not questions about changing everything," Stan said. She hadn't planned to say anything about any of this, but suddenly she couldn't help herself.

"It is about the wedding," Patricia said

stiffly. "But it's not about the location. Or the food."

"The food? What about the food? Mom —"

"I'd like it if Tony could walk you down the aisle," her mother interrupted.

CHAPTER FIFTY-ONE

Stan sat back against the chair, her mouth forming an *O*. This was not what she'd been expecting. Another demand about decorations, or the pub versus a respectable church, or debating the benefit of her mother's gardens as the perfect reception area. But . . . Tony walking her down the aisle? Never mind the fact that she didn't want an aisle in the first place. She hadn't planned on anyone doing that. Mostly because her dad was gone, and he'd been the only one she could imagine having that honor.

Maybe that was why she'd fought so strongly against an aisle. Just one more reason why the pub was so perfect. No need to worry about all that.

Her mother still watched her, waiting for an answer. One that Stan didn't want to give. Yes, she'd changed her mind about Tony. One hundred percent. But that didn't mean they were so tight that he could slip right into that role. They'd only known each other a little more than a year, for goodness' sake.

"Mom. We aren't changing the venue," Stan said. "Which means I won't have much of an aisle to walk down in the pub."

"Nonsense," Patricia said, brushing her argument away with a sweep of her hand. "I told you Pastor Ellis rearranged his schedule to accommodate you. And that your extended family is coming. We need to move the ceremony to the church."

"Right. You told me all that. Just because you told me doesn't mean it's happening. Look, Mom. Tony and I are in a good place. We've both made the effort to get there. But I'm not sure that means we're close enough to share that moment. Does he even want to do this? Or is it something you're demanding we both do?"

"*Demanding?*" Patricia pressed her lips together so hard they nearly disappeared. When she finally spoke her voice dripped icicles. "I've been trying to make this wedding of yours something to remember. Something well-organized and classy. Worthy of a Connor. I've offered you our home, I've offered to pay for someone to plan it, I've bought you a dress. But you're trying

369

to thwart me at every turn. Honestly, Kristan, you're quite ungrateful. And most of the time I think you're still doing it to spite me." Patricia stood.

Stan stood too, all the pent-up anger in her chest finally threatening to boil over. "That's not fair. I want you to be involved. I just want you to be respectful of what I actually want. Since this is *my* day. You never once asked me if I wanted any of the things you've been proposing!"

Patricia stared her down, her lips pressed tightly together, back stiff and straight as a board. "I'll give you some time to think about this," she said after a minute, as if Stan hadn't spoken. "And I won't tell Tony about your reaction, mainly because I don't want to hurt his feelings. But you really should think long and hard about your behavior. It's quite rude."

And with that, she sailed out the front door. Stan heard the final click as she closed it behind her. No slamming doors for Patricia Connor. It wasn't ladylike or appropriate.

Stan remained rooted to the same spot. She wasn't sure why she felt guilty and upset. Her rational brain knew she had no reason. Her mother was trying to control everything, like she always did, and using her master manipulation techniques when she wasn't getting her way. They could go back in time and apply this scene to pretty much everything major Stan had done — boyfriends, college, career choice. But this . . . Stan wasn't wrong. And she wasn't giving in.

Stan headed upstairs. She had better things to do than waste time thinking about her mother's crazy. She was going for a run to clear her head.

Stan burst into her closet to find a pair of shorts and a T-shirt. She took a second to realize something wasn't right. Her gaze traveled to the closet floor, to the sea of white. There wasn't supposed to be a rug here. She gasped when she realized the white was the fancy wedding dress her mother had bought her. Crumpled in a heap on the floor. And right in the middle of the heap was a pile of cat vomit.

And not just regular vomit. This was true, hardcore vomit. The hairiest of hairballs. In that disgusting green-black color suggesting that the culprit had been saving this up for a long time.

"Oh. My. God." She stared at the scene, which could have come out of a horror movie. Stan realized she was being watched. A pair of brilliant green eyes peered at her from behind the white mess. Nutty. Still defiant, but maybe a little anxious about the situation.

Stan sat back on her heels and regarded him. He blinked slowly.

"Did you do this?" she asked.

He continued to stare. Benny popped up beside him, his sweet orange face also looking concerned. He purred.

Stan's gaze traveled from one furry face to the other. "Which one of you pulled the dress down? And threw up on it?"

Nutty stood, flicking his tail, and sauntered over to her, rubbing against her leg.

"Did you do it because you knew I didn't like it?"

He purred. Benny meowed plaintively. Stan couldn't tell if he was trying to save his brother and take the blame himself, or throw Nutty under the bus.

Stan had her suspicions, though. She and Nutty had always been on the same wavelength. Was it really any surprise that he'd pulled this dress off its hanger, made a bed out of it, then threw up on it?

Not really. He'd probably done her a favor. One more reason she shouldn't do this wedding the way her mother wanted.

"Stan? She gone? What happ— oh." Nikki, who'd come into the room, stopped and stared. "Crap. Is that —"

"My wedding dress? Yeah. Sure is."

"Oh." They both stared at it for a few more minutes. "Well, maybe we can get it cleaned," Nikki said. "Let's call Char. I bet she can help."

Stan didn't know whether to laugh or cry.

"Nik," she said when she trusted herself enough to speak. "I love the positivity, but did you see this? I mean, this is . . . bad. And, it looks like he kneaded a nice little bed in the lace before he puked on it." Stan pointed to the shredded pieces of lace surrounding the masterpiece. "Let's face it. This puppy is pretty much ruined."

"Yeah." Nikki sat down heavily on the floor next to her. "So now what?"

Stan looked at her friend, the first genuine smile in a week breaking out on her face. "Now I don't have to wear it. I knew cats were the most amazing pets ever! Sorry, Scruffy. You know what I meant," she added hastily, noting the crestfallen look on her little dog's face. "You should've peed on it first. Just to make sure it wasn't fixable."

CHAPTER FIFTY-TWO

When Jake got home with the Thai food, she and Nikki were sitting in the sunroom. She'd brought the ruined dress down and laid it on the table in front of her, as a reminder to stay strong for what she was going to ask Jake. Scruffy and Henry were at her feet, watching her with some concern. She'd tried to wipe the puke stain out just to say she'd given it a shot, but she'd really just made it worse. Nutty didn't get hairballs often, but when he did, it was never pretty.

"You're really going to ask him?" Nikki asked when she heard the door.

Stan nodded. "I have to give it a shot."

"Okay. Let me know how it goes." Nikki rose. "I'm going to take a quick walk around the green before dinner," she said as she passed Jake in the hall, practically running for the front door.

Jake stopped and watched her go, then

turned back to Stan suspiciously. "What's that about?"

"Nothing. She, uh, wanted to get a work-out in before dinner."

"Really. What are you doing? How was the visit with your mother?" Jake came to the doorway, eyes traveling to the dress. "Is that your —"

"Wedding dress. Yup." Stan tossed the lacy bundle aside. "Sure is. So I've been thinking."

"Yeah?" He came over and sat next to her. She could read the concern in his eyes. She didn't blame him. She must look like an unhinged maniac right now. She could feel the wild look in her own eyes.

"I need to ask you a favor. And I really need you to say yes."

"What kind of favor?" Jake asked carefully.

"Say yes first," Stan commanded.

"Babe." Jake took her hand, ran his thumb over her knuckles. "Why don't you tell me what's wrong first? I know you've been under a lot of stress lately. What happened?"

"Can't you just say yes? I didn't think you were going to fight me too!" She yanked her hand away, kicked the dress aside and got up, stalking around the small room like a caged animal. "I want to elope."

"Elope?" Jake stared at her. "For real?"

"Yes, for real. Do you think I'm asking you for my health? Well, maybe I am, now that I think about it." She stopped and considered that. "Since I might have a nervous breakdown if I have to deal with any of this for another minute." She turned and faced him. "Come on. Please, Jake. This is not enjoyable for me right now, and I don't want our wedding to feel that way." She was mortified that her eyes were filling with tears coming too fast and furious for her to blink away.

Jake went over and pulled her close as they spilled over onto her cheeks. "Honey. What's going on? Is this about your mother? I didn't step in earlier because I figured everything she was pushing didn't matter that much, but I guess I was wrong. Tell me what you want me to do."

She wiped her face on his shirt and looked up at him. "I want you to run away with me tonight and elope." She squeezed him tighter. "Please?"

He rested his forehead against hers. "What did she do?"

"On top of everything else?" Stan sniffled and wiped away a fresh tear.

"Oh, boy. What now?"

"She wants Tony to walk me down the aisle."

"Wow." Jake lifted his head and regarded her seriously. "That's kind of huge."

"I know."

"Did Tony ask? Or was this her idea?"

"I asked the same thing. She said they both talked about it. I'm not sure what that means. I hope she's not forcing him because that would be so awkward for everyone, right? I mean, knowing her, he probably doesn't even know she asked me. I hate this. He probably feels like I do — like she's forcing him into something. I can't put either of us through that. And I don't want a wedding like that! But she never listens. It's like, she doesn't even care what I want."

"Stan. I know you've been struggling with your mother. I understand you want to push back on this stuff. But the Tony thing — you need to talk to her about that. About how you really feel. Because I'm guessing that you're already sad about your dad not being here for this, and that's probably why you don't want to go the traditional ceremony route. Am I wrong?"

Stan stuffed her hands in the back pockets of her jeans. "No. You're absolutely right. As usual. You always get it. You always get *me.*" The tears started fresh again. "That's why I think it's silly that we can't just elope . . ."

"Sweetie. My parents would be devastated. Never mind Jessie and Brenna. And Liam and Izzy and Nikki and Char and Ray. And the rest of my extended family." He winced a little bit. "And that's not even half the people. You heard Cyril. This is going to be his whole Sunday front page the day after the wedding. The whole town is so excited about this. *We're* excited about it." He squeezed her shoulders. "Aren't we?" His eyes searched hers.

She couldn't resist him. Ever. And he always seemed to bring her back to center. "Yeah, we are. I know, I'm overreacting. I'm sorry." Stan dropped back onto the couch. "I have to stand up to her. But I have to do it nicely, you know? That's my problem. I've been letting this whole situation make me feel sixteen again, so she's treating me like I'm sixteen. It's a problem."

He nodded. "But you're right. If you have an adult conversation with her, and explain how much you appreciate everything she's trying to do, and tell her your side, it will be fine. I guarantee it."

"Yeah," Stan said, with false bravado. "It will be fine."

She wished she felt as confident as Jake.

CHAPTER FIFTY-THREE

"I have to go talk to her. And I think I'd rather deal with the stalker." Stan stood at Izzy's counter the next morning, filling her friend in on yesterday's events. Izzy hadn't been able to help herself when Stan described the vomit-covered Vera Wang masterpiece — she had to stop pouring coffee for a minute, she was laughing so hard.

"That's pretty bad." Izzy wiped off the steam wand on her espresso machine and placed the cup in front of Stan. "You really asked him to elope?"

Stan nodded, accepting the cup. "Thanks. Yeah, I did. Figured it was a long shot, but I was kind of at my wits' end."

"Understandable," Izzy said.

"So what do I say to her? My approach sounded good when I said it to Jake, but I don't know if I can talk to her about this without feeling sixteen." Stan felt miserable. "And what do I do about this stupid dress?"

"Stan. Take a breath. Eat this." Izzy handed her a plate with one of her famous chocolate croissants on it. "Get some sugar and caffeine in you and you'll feel a whole lot better. Okay?"

"I guess." Stan took the plate and sniffed. "So you're saying I don't need a dress because you know I'm going to be too fat to fit in it?" She frowned at Izzy's steely stare. "You know I love these, right?"

"That's why I make them," Izzy said. "Go sit and eat."

Stan took her breakfast and headed to a window seat. A couple sips of her latte and a bite of her croissant instantly put her in a slightly better mood, and she relaxed enough to get out of her head and into the café. The three women at the table behind her were talking, and she couldn't help but listen. Then she wished she hadn't.

Because of course, they were talking about Perry Puck's funeral.

"I think it was both of them," one of the women said conspiratorially.

"Both of them? The girlfriend and her crazy friend? Oooh, that's a thought," her friend said. "Kind of like that girl who went to Italy and sliced up her roommate!"

A silence. "Not exactly like that," the first woman said after a minute. "I mean, unless

380

the two girls were seeing each other and had to get rid of the boy!"

The three of them giggled. Stan pushed her plate away, her appetite curdling. On second thought, she grabbed the last piece of her croissant, picked up her latte, and left.

When Stan got to her shop she found Jessie leaning against her car in the back lot, waiting for her. And she didn't look happy.

"Oh no. Now what?" Stan climbed out of the car and paused in front of her.

"She didn't do it."

"Who didn't do what? Come inside." Stan unlocked the back door and led them in.

"Marcy. Our crazy stalking funeral crasher. She didn't kill Perry. And I'm right back to where I started." Jessie walked around the kitchen straightening Stan's various cooking and baking paraphernalia.

Stan dropped her purse. "Wait. What do you mean she didn't do it?"

"I mean, she didn't kill him. She was at the gym on Friday night. With an entire class of Zumba freaks as witness." Jessie looked almost as disgusted at the thought of Zumba as she did at the prospect of being back to square one in her investigation. "She did, however, stalk him. And you."

"She was my stalker." It was surreal to think she'd had a stalker. "How did she . . ."

"Apparently, she pilfered Brenna's keys when my sister was over trying to take care of Andrea, and had copies made. Of all of them, because she didn't know which was yours or your shop's."

"But . . . why?"

"Why did she stalk you? Because she's got problems. Clearly. She's at a hospital under evaluation by a shrink. I'm going to charge her with stalking and trespassing, but likely she'll get some lame community service and maybe probation. Unless her family can get a judge to drop the charges because of the psychiatric care or something."

Jessie sighed. "She blames you for Perry ending up dead. Since it happened at your party. And even though she was stalking him, apparently she was in love with him. And he with her. He just didn't know it yet. How do these nuts end up in my town?"

"So what was in her backpack?" Stan asked.

Jessie barked out a laugh. "A poem. That she'd written for Perry. She wanted to read it at the funeral."

"But everyone thought she was going to blow the place up."

"Well, yeah. She was completely unhinged." Jessie stopped and leaned against the counter, scrubbing her face with her hands. "I guess I'm back to twenty-four-hour shifts until I figure this out. Unless it really was Andrea."

"Back to her, huh," Stan said. Apparently, Tyler hadn't come clean, thinking they were in the clear with Marcy's arrest. But what she didn't understand about Andrea was why she'd rather be a murder suspect than have people know she cheated on her boyfriend.

People were weird.

"Yeah. Back to her. Unless I can prove his family put out a hit on him or something. I gotta go. Just wanted to tell you that she's in the hospital indefinitely, so you don't need to worry about her showing up on your doorstep."

Jessie turned to go, then paused and turned back. "She actually told me she watched *Fatal Attraction* three times last weekend just to get prepared for the big scene. She was going to throw a stuffed animal into the pot, but she said she came in and found the chocolate one sitting out on the counter and thought it was perfect. She also said she was kind of worried the stuffed animal could've caught fire. So she was glad she didn't have to do that."

Chapter Fifty-Four

Despite her attempt to make a joke out of the stalker thing, the reality that Marcy hadn't killed Perry sent Stan into a spiral of emotions. There was no resolution yet, and the killer was still out there.

Cyril would be happy. All of these twists and turns would keep him in front-page stories for the foreseeable future.

But it didn't make Stan happy. It frustrated her. And, though she hated to admit it, she was still scared. And mad, that her wedding was probably going to be overshadowed by all of this. Brenna also didn't take the news well when Stan filled her in, especially because she saw that the blame for the murder pointed right back to Andrea. Since neither Tyler nor Andrea had yet come clean about her alibi.

Between the two of them, the shop was subdued.

Stan knew she needed to tell Jessie, despite

her promise to Tyler. She'd give him one more chance to do the right thing. She tried to call him twice but got no answer. She finally called the *Holler* offices, but no one was there, either. "So frustrating," she muttered.

"Hmmm?" Brenna looked up from where she was boxing up some cookies for a to-go order.

"Nothing," Stan said, looking up as the bell on the door jangled. Her eyes widened as Tony Falco stepped into the shop. He looked around, spotted her, and waved, making his way to the counter.

"Hi, Stan. I wondered if you had a few minutes to talk?" He looked like he'd just come from the office, even though it was Saturday.

"Of course," Stan said. "Is everything okay?"

"It is. I just . . . wanted to come see you. I had a meeting at the office, and you were on my mind."

He seemed nervous. Stan wondered if he was going to reprimand her for callously tossing aside her mother's feelings and giving her a hard time about the wedding stuff. Or maybe her mother had told him about her reaction to the request that he walk her down the aisle after all. She swallowed, trying to calm her suddenly pounding heart. She hated family confrontations.

"Sure. We can go out back. Let me get Brenna. Do you want coffee or tea?" she asked.

"Tea, please," he said. "Trying to cut back on the coffee."

"Oh. Good luck with that," Stan said, smiling. "They'll have to pry my coffee cup out of my cold hands when I die." Too late, she realized that may not be the best thing to say right about now. "I have Earl Grey, peppermint, chamomile?"

"Peppermint," he decided.

She filled two cups with hot water and added the tea bags, then motioned for him to follow her. "Hey Bren," she said. "I'll be back out in a few."

"Take your time. Hi, Mayor Falco."

Tony greeted her, then followed Stan to their little table in the kitchen. They both sat.

"Tony," she began, at the same time he said, "Stan, could I —"

They both paused, then laughed awkwardly. "Go ahead. Please," Stan said.

"Thank you. I just wanted to come and tell you that you needn't feel bad, or obligated, or anything else you may be feeling about your mother's request," Tony said bluntly. "She meant well, but I told her it was too soon. But you know her." He smiled a little. "She very rarely listens to anyone."

Stan felt a giant weight lift off her chest. "Believe me, I hear you. Tony, I don't want you to think that I have any reservations about our relationship, or that I don't want you to be part of my wedding," Stan said. "I really didn't want the traditional wedding format anyway. She was pressuring me to do that."

Tony held up a hand. "You don't need to explain anything at all. I know you've been feeling overwhelmed with all the proposed changes to your plans. So I hope you'll forgive me for inserting myself, but I spoke to your mother. To suggest an alternative to her alternative plans."

"Really." Stan couldn't hide her surprise. Tony had stepped in on her behalf? "What kind of alternative?"

"That the wedding take place as you two planned it, then when you return from your trip we have a party for you at our house. Basically the reception she was planning for the day of."

"And she agreed?" Stan asked.

Tony nodded. "She did. I'm sure she'll want to tell you herself, so please don't ruin the surprise." He winked. "Anyway," Tony said, finishing his tea. "That's all I wanted to say, Stan. I do treasure our relationship, and I wanted to make sure we were okay."

"Thank you," Stan said, touched. "It really means a lot, Tony."

She followed him outside. He paused. "I know things have been a bit crazy on all levels, but I hope now you can take the rest of the time leading up to the big day and enjoy it a bit more."

"I hope so, too," Stan said. "Thanks for coming."

Stan stood there for a long time after he left, watching her little town go about its day around her. And then she went inside and called Jessie to tell her she needed to go talk to Tyler.

CHAPTER FIFTY-FIVE

After they closed the shop, Stan drove home and called Nikki from the driveway.

"I'm outside. Let's go," she said when Nikki answered.

"Where?"

"I'll tell you on the way. We have to make a couple stops."

"I'll be right out." Nikki ran out a minute later and hopped in. "So what's the big mystery?"

"We're going dress shopping."

Nikki whipped her head around, a grin breaking out. "Really?"

"Really."

They drove out of Frog Ledge and headed west. Nikki settled back against the seat. "So where is this place?"

"It's about an hour away," Stan said. "It's a cute dress shop I found when I was out that way picking up some supplies. I liked it because it didn't sound overly fancy, but it definitely looked trendy. And . . ." she hesitated, glancing over at Nikki. "It's near one of the Pucks' organic markets. The first one, in fact. I actually was in there the last time I came to the shop because it's got a great café in it."

"Oh, man." Nikki covered her face with her hands. "So this *isn't* about your wedding dress."

"It totally is," Stan protested. "It's just convenient. Because I really want to see Perry's sister again."

"Why?" Nikki asked.

"I don't know. Call it my gut instinct. But I just want to have a conversation with her." She glanced at Nikki. "Trust me, okay?"

Nikki sighed. "What choice do I have?"

"Anyway, I have bigger news. Tony came to see me today." She filled Nikki in on that conversation, which took almost the whole rest of the drive.

When they finally pulled into the dress shop's parking lot, Stan drove up to the front window. Her face immediately lit up into a smile. "Look." She pointed at the window. "That's it. It's still here." The dress was perfect. It was simple, fitted, with beads on the bodice and a short train.

"It's exactly your style," Nikki said. "I love it."

They went inside. The place was empty. The girl at the counter waved at them. "Hey. Can I help you?"

"Yes. I'd like to try on the dress in the window." Stan pointed.

"Oooh, that's a beauty. I'm surprised it's been here so long," the girl said, going to fetch it.

"It was waiting for you," Nikki murmured. "I'm not surprised."

"I tried it on before," Stan said when the girl returned with it. "I'm so happy it's still here."

"Well, so am I! Let's get you a room. I'm Jen, by the way. Holler if you need me." She set Stan up in a fitting room and left her to it.

Nikki waited anxiously outside the door. Stan came out a few minutes later, smiling from ear to ear, and swore she saw her very stoic best friend's eyes fill with tears.

"You like?" Stan asked anxiously.

"Like? I love." Nikki blinked furiously, then came over and hugged her. "It's perfect. It's *you*. Stan, you have to get it."

"Yeah." Stan gazed into the mirror. "I do, don't I?"

"You sure do," Jen exclaimed, materializing beside them. "Beautiful! Should I wrap this up for you?"

"Actually," Stan said, still looking at her reflection, "can you hold it for me?"

"What?" Nikki nearly yelled. "You have to get that dress! Your wedding is . . . *soon!*"

"Relax," Stan said. "I know. And I'm going to buy the dress. I'll pay you for it now," she said to Jen. "But I need to come back for it."

"No problem," Jen assured her. "It will be here waiting for you."

Nikki waited until they were in the car before she said anything else. "So explain why you don't want to bring the dress home now? Are you afraid the cats will destroy it?"

Stan laughed. "No. I just thought . . . since you got to pick it out with me officially, maybe someone else would like to unofficially pick it out with me. Not that she needs to know all the history."

It took Nikki a second, then it dawned on her. "Oh! You're bringing your mother back to get it."

Stan nodded. "You think that's stupid?"

"Not at all. I think it's sweet. I'll never tell." She pantomimed zipping her lips together, then turned and looked at Stan. "Did you tell her yet? About her dress?"

"No. I figure she wants to make the first move to talk, given what Tony said about her wanting to tell me herself about the new proposal. Unless he read her wrong and she's going to freeze me out until I cave."

"I bet she's just busy. You know, being the mayor's wife and all."

Stan wasn't so convinced, but she pushed it out of her mind as the sign for the Greenery appeared in front of them. She pulled into the parking lot and looked expectantly at Nikki.

"Well, let's see what we can find out."

Chapter Fifty-Six

"Do you really think she's going to be in here?" Nikki asked. "Doesn't she run the place? And aren't there more than one?"

"There are, but this is the main one. Her husband said this is where they spend the most time. And I don't think her running it is official yet."

They went inside and stood for a moment, scoping the place out. It had a good vibe to it. There was a bakery counter immediately as you walked in, with today's gluten-free, dairy-free, organic treats. The café menu also offered hot breakfast, lunch, and juices. There were about ten aisles of groceries, and a lovely little produce section.

"Cool place," Nikki remarked, then made a beeline for the essential oils. Stan turned to the woman behind the café counter and smiled. "I'm looking for Sydney. Is she here?"

"Syd? Sure, she's out back. One second."

The woman picked up a phone and said, "Can you send Syd out?" She listened, then huffed out a breath. "Well, can't *you* finish the Strawberry Supreme? She has a visitor." She hung up and smiled at Stan. "She'll be right out."

"Thanks." Stan took the opportunity to peruse the case, her gaze falling on the pumpkin spice gluten-free donut. Pumpkin was her favorite, no matter what time of the year.

"It's delish," the woman behind the counter said. "Syd makes those herself. There she is now." She nodded behind Stan.

Stan turned and saw Sydney walking toward her. She wore an apron stained with the aforementioned strawberries, and she wore leggings and a T-shirt underneath. Very different from the high-end look she'd sported the night of the murder. A look of recognition passed over her face when she saw Stan, but she didn't smile.

"Hi," Stan said as she approached. "I'm not sure you remember me, but I'm Stan Connor."

"Of course I remember you." *My brother got murdered at your party.* The unspoken sentence hung between them, until Sydney broke the awkward silence and motioned toward the seating area. "Want a cup of coffee?"

"I'd love one." Stan looked around for Nikki, but she was having an in-depth conversation with one of the workers about some oil or another. "And I might try one of your pumpkin spice donuts."

"Those are the best." Sydney grabbed two donuts and poured two cups from the pot behind the counter and carried them over to a table. "So what can I do for you?" she asked with unabashed curiosity once they'd sat.

"I was in the neighborhood and I saw the store. Came in on the off chance I would find you." Stan took a breath. "Sydney. The woman they thought killed Perry didn't."

"I know." She looked down into her cup. "I heard."

"There were a couple of other people at the farm he'd been having a hard time with, but they didn't do it, either. Mostly everyone at the top of the suspect list has an alibi."

"*Mostly* everyone? What does that mean? What about Andrea? I thought she was so nice, but my husband told me how she freaked out on him the other day. It's crazy. And how do you know all this, anyway?"

she asked, eyes narrowed. "You're not a cop."

"No," Stan said. "Small town. You know that. We all know stuff. And the thing with Andrea was terrible. Please apologize to Jason again for me. But Sydney — people are talking about your parents." It was a white lie, but she guessed on some level it was true.

"What about them?"

"About how they didn't want to talk to the police. That everyone's heard they gave Perry a real hard time about his life."

She shrugged. "It's all true. It's mostly my father. He's obsessive about this place. And my grandfather expected Perry to take over, so my father rode Perry even harder because he wanted Perry to get control, thinking if he did, *he* would finally get control. I know, it's all very convoluted."

"So does your grandfather still run the business?"

Sydney laughed. "No. He just holds the purse strings. My father technically runs it, but he never makes really big decisions. He's kind of a figurehead. Grandpa never gave my father much power." She leaned forward, lowering her voice. "It's a big secret, but my father was a screwup too. But, he was the only child, so . . ." she shrugged. "But Grandpa saw how smart Perry is — was. That's why he wanted him in charge. And my father was worried that Perry was never going to fall in line, and the business was going to cave and he'd lose his *status*." Sydney shoved her cup aside, almost knocking it over. "That's all he cared about."

"So it was in his best interest to keep Perry alive," Stan murmured.

Sydney gave her a strange look. "Of course it was. Why, do you think my dad killed Perry?" Now she laughed out loud. "He wouldn't have the stomach for it, believe me."

"So you're going to take it over," Stan said.

The smile vanished from Sydney's face. "Don't remind me. I actually got a call from the Frog Ledge newspaper today. They want to do a whole profile on me." She rolled her eyes. "I mean, it's a nice thought, but I don't want this."

Stan stared at her. "What do you mean you don't want this?" That was a very different story than her husband had told.

"Just what I said. Don't get me wrong, I love the business. Way more than my brother did. But I want to be out back cooking and making strawberry smoothies." She smiled a little. "I clean up good, but I have no desire to run the place. That's my husband. He's been kissing up to my grandpa for years, hoping for this. Honestly? This whole family business thing is a noose around my neck. Just like it was Perry's. I'm actually looking for my own way out." She smiled, but it reminded Stan more of a grimace. "Although short of getting myself murdered, I don't see how it's going to happen."

Chapter Fifty-Seven

"So did she have anything to say?" Nikki asked when they got back in the car. "That's a great market, by the way."

"Actually," Stan said, "she did." Stan pulled out her cell phone and called Jessie.

"You need to talk to the sister again," she said without preamble when Jessie answered.

"What's with you and all the info today?" Jessie asked. "Thanks for the Tyler tip, by the way. I have no idea why Andrea would keep that a secret, given everything else. People are crazy, aren't they?"

"They are. Is it enough to get her off the list?" Stan asked.

"No," Jessie said. "Because Tyler could be covering for her. But it gives her some wiggle room. What else is up?"

"There's something weird going on with the sister. The husband told me all about how Sydney has been dying — no pun intended — to take over the business. But my mother said Mrs. Puck made a comment to her that neither kid was into it. And I just left Greenery. I had a conversation with Sydney. She's trying to figure out how to get out of running the show."

"Really," Jessie said. "I did try to have another conversation with her, but the family lawyer declined on her behalf."

"Well, you might need to pull out the big guns," Stan said. "And make sure to include the husband in the conversation."

Stan dropped Nikki off and drove to her mother's house. She didn't want to wait for her mom to call. Perry's murderer might not be behind bars yet, but she was determined to make the next two weeks as pleasant as possible. Which meant getting along with her mother, and if that meant making the first move, well, then, she would.

But when she pulled into the driveway, there was a car already there. A black Honda sedan. "Cyril?" she asked in disbelief. What was he harassing her mother about?

Stan went up to the house. The inner door was open, and she could hear voices. She pressed the bell.

Her mother appeared a moment later.

"Kristan. Hello." Patricia opened the screen door, leaning forward to give her a distracted air kiss. "Come on in. Cyril and I are working on something."

"You and Cyril are working on something?" Stan repeated, following her into the dining room.

Cyril turned from his seat at the dining room table. There were papers spread out, and a couple of his ever-present steno pads. "Hey, Stan."

"Hey Cyril. I didn't know you were interviewing my mother."

Cyril shrugged. "I didn't think I needed to clear it with you."

"Well, what are you two doing? Mom, I have to tell you, if it's a sensitive subject, you should know better —"

"Honestly, Kristan," Patricia interrupted. "I'm perfectly aware of how to handle myself with the media." She turned to Cyril. "Should we tell her?" Her face was serious, but Stan detected a teasing tone.

Cyril considered. "We could just let her read about it."

Stan was slowly losing her patience. "Read about what?"

"She gets this way sometimes," Patricia said to Cyril. "Very impatient. I have no idea where it comes from."

"Mom."

Patricia sighed. "If you must know, I'm helping Cyril with his story on domestic violence survivors. He thought it would be a fitting tribute to Perry, and to Gabrielle."

Stan stared at Cyril. "You are?"

Cyril nodded. "It's a great story. The whole premise behind Party Pleasers is brilliant. I'm trying to figure out how to do it without giving away the location. The people who use the services depend on anonymity," he told Stan. "And you better read the story."

"I swear on my firstborn," Stan said dryly.

"So you are going to have kids?" Patricia beamed. "I was wondering. That's wonderful news!"

"It's just a phrase, Mom," Stan said. "But I never said I wasn't," she added hastily as her mother's face fell. "Anyway. Can we get back to the point? How did you end up as an interview subject?"

Patricia shrugged. "I'd had a few conversations with Cyril, and I mentioned knowing Gabrielle from the board, and how much the cause meant to her. Her best friend was killed by her husband," she added. "Gabrielle was very passionate about this. And Perry got very involved."

"I'll say," Stan said. "So he donated his

stripping profits to the cause?"

"Half of every job," Patricia said. "Which is why Gabrielle couldn't say much about it, even when her husband was having fits."

"It's like the Underground Railroad," Cyril said, his voice filled with admiration. "They have a whole network of people transporting the clients around. Some of the strippers are even transporters. Their goal is to get people to new locations, far away from their abusers. It's quite complex when you think about it."

Patricia nodded. "And the best part is, they created this other business as a front, which helps them stay under the radar. It's quite brilliant."

"Did Gabrielle tell you all this?"

Patricia nodded. "Jessie was right. She did eventually need someone to talk to. She got tired of fighting with her husband on everything — especially parenting — and has been living a separate life for years. They barely speak. Yet he called the shots when it came to handling the fallout from Perry's murder, because of his family's business. I feel terrible for her. She's thinking of leaving him. The way he handled this situation nearly put her over the edge."

"Pretty messed-up family," Stan said, meeting her mother's eyes. A silent apology.

"Yes, well," Patricia said. "With some families, it gets to be too late to fix things. And that's really a shame, isn't it?"

CHAPTER FIFTY-EIGHT

Cyril left after promising to circle back with Patricia early in the week with any additional questions.

"See you later, Stan," he said, shrugging on his trench coat.

"Hey, will you be at the office later? I need to talk to you," Stan said. "You saved me a call by being here."

"You do? I'm intrigued." He smiled. "I'll be there late. Working on this story."

Stan shut the door behind him and returned to the dining room. "I'm impressed, Mom," Stan said. "You've been busy."

"Well," Patricia said. "I couldn't stop thinking about Gabrielle and Perry and how odd the whole thing was. So I did a little digging on my own." She shrugged modestly. "And Cyril is a great thinker. Very smart."

"I guess so," Stan said. "So did Gabrielle talk about her daughter at all?"

Patricia nodded. "She did. They don't seem close. I got the sense she was closer to Perry, despite her husband's issues with him. And she definitely does not care for Sydney's husband."

Stan paused. "Did she say why?"

"She didn't *say* much at all. It was more her tone when she spoke about him. But she did say he was very serious about the business. Whereas her own two children weren't that excited about it. Anyway. Enough about the Pucks. Did you have something you needed to talk about?"

"Yes, actually, I did. Can we sit?"

Patricia nodded. "We can go in the living room. Would you like tea?"

"No, thanks." Stan walked into the living room, but before she could sit she turned and faced her mother. "Mom. I'm sorry. I'm sorry I didn't want to have the wedding in a church, and that I didn't want anything fancy, and that I fired Chelsea. And that Nutty puked on the dress you bought me. And ripped it. I've been meaning to tell you. I really appreciate you wanting to make the wedding amazing, and memorable. But I really need you to understand that it means the world to us to have the wedding at the pub." She paused to take a breath. "Are you mad?"

Her mother was silent for so long, watching her, that Stan started to fidget. "Well? Say something! You always have something to say," she said, shoving her hands on her hips.

Patricia sighed, then came over and put her arm around Stan, leading her to the couch. "Of course I have something to say."

"Well, good." Stan sat, crossing her arms over her chest. "So talk."

"I want you to have the wedding you want," Patricia said, sitting down across from her. She crossed her legs and clasped her hands together around one knee. "I've been meaning to call you, but I got very busy with Cyril. I wanted to propose an alternative. You have your wedding as planned, and when you come back from your trip, we throw you a party. Here, in the gardens. It will be lovely." She sat back and smiled. "What do you think of that?"

Tony had told her, but part of her hadn't believed it until she heard it with her own ears. Part of it was because she had to gauge her mother's expression, and her tone of voice, for herself to see if she truly meant what she said, or if she just felt like she had to say it.

"I think . . . that sounds lovely. So let me get this straight," Stan said. "We're getting married at the pub. And having the party there. People might be crowded. And Chelsea isn't planning it. You're fine with that?"

Patricia smiled. "I think it's lovely, if that's what makes you happy. I'm sure we'll all have a lovely time."

"And the dress," Stan went on. "The dress got ruined. So I have to get a new dress, and it won't look like the one you picked."

"I heard you. It's a shame the dress got ruined, but things happen."

"Things . . . okay, then. But there's one problem."

"There is?"

"Yeah. I need a new dress."

"It seems so," Patricia agreed.

"Well, there's a little shop about an hour from here. Would you . . . like to go with me tomorrow?"

Patricia paused, then smiled. "I would love to."

"Great." Stan made a mental note to call the shop and have them hang the dress back in the window. "And Mom? One more thing."

Patricia waited expectantly.

"I know we don't have a traditional aisle in the pub, but I wondered if you and Tony both wanted to walk me down whatever aisle we can finagle? It might be made of pub tables, but it will do the trick."

Stan wasn't sure, but she could've sworn her mother's eyes got a little watery. And for once in her life, Patricia Connor didn't have anything to say. Instead, she came over and hugged Stan.

"Well," Stan said, blinking her own watery eyes. "I'll take that as a yes."

CHAPTER FIFTY-NINE

The *Frog Ledge Holler* offices were in the same building as Izzy's bookstore. When Stan arrived later that evening, the parking lot was crowded. She had to smile. Everyone who wasn't at the pub seemed to be over here. It was great for her friend.

Stan parked on the street and hurried inside, skidding to a stop when she realized Jessie was in there with Cyril. And they weren't yelling at each other. They looked pretty cozy, heads bent close together, Jessie reading something on the computer over his shoulder. She stopped talking when Stan came in.

"Hey," Stan said, looking from one to the other. "What's going on?"

"What are you doing here?" Jessie asked.

"I could ask you the same thing," Stan said. "But I have a hunch."

Jessie narrowed her eyes. "What hunch?"

"I think we're here for the same reason.

This interview tomorrow with Sydney and her husband."

Jessie said nothing.

"You can't get to them without the lawyer stalling you, so you're entering an unholy alliance to get it done. I love it."

"I never said that's what I was doing," Jessie said through gritted teeth.

"But it totally is." Stan came over and peered over Cyril's shoulder too.

"Hey!" he said. "You don't read a reporter's story until it's in the paper."

"That's not a story. Those are interview questions. I knew it!" Stan said triumphantly. "I'm impressed, Jess."

Jessie turned back to the screen, dismissing her. "Hey, I gotta solve this case. It's killing me. And Stan, when you called me earlier and told me about your conversation with Sydney, I knew I had to do it. Otherwise, I was going to be spinning my wheels talking to a hundred fifty people at some party they were supposed to be at Friday night until one of them 'fessed up that they weren't really there. I'm so over rich people," she muttered. "Anyway, the husband is looking pretty guilty to me right now."

"I thought so too," Stan said. "Unless they did it together."

The three of them pondered that thought.

"So how are you going to do it?" Stan asked Cyril. "Lure them in with happy questions? Or do the real interview then just flat-out ask?"

"Do not talk about it," Jessie instructed Cyril. "You don't need to worry about it, Stan. We've got it covered."

"Jeez. It was my idea," Stan said indignantly.

"Hardly," Jessie said. "I got here first."

Chapter Sixty

Stan knew there was no way Jessie would let her hide in the *Holler* offices to listen to the interview. But she figured she could get her to let her sit in the police car with them outside and listen.

And she didn't ask her first. She just drove to the *Holler* offices in the morning, two hours before the interview was scheduled, with coffees and muffins from Izzy's. As she suspected, she found Jessie and Lou in Lou's personal car across the street, getting the audio all set up and tested.

She parked a little ways away and rapped on the passenger window, causing Jessie to jump a foot.

Jessie turned and buzzed the window down. "You're lucky I didn't shoot you," she said.

"Sorry. I wanted to come listen in with you guys. And I brought you coffee. And muffins."

"No! Well, yes to the coffee and muffins. And how'd you know we'd even be doing it this way?" Jessie asked.

Stan shrugged. "A good guess. And why not?"

"Yeah, why not?" Lou wanted to know. "She's pretty invested in this whole thing at this point. Just sayin'," he mumbled when Jessie turned her death glare on him.

"Come on, Jess. I tipped you off," Stan reminded her.

Jessie huffed out a breath. "Fine. Sure. Sit in. Bring a friend. Maybe we can get some popcorn too. It's not like this is official police business or anything." She went back to what she was doing.

Lou winked at Stan. She mouthed *Thank you* as she climbed into the backseat. "Cappuccino muffin?"

Stan watched as they had Cyril test the microphone they'd planted on him in a dozen different scenarios. Satisfied they could hear everything, they finally settled back to wait.

And then Jason and Sydney drove up in Jason's fancy black Beemer. Stan poked Jessie. "Look."

They watched as he helped his wife out of the passenger side. Sydney laughed at something he said, and he leaned over and kissed her.

"Maybe the whole together thing isn't so off base," Stan said softly.

Jessie grunted. They all listened anxiously until they heard Cyril say, "Good morning. Come on in, have a seat."

"Hi there," Sydney Puck's voice. "Thanks for having us."

"Of course," Cyril said. "Hello, Jason."

"Hi," Jason said. "Thank you so much for this opportunity. Syd and I are really excited."

"Coffee?" Cyril asked.

Jessie rolled her eyes. Once they got the pleasantries over with, Cyril got right down to business.

"Okay," he said. "So out of tragedy comes a new direction for the Puck family. I'd love to talk to you both today about your plans for the business. Jason, I assume you'll be just as involved as Sydney. The Pucks do like to keep it in the family, right?"

"Absolutely," Jason said, before Sydney could even respond. "We have a lot of plans for the business."

Stan leaned forward, hanging over the seat back. They listened as Jason, with a few minor inputs from his wife, described the direction they wanted to take the markets, their goals for expansion, and how they planned to navigate the first year after taking the reins.

Jessie looked like she was about to jump out of her skin after half an hour of this.

"Relax," Lou said. "They'll get there."

"Yeah, well, I'm getting old," Jessie said.

And then things got interesting.

"So," Cyril said. "If Perry hadn't . . . passed away, would you have been able to take over the business if he'd chosen not to?"

A pause. "What do you mean?" Sydney asked finally.

"Well," Cyril said. "We've heard that your grandfather was adamant about Perry's role in the business."

"He was," Sydney said. "I don't know, I never asked my grandpa about it."

"Why not?" Cyril asked.

Another pause. "I don't know," Sydney said. "I never gave it much thought. Honestly, I was fine with him being Perry's champion."

"But you've both worked there for a long time," Cyril said.

"You bet we have," Jason said. "I've been in a management position for ten years. And I've been working there a lot longer. It's how Syd and I met."

Stan shot Jessie a questioning look. She

hadn't known that. Jessie shrugged.

"So you want this to be a career thing," Cyril said, presumably to Jason.

Lou fumbled with the volume, turning it up.

"Absolutely. This is where I belong," Jason said.

"And how far would you go to get there?" Cyril asked.

Another silence. Then, "Excuse me?"

"I'm just curious. Off the record, of course," Cyril said. "Frankly, you seem like you're the most logical suspect in this murder. If Perry were still alive, you'd still be relegated to managing the cafés, right?"

Sydney's gasp was audible. "What the . . . Jason, what is he talking about?"

They heard a nervous laugh. "No idea, hon. He's obviously crazy. Come on." Stan heard the scuff of a chair being pushed back and the rustle of clothing.

"Shoot." Jessie had one hand on the door handle. "Not enough. He didn't say anything."

But for once, Cyril's tenacity was welcome. He wasn't letting his interview subjects off the hook that easily.

"Sydney," he said. "Can you comment on your admission that you didn't want the business?"

That caught Jason's attention. "What?" he asked. "Who did you say that to?"

"I . . . no one," Sydney stammered.

"If you don't want it, but your husband is telling people that you do — that in fact, you've been waiting for it your whole life — that sounds like you two might not be on the same page," Cyril went on.

"Jason. Who are you saying that to?" Sydney asked. "And why?"

"Syd, he's crazy. Let's go." Jason's voice faded, presumably because he was walking toward the door.

"But you knew neither of you would get it with Perry still alive, right?" Cyril continued.

Lou's hand hovered over the volume button. They all leaned in closer.

"You have a lot of nerve," Jason shot back. "Sydney. Let's go, now!"

"Bossy," Jessie muttered.

"Jason. I have a source who tells me you never made it to the Hartmans' party Friday night," Cyril said.

Jessie's eyebrows shot up. "He's good."

"Is it because you were in Frog Ledge, waiting for your opportunity to get rid of your brother-in-law?" Cyril continued.

Silence. Then Sydney's voice, small as a church mouse. "Jason?"

And then everything happened at once. Over the wire, Stan heard what sounded like a door crashing into a wall. Jessie and Lou shot out of the car at the same time as Jessie yelled over her shoulder at Stan to stay put. And then Jason flew out of the building and raced to his car.

He didn't even get to beep it open before Lou was on him. Jason didn't put up much of a fight, and they had him handcuffed before Stan even blinked.

The whole thing had taken less than two minutes.

Stan scrambled out of the car and went over to where Cyril had just emerged from the building with Sydney. She wasn't hysterical this time. She was white-faced and shaking, and silent tears were pouring down her face. She saw her husband in handcuffs and started to cry, her shoulders shaking.

"You're under arrest," Jessie said to Jason. "For the murder of Perry Puck. You have the right to remain silent —"

"Oh, please," Jason spat. He glared at her. "He was useless. I was meant to run that place. Me and my wife. We put the time in. We cared! Perry didn't care. He was a selfish, vain jerk. But it didn't matter to old Grandpa. Perry could do no wrong. So I had to take matters into my own hands."

Jessie shook her head. "Take him to the barracks," she said to Lou, and marched over to Sydney and Cyril. "Well done," she murmured to Cyril, then turned her attention to Perry's sister. "Sydney," she said, her tone unusually gentle. "Why don't you come with me?"

Sydney let herself be led. "Did he really kill my little brother?" Stan heard her ask Jessie.

"Is there someone I can call for you?" Jessie asked as they walked away.

Stan stood silently with Cyril as people started to gather on the street, bookstore customers and other townspeople, watching the drama play out. For once, Cyril didn't even look excited about a potential story.

"Families," he said, finally, to Stan. "You gotta wonder how they get so messed up."

Chapter Sixty-One

Their wedding day dawned perfectly, as Stan had always known it would. Blue skies, bright sun, a light breeze.

"I can't believe this weather," Nikki said, opening the front door wide and stepping onto the porch. "What an amazing day."

"It really is." Stan took a breath of the fresh, beautiful air and smiled. "It's perfect." The wedding was at four, so they'd have the benefit of photos in the sunlight before the party. She couldn't have asked for a bluer sky. And it wasn't too hot, either, which was important for photos.

"And you look perfect," Nikki said, stepping back to look at Stan from head to toe. "That dress was made for you."

"I feel perfect." Not one to spend a lot of time in front of the mirror these days, Stan had taken a few extra minutes to admire her dress. It *was* perfect. This whole day was perfect.

"Come on," Nikki said. "Your car's here." She pointed at the white limo waiting in the street. "Liam's coming by to get the dogs now. They'll meet us at the pub."

Stan felt like a princess driving around the green in her limo. People had gathered on the green to watch her go by. She felt a little bit like she was in a royal wedding.

It felt amazing.

When the limo rolled up to the pub, she almost didn't recognize the place. It had been completely transformed into a fairyland of decorations and lights that she could tell were going to be brilliant later when night rolled around. She was just so happy to be here.

Tony materialized at her side when the limo stopped. "My dear," he said, offering his arm. "I'll escort you inside."

When she and Nikki stepped through the front doors, Stan swore the entire town was there. The pub was lined with people — her friends, her family, and the people she'd come to know as her second family over the past two years. She felt truly blessed.

And the pub didn't look like a pub. Kyle and Caitlyn and the team they'd assembled had done an amazing job setting up and decorating the room. Candles of all lengths and sizes covered nearly every surface that didn't have flowers — purple ones — covering it already. Stan had her aisle, which led up to the stage where Pastor Ellis would preside over their ceremony. Stan had to smile. Her mother had gotten the pastor to officiate a wedding in an Irish pub. It was kind of hilarious.

Char and Ray stepped out of the crowd to give her a giant hug. "You look beautiful," Ray told her, dabbing at his eyes with his hanky.

"Of course she looks beautiful, Raymond! Did you expect otherwise?" Char tsk-tsked at him. She kissed Stan's cheek. "I'll save my big hug for after pictures. Don't want to smudge your makeup."

"Thanks, Char." Stan blew her a kiss. Izzy sidled up to her, a giant smile on her face.

"You look happy," Stan said.

"I'm so happy. I'm happy for you. And I'm happy for me," she added, holding out her left hand.

Stan's mouth dropped open at the gorgeous, square-cut diamond on her ring finger. "Izzy!"

"I know," Izzy squealed. "I don't want to take away from your day, but I had to show you!"

"Congratulations. I'm so happy." Stan hugged her, trying to hold the tears at bay.

Izzy was going to be part of her family officially. That was the icing on today's cake.

The music started to play. Stan saw the dogs sitting at the front of the pub, waiting expectantly for her. Next to Jake. Who looked so amazing. She felt like running down the aisle toward him.

Her mother and Tony materialized on either side of her, each of them taking her arm. "Ready?" Tony asked.

Stan looked at her mother, who was having a hard time keeping the Patricia Connor composure she was famous for. Stan leaned over and hugged her, then smiled at Tony. "Ready."

After the ceremony, as Kyle, Liam, and Ray frantically rearranged the room to accommodate the party, Stan stood at the makeshift altar with Jake, enjoying one more moment before they got pulled into the fray.

She admired her simple wedding ring, then turned and kissed him again. "Can you believe we made it?" she asked.

He laughed. "I was starting to worry over the last few weeks. But it was definitely worth the worry. I just hope we can get on the plane for our honeymoon without any other incidents."

"That's a jinx if I ever heard one," Stan

teased. "Actually, I think things might start to calm down in Frog Ledge." She leaned against Jake and looked out over the crowd. Her perfect town. Her perfect life.

"Yeah? How do you know?" Jake asked.

She turned and smiled up at him. "Just a feeling."

ACKNOWLEDGMENTS

I'm so blessed to have this writing career, and all the amazing people who've made it possible. Thank you to my agent, John Talbot, for helping me dream up this series back in 2011, and for being such a wonderful support system. To my editor, John Scognamiglio, and the rest of the Kensington crew, for all their hard work in putting out this book, and this series. I am so grateful.

I'm extremely lucky to also be part of such a fabulous writing community, especially the Wickeds, my sisters in crime — Jessica Ellicott/Jessie Crockett, Sherry Harris, Julie Hennrikus/Julia Henry, Edith Maxwell/ Maddie Day, and Barbara Ross — love you girls. Thanks for going on this ride with me.

And to the loyal readers, thank you from the bottom of my heart. I couldn't do this without you. See you at the bookstores.

GOURMET PET FOOD RECIPES

STRAWBERRY BISCUITS

1 1/2 cups Bob's Red Mill Gluten-Free
  1-to-1 Baking Flour
2/3 cup oatmeal
1/4 cup flax seed meal
1 cup strawberries
1/2 cup vanilla Greek yogurt (or coconut
  yogurt for a dairy-free option)
1/2 cup water

Directions
Combine all dry ingredients in a large bowl.
Add wet ingredients and mix well.

Using a cookie scoop, drop tablespoon-size
amounts of mixture onto a lightly greased
cookie sheet.

Bake 18 minutes at 350°F.

Note: Cookies may be dehydrated for a

longer shelf life.

COCONUT-CAROB COOKIES*

1 cup oat flour
1/2 cup old-fashioned oats
1/2 cup shredded unsweetened coconut
1 tablespoon vegetable oil
2/3 cup water
1/4 cup carob chips

Directions
Combine all ingredients except for carob chips. Using a cookie scoop, drop batter onto a lightly greased cookie sheet. Bake for 25 minutes at 350°F.

While cookies are baking, slowly melt carob chips. This can be done in the microwave, heating carob in 10- to 20-second intervals, or on the stovetop, using a double boiler on a low heat. Carob can be thinned out with a drop or two of vegetable oil to help bring to desired consistency.

Once cookies are done and have cooled, drizzle melted carob over the top. This can simply be done with a spoon and a light

*This recipe previously appeared in The Recipe Library.

hand — no pastry bag necessary.

Allow a few minutes for carob to harden and then feed to drooling doggies!

Note: Cookies can be dehydrated prior to topping with carob for a longer lasting shelf life.

Makes approximately 18 cookies.

Peanut Butter and Bacon Homemade Dog Treats*

1 cup creamy natural peanut butter
3/4 cup milk
1 large egg
2 cups plus 1 tablespoon whole-wheat flour
1/2 tablespoon baking powder
4 strips bacon, cooked and crumbled
1/2 cup old-fashioned oats

Directions
Preheat oven to 325°F. Line a large baking sheet with parchment paper and set aside.

In a large bowl, add the peanut butter, milk, and egg. Stir until well mixed. Add the flour and baking powder. Mix well to incorporate

*Recipe courtesy of Chris Carrington.

all of the ingredients.

Knead the dough until it is firm and elastic. You can knead directly in the bowl or, if you prefer, on a level workspace. Sprinkle 1 tablespoon of flour onto your workspace and place the kneaded ball of dough on top. Flatten the dough a bit and sprinkle the crumbled bacon and oats on top. Knead the dough four or five more times to distribute the bacon and oats.

Drop by spoonfuls onto prepared baking sheet. Bake for 20 minutes and cool on a wire rack.

You can store these peanut butter and bacon dog treats in an air-tight container in the refrigerator for up to 1 week, if they last that long. You can also freeze them for up to 1 month.

ABOUT THE AUTHOR

Liz Mugavero is a corporate communications consultant and animal lover from the Boston area, whose canine and feline rescues demand the best organic food and treats around. She is the author of *The Icing on the Corpse, Kneading to Die, Murder Most Finicky,* and *A Biscuit, A Casket;* her short stories have been published in the UK and Australia; and her essays have appeared in national publications *Skirt!* and *Sassee Magazine for Women.*

The employees of Thorndike Press hope you have enjoyed this Large Print book. All our Thorndike, Wheeler, and Kennebec Large Print titles are designed for easy reading, and all our books are made to last. Other Thorndike Press Large Print books are available at your library, through selected bookstores, or directly from us.

For information about titles, please call:
(800) 223-1244

or visit our website at:
gale.com/thorndike

To share your comments, please write:
Publisher
Thorndike Press
10 Water St., Suite 310
Waterville, ME 04901